ROKKA:
Braves of the Six Flowers

1

ISHIO YAMAGATA

ILLUSTRATION BY
MIYAGI

ROKKA: Braves of the Six Flowers 1

ISHIO YAMAGATA

Translation by Jennifer Ward
Cover art by Miyagi

This book is a work of fiction. Names, characters, places, and incidents are the product of the author's imagination or are used fictitiously. Any resemblance to actual events, locales, or persons, living or dead, is coincidental.

ROKKA NO YUSHA
© 2011 by Ishio Yamagata, Miyagi
All rights reserved. First published in Japan in 2011 by SHUEISHA, Inc.
English translation rights arranged with SHUEISHA, Inc.
through Tuttle-Mori Agency, Inc., Tokyo.

English translation © 2017 by Yen Press, LLC

Yen On
1290 Avenue of the Americas
New York, NY 10104

Visit us at yenpress.com
facebook.com/yenpress
twitter.com/yenpress
yenpress.tumblr.com
instagram.com/yenpress

First Yen On Edition: April 2017

Yen On is an imprint of Yen Press, LLC.
The Yen On name and logo are trademarks of Yen Press, LLC.

The publisher is not responsible for websites (or their content) that are not owned by the publisher.

Library of Congress Cataloging-in-Publication Data
Names: Yamagata, Ishio, author. | Miyagi, illustrator. | Ward, Jennifer (Jennifer J.), translator.
Title: Rokka : braves of the six flowers / Ishio Yamagata ; illustration by Miyagi ; translation by Jennifer Ward.
Description: First Yen On edition. | New York, NY : Yen On, 2017—
Identifiers: LCCN 2017000469| ISBN 9780316501415 (v. 1 : paperback)
Subjects: | CYAC: Heroes—Fiction. | Fantasy. | BISAC: FICTION / Fantasy / General.
Classification: LCC PZ7.1.Y35 Ro 2017 | DDC [Fic]—dc23
LC record available at https://lccn.loc.gov/2017000469

ISBN: 978-0-316-50141-5

10 9 8 7 6 5 4 3 2 1

LSC-C

Printed in the United States of America

CONTENTS

Prologue	The Forest of Peril	1
Chapter 1	A Departure and Two Meetings	9
Chapter 2	The Six Braves Convene	51
Chapter 3	A Trap and a Rout	83
Chapter 4	Counteroffensive	127
Chapter 5	When All Is Explained	183
Epilogue	The Next Mystery	211

Prologue

The Forest
of
Peril

The legends speak of a time when evil will awaken from the depths of darkness to transform the land into hell. They say that the Spirit of Fate will select six Braves and bestow upon them the power to face this great danger.

The story that follows is about those Braves, destined to be the saviors of the world. But the most important point concerning their story is this: There are most definitely *six* Braves chosen to save the world. Not five, not seven. Only six.

A boy ran through a forest enshrouded in deep fog. He was a young swordsman, his long red hair fluttering behind him. He wore light leather armor over hempen clothes, with an iron-plated headband tied about his forehead. In his right hand, he grasped a rather small but sturdily made sword. Most noticeable, though, were the four wide belts wrapped around his waist. Affixed to those belts were a few dozen small pouches.

The boy's breath was ragged. He was wounded. His coarse clothes were torn in a number of places, exposing sharp gashes in his skin. His leather armor was charred, and both arms were covered in burns. Blood poured from his wounds, dyeing his shoes bright red. Wounds of this degree would have long since brought a normal man to his knees.

The boy's name was Adlet Mayer. He was turning eighteen. As he ran, he looked nervously over his shoulder. The fog and dense leaves obstructed the light, making the forest dark. He could just faintly pick out a figure through the murky fog. He was being followed. His pursuer pressed closer, only about thirty meters behind. *This is bad*, he thought, and it was that moment when a voice echoed through the forest.

"There you are!" The cry came from a girl. Her voice was high and soft, like the trill of a baby bird.

"*Ngh!*" Just as Adlet heard her, a blade sprouted at his feet. It was silver, about three meters in length, springing up from empty ground, its point aimed precisely at Adlet's heart. He swung his sword with a backhand stroke. The quartz decoration fitted into the hilt of his weapon just barely protected him from being skewered. The impact threw him backward, and the blade that had assailed him shattered into fragments. As he rolled away, he plunged his sword into the ground. Then, lifting his body with the strength of his arms, he leaped. Three more blades immediately rose from the ground. Adlet just barely skimmed over their tips.

"Did I get him?" asked his pursuer.

Adlet landed on the ground and replied. "Not even close. When you're trying to finish someone off, you've got to be quieter about it," he said, setting off running once more. He ran until his tormentor disappeared into the fog and he couldn't see her anymore. "Try harder! You're not gonna catch the strongest man in the world like that!"

"You just won't give up!" The girl persisted in her pursuit.

Adlet cradled his right arm as he ran. To be honest, he hadn't fully dodged that last attack. Blood flowed from a gash in his upper arm. That bragging had been the most he could manage, a bluff for the sake of hiding his injury.

As Adlet fled, he looked at the back of his right hand. A strange crest was tattooed upon it. Roughly the size of a baby's palm, the design was a filigree circle with a six-petaled flower in the center. The crest glowed faintly, a pale shade of crimson. Gazing at it, Adlet muttered, "I'm not gonna get killed. A Brave of the Six Flowers isn't gonna die in a place like this."

The crest on Adlet's right hand was commonly referred to as the Crest of the Six Flowers. It was proof that he was one of the chosen Braves fated to save the world.

The legends speak of a fearsome creature that slumbers at the westernmost tip of the continent. It is said to have a repulsive shape and power far beyond human comprehension. Its only purpose is to kill. When this creature awakens, it—in the company of tens of thousands of servants known as fiends—will overrun the world, transforming it into hell. This creature has no name. It is referred to only as the Evil God.

The legends speak of a time when the Evil God ends its enduring dormancy and rises once again. It is then that the Spirit of Fate will choose six Braves. They say that a crest in the shape of a flower appears on the bodies of those so chosen. These six are the only ones capable of defeating the greatest threat humanity has ever known.

And now, Adlet Mayer has been selected as one of the Braves of the Six Flowers. And so, he sets forth on a journey to defeat the Evil God. He heads for the land where the dangerous creature once slept to find the other Braves, those similarly marked by fate.

But...

"You still won't give up?"

The voice of his pursuer drew nearer on his heels. Blades continued to vex him from beneath. Adlet ran desperately to evade both. Blood loss clouded his eyes. His fingertips were frozen, and his feet stumbled. But he couldn't stop. If she caught him, she would kill him.

What am I doing in a place like this? Adlet wondered. What he should have been doing right about then was attacking the lair of the Evil God. He should have been fighting the fiends that blocked his path, together with the others chosen by fate. But instead, this girl was chasing him down, and he was going to die.

"I'll get you this time!" The girl fired off attacks in Adlet's direction in rapid succession. Cold steel skimmed by his hair, slicing his armor.

"*Ngh!*" He threw himself to the ground to avoid the blade careening at his chest and then stood again immediately, breaking into a sprint. The next blade came from directly underneath. He dodged it with a leaping roll to the side. Her aim wasn't precise, but her attacks were fierce. Out of every few dozen, one or two would come right at him. With each attack he dodged, little by little, the margin of error grew smaller.

"!" Two blades came at him from both sides. One of them gouged into his torso. It sliced through his ribs, the impact sending him tumbling to the earth. Blood spurted from his throat and mouth. Adlet pressed his injured side, curling up. He couldn't even stand anymore.

His pursuer was already so close that Adlet could see her clearly. "I've finally caught you," she said. The shape of a girl emerged from the shade and fog that hung beneath the trees. Her appearance was dazzling. She was clad in white armor, and the hilt of the slender sword she held was inlaid with jewels. On her head, she wore a helmet designed to resemble rabbit ears. Bright flaxen hair, large red eyes, full lips, beautiful, distinctive features—just seeing her standing there, he could sense her nobility and dignity. Everything about her was elegant.

Adlet called her name. "Nashetania." Adlet knew—he knew that on her chest she bore a Crest of the Six Flowers, just like the one on Adlet's right hand. He knew that she was also one of the six Braves chosen to defeat the Evil God. And now, he was about to be killed by one of his own, a comrade he was supposed to be fighting alongside.

"Listen, Nashetania."

"To what?"

"I'm your ally."

Nashetania giggled and then pointed her slim sword at Adlet. Its blade extended to pierce Adlet's ear. "It's far too late for that sort of nonsense." Nashetania was smiling, but she regarded him as if he were vermin. "You're a fool. If you had only surrendered and confessed, you could have had an easier death."

"I'm not gonna confess to anything. I haven't done a single thing wrong."

"It's no use. You won't deceive me again." Nashetania quietly sighed. "You hatched a plan to trick us. You fooled us all and even hurt us. It's quite clear that you are the impostor."

"I'm not lying. You're the one getting tricked. The enemy is using you to try to kill me." But she wasn't listening. "I haven't killed any of our allies. I'm not scheming to trap everyone, either."

"I've told you, you shan't fool me anymore."

"I'm not lying to you! Listen to me, Nashetania! I'm not the seventh!"

The tip of Nashetania's blade hovered over Adlet's heart. "No. You *are* the seventh."

The legends speak of a time when the Evil God will rouse from its deep sleep. It is then that the Spirit of Fate will choose six Braves. On the bodies of these six Braves will appear a crest in the shape of a flower. Only the Braves of the Six Flowers are capable of defeating the Evil God and protecting the world.

But...

When the time came, there appeared *seven* warriors bearing the Crest of the Six Flowers. All seven warriors bore crests that were genuine. Why was there one extra? Adlet knew why. One among those seven was the enemy—plotting the downfall of the true six, infiltrating their number in order to kill them. But among the seven Braves who had come forth, who among them was the enemy? Adlet still didn't know the answer.

Chapter 1

A Departure
and
Two Meetings

Three months earlier, Adlet Mayer had been in the Land of Bountiful Fields, Piena, situated in the center of the continent. It was the greatest nation by every metric—in landmass, population, military strength, and also the prosperity of its inhabitants. Regardless of the category, no other country surpassed its grandeur. The royal family's influence echoed throughout the entire continent, and it was fair to say that Piena was the preeminent power in the land, effectively reigning over all.

At that time, the annual Tournament Before the Divine was being held in the royal capital of Piena. Since the greatest country in the world was hosting this tournament, the scale was of course grand. Competitors included knights of Piena, tough-guy infantrymen, well-known representatives of every nearby nation, famous mercenaries, and finally, Saints bestowed with the power of Spirits. Even unaffiliated fighters and city dwellers with confidence in their abilities were participating. The tournament opened its doors to all sorts of people, with the number of competitors exceeding fifteen hundred.

However, Adlet Mayer's name was not on the tournament list.

"And for the semifinals! On the western side, Batoal Rainhawk, captain of the royal guard of the Land of Bountiful Fields, Piena!"

An old, gray-haired knight emerged from the western side of the coliseum. The arena filled with cheers.

"And on the eastern side! Representing the Red Bear mercenaries, Quato Ghine of the Verdant Land, Tomaso!"

A man so gigantic he could have passed for a bear emerged from the east to face the knight. The cheers for him were no less enthusiastic than those for the old knight.

The monthlong tournament was finally approaching its finale. There were only three competitors and two matches remaining. The stands were packed with an audience of more than ten thousand.

The coliseum sat in a temple adjacent to the royal palace—in fact, you might even say that this arena was itself the temple, where the Spirit of Fate was worshipped. A statue of a holy woman holding a single flower stood at the southern wall, warmly watching over the two warriors.

"To both combatants: Know that this is not a regular duel. You battle before the great king of Piena, and before the Spirit of Fate that safeguards the peace of our world. We wish for a fair and noble battle, one worthy of the Spirit's witness," the high chancellor instructed them, facing the pair.

But neither of the warriors paid any heed. They glared at each other with enough intensity to generate sparks, or so it seemed. As the audience looked on, they, too, were gradually drawn into the tension. This year's tournament had special meaning. There had been plausible-sounding rumors that the winner would be chosen as one of the Braves of the Six Flowers.

"As you know," continued the high chancellor, "he who wins this battle will fight the victor of last year's tournament, Her Highness Princess Nashetania. The cowardly and the base are unworthy of facing her. So both of you must..." The high chancellor of Piena droned on for quite some time. Few noticed the rather quiet, unusual event that occurred as he spoke.

A single boy approached from the coliseum's southern gate. The guards made no attempt to stop him. The high chancellor's personal retinue scrutinized the boy but didn't make a move, either. Nor did the audience pay him much mind. His demeanor was so casual, people believed stopping him would have been out of line.

Long red hair spilled off his head. He wore plain clothes—no armor, no helmet—and a wooden sword was slung over his back. Four belts were strapped about his waist, with a number of little pouches fastened to them. The boy wedged his way in between the two warriors and said, smiling, "Pardon me, guys."

The high chancellor, shocked at the sudden intrusion, berated this interloper. "Who are you?! This is beyond rude!"

"My name is Adlet Mayer," the boy replied. "I'm the strongest man in the world." The two warriors who had been about to fight the decisive semifinal match glowered at this upstart—Adlet Mayer. But Adlet paid them no mind. "I'm here to notify you of a change in the matchups. It's gonna be Adlet, the strongest man in the world, versus you two."

"Just who do you think you are?! Are you mad?!" The high chancellor's face was turning red.

But Adlet ignored him. At this point, the audience broke into murmurs, finally noticing that something was amiss.

"Come on, hurry up and kick this idiot out," said the mercenary, irritated his fight had been interrupted. Finally, the high chancellor's personal guard remembered their duties and lifted their clubs.

Adlet grinned. "Aaand the match begins!" His hands moved faster than the eye could see. Something flew from his fingertips, hurtling at the faces of the four guards. The soldiers clutched their faces and began moaning in pain.

"You guys really are good," said Adlet. He wasn't looking at the honor guard. His eyes were on the old knight and the mercenary who stood on either side of him. Both of them held, pinched in their fingers, the poisoned needles Adlet had thrown. The points had been dipped in a nerve toxin that stimulated pain receptors. The poison was mild, but it would cause pure agony for about thirty minutes.

The mercenary and the old knight drew their swords simultaneously. It seemed they had finally realized that the intruder was not just any idiot. The mercenary swung at Adlet, holding nothing back. Though his weapon was simply a dull practice sword, the blow would most certainly mean instant death if it connected.

"Heh!" Adlet chuckled, ducking the attack. Without waiting even a second, the old knight charged him from behind. But Adlet reached into the pouches on his belt with blinding speed. He produced a tiny bottle with his right hand and turned to toss it.

The old knight grunted, slapping away the bottle with the flat of his sword. The little bottle had only contained water, but it was distraction enough to give Adlet an opening. The old knight and the mercenary went on the defensive, putting some distance between themselves and Adlet as they occupied positions to his front and rear. If this were a regular fight, the situation would have spelled inevitable defeat. But Adlet had found a sure way to win.

He pulled a small ball of paper from one of his pouches and threw it on the ground. Instantly, there was an explosion at his feet. Smoke surrounded Adlet, concealing him.

"What the hell?!"

"What trick is this?!"

The old knight and mercenary simultaneously voiced their astonishment.

Of course, neither of them would be undone by mere sleight of hand. Adlet moved fast. Exceptionally so. Within the cloud of smoke, he extracted another tool from one of his pouches. While his two opponents were still baffled by the smoke, he laid the groundwork for his victory. First, Adlet leaped at the old knight, pulling out the wooden sword at his back as he struck.

"Not good enough!" the knight yelled.

The moment the old warrior blocked his attack, Adlet released the wooden sword. He used both hands to hold down the old man's arms, moved his face close, and then clacked his teeth together.

Perhaps the old knight hadn't seen the striking flint set on Adlet's teeth or the spray of high-purity alcohol that spurted from his mouth.

"Gah!" the old knight cried out as flames erupted in his face.

Still grasping one of the old man's arms, Adlet turned his back to his adversary, then hurled him over his shoulder. The knight's back hit the ground, and he could move no more. Adlet immediately spun around, but not to face his remaining opponent. His attack was already done.

Slowly, the haze of the smoke bomb cleared. The mercenary was crouching low within the cloud, holding his legs as he shrieked in anguish.

"Sorry. Those poison needles hurt, don't they? I would've preferred defeating you with different methods, if I could." Adlet furrowed his brows as he smiled audaciously.

Something resembling large thumbtacks was scattered in the spot where Adlet had been standing scant moments earlier. They weren't really noticeable unless you were looking for them—they were painted a pale gray, the same color as the ground in the coliseum. The points of the tacks were coated with that same nerve toxin that inflicted horrific pain. The mercenary had charged through the smoke, intending to catch Adlet from behind, only to step on those spikes. Had he been wearing iron leggings or sturdy leather footwear, the attack might easily have been deflected. However, it seemed the mercenary valued quick footwork in particular, as he wore light and nimble cloth shoes. When Adlet had first sized up his opponents, he had paid special attention to their feet.

"How do you like that? I win!" Adlet yelled.

The audience was dumbstruck. Just hearing his announcement apparently wasn't enough to make them believe that some nameless interloper could come in and defeat two top contenders at the tournament in under ten seconds.

"Wh-what are you all doing?! Come here, now! Surround him! Surround him and capture him!" The high chancellor, panicked, yelled at the soldiers encircling the arena. The soldiers needed no additional prodding—they removed the covers from their spears, advancing toward the center of the coliseum.

Right before their attack, Adlet turned to the holy statue that watched over the battle and shouted, "My name is Adlet Mayer! I'm the strongest man in the world! Do you hear me, Spirit of Fate? If you don't choose me as one of the Braves of the Six Flowers, you're gonna regret it!"

The guards charged Adlet. At this point, the audience finally seemed to realize what was going on. "Royal guard! Draw your swords! Catch the boy!" The audience in the spectators' seats spilled into the arena as well. The fallen knight and mercenary rose and faced Adlet once more. This arena for sacred battles, where warriors demonstrated their strength before the Spirit, was now host to a chaotic brawl.

And so, from that day forth, Adlet Mayer's name resounded throughout the land...as the Wicked Trickster Adlet, the Cowardly Warrior Adlet, the worst Brave candidate in all of history.

One thousand years ago, a monster appeared on the continent. Little was known about the creature, such as where it came from, why it was born, what it felt, what it wanted, or even if it had will or sentience in the first place. No one even knew if it was actually alive. The beast just appeared suddenly, without warning.

Some testimonies remained from the very few who had encountered the creature and survived. The monster was a few dozen meters in length. They said that it did not have a static form, but rather resembled living, shifting mud. It was the only one of its kind that had ever appeared in the world. Its body emitted toxins; acid that melted everything it touched oozed from the beast's tentacles. Then it began attacking humans. It did not eat them or play with them. It simply killed for the sake of killing. It divided its own body, creating monsters to serve as its minions, and killed even more. This foul pestilence had no name, because there was no need to give it one. There was no other creature that could even occupy the same category. This monster was simply called the Evil God.

At the time, the continent was ruled by the great Eternal Empire of Rohanae. The empire dominated the whole world, but even after bringing the strength of its entire army to bear, it had been unable to defeat the Evil God. The nation was laid to waste, its royal line died out, and its towns and villages were razed to the ground.

Just as the people despaired, accepting that it was their fate to be destroyed, a Saint came to them. With a single flower as her only weapon, the Saint stood against the Evil God. She was the only one in the world who could fight it.

It was a long, long battle. Finally, the Saint chased the Evil God to the westernmost tip of the continent and defeated it. When she returned, the Saint said, *The Evil God is not dead. One day, it will awaken from its slumber in the west and transform the world into a hell.* And so she prophesied: *When it reawakens, six Braves will appear to inherit my power, and they are destined to subdue the Evil God once more.* She described how the crest of a six-petaled flower would appear on the bodies of the chosen warriors. And that is why they were called the Braves of the Six Flowers.

Twice the Evil God rose from its dormancy, and twice, six Braves appeared—just as had been foretold—and sealed it away once more.

To be chosen as one of the Braves of the Six Flowers, there was a condition: A Brave-to-be had to demonstrate his or her power at one of the temples to the Spirit of Fate that the Saint of the Single Flower had constructed. There were thirty of these temples across the continent. Easily more than ten thousand candidates would come from all over the land to demonstrate their strength at these temples. When the Evil God woke, the best six among them would receive the Crest of the Six Flowers. To be chosen as one of the Braves of the Six Flowers was the greatest honor for a warrior. They all dreamed of being chosen as one of the Braves, and Adlet was no exception.

Rumor held that the Evil God's resurrection was nigh. Over the past few years, a number of omens had been observed. It could happen as late as the end of the year or as soon as the very next day.

"……I regret my actions. I accept that I've done wrong." It was three days after the semifinal match of the tournament, and Adlet was imprisoned in a jail for the most heinous of criminals. The high chancellor stood on the other side of the bars, a sour look on his face.

Adlet was seriously injured. His head, shoulders, and both legs were wrapped in bandages, and his right arm hung in a sling. Even Adlet couldn't have escaped unscathed when so outnumbered. He took a seat on the cold bed, faced the high chancellor in front of his cell, and spoke. "Just so you know, I did want to enter the tournament legitimately. But there were these rules and stuff, and they just wouldn't let me into the arena," he grumbled. The Tournament Before the Divine had rules. The weapons allowed were limited, permissible tactics were restricted, and foul play or attempts to catch one's opponent by surprise were forbidden. Had he followed the rules, Adlet would have been useless. "As you know, I'm the strongest man in the world, but those rules kinda cramped my style. So I had no choice but to ignore them and invite myself in."

"What is your goal?" demanded the high chancellor.

"Duh. To be chosen as one of the Braves of the Six Flowers."

"A Brave? *You?* A scoundrel like you, chosen as one of the honorable Braves of the Six Flowers?"

"Oh, I'll be chosen. Of course I will. 'Cause I'm the strongest man in the world." Adlet smiled, and the high chancellor struck the iron bars. *This old guy sure lacks self-control,* thought Adlet.

"You feel no remorse at all!" the old man accused.

"Yes, I do. I really do. I injured a lot of people, like the soldiers in your personal guard and the royal guard."

"And how do you feel about having made a mess of this sacred tournament?"

"What does that matter?"

The high chancellor emitted an incomprehensible sound and drew his sword. His bodyguards desperately restrained him as he attempted to pry open the lock of Adlet's cell. "Listen, you! You'll stay in here forever! You're headed for the noose! Absolutely!" With his soldiers escorting him, the high chancellor exited the jail.

Adlet sprawled out on the bed and shrugged as if to say, *What a mess.*

He remembered his confrontation with the old knight and the mercenary three days earlier. Both had been terrifyingly strong. If Adlet had made even one wrong move, he would most likely have lost. But he'd still managed to pull off a victory. It hadn't been a pretty fight, but still, he had won. That was proof enough that he was the strongest man in the world.

"Now that I think of it, that was the only letdown," Adlet muttered as he rolled around on his bunk. He was thinking about Princess Nashetania—Nashetania Rouie Piena Augustra, the crown princess of the Land of Bountiful Fields, Piena. She was of noble birth, first in line to inherit the crown, and also the strongest warrior in Piena. He had heard she was a Saint, wielding power she had received from the Spirit of Blades, and capable of conjuring blades from thin air at will. Nashetania had been the victor of the sacred tournament the previous year. The winner of the match that Adlet had interrupted would have competed with her in the final round. Adlet had wanted to battle Nashetania. Even if he couldn't fight her, he'd at least wanted to see her face. He'd figured that if he defeated the two men, with any luck, she might have turned up. But in the end, she was a no-show. *Well, it doesn't really matter, anyway*, he thought, yawning.

"Oh. I found you." Just then, a voice addressed him from the other side of the bars. The person standing there looked out of place in the somber prison.

"Who're you?" asked Adlet.

The maiden was beautiful and blond with a wonderful, soothing smile. She wore a maid's black uniform, but it didn't suit her. It would have been more fitting on a plainer girl. "You're Adlet, right? Pardon me, but could you come over here?" His visitor beckoned him to come close.

Confused, Adlet got up, moving toward the bars. When he approached her, a sweet smell like apples wafted toward him. It was a pleasant, enchanting scent that he had never smelled before.

"Please, shake my hand." Suddenly, the girl passed her hand through the space between the bars.

"Huh?"

"I apologize for the sudden intrusion. You put on such a show in that fight three days ago. It left quite an impression on me. You've made me a fan."

"…Huh? What?" The girl's scent had melted all the circuits in his brain, and that was all the reply he could muster.

"Please shake my hand. Come on."

Adlet did as he was told and lightly grasped the hand she extended. It was so soft, he marveled that such suppleness could even exist.

Lightly pressing her palm in his, the girl said, "You're really anxious, aren't you, Adlet? Is this perhaps the first time you've ever held a girl's hand?" She covered her mouth as she gave him a mean smile.

Adlet panicked and released her hand. "Wh-what're you talking about? I'm totally calm. I've held girls' hands lots of times."

His guest giggled. "You're blushing."

When she laughed, it felt like the apple scent she exuded became even stronger. Adlet looked away, covering his flushed cheeks.

"You're such a great fighter, but you can't handle girls?" she teased.

"Come on. Adlet Mayer is the strongest man in the world. There's nothing the strongest man in the world can't handle."

"I'm glad I came down here. You really are interesting." She laughed. "I want to know more about you. Can we talk?"

Adlet nodded. The apple-scented girl gave him a mischievous smile. Suddenly, Adlet realized that he still hadn't asked her name.

Adlet Mayer was turning eighteen that year. He hailed from a small, remote country in the west, the Land of White Lakes, Warlow. When he was ten years old, circumstances had caused him to leave the village he called home. He had no lover and no friends. His parents had passed away when he was young. For a very long time, he had secluded himself in the mountains with his master, spending his days training to defeat the Evil God. He had refined his swordplay, honed his body, and learned how to make and use all sorts of secret gadgets. He practiced a unique form of combat that combined swordsmanship with the employment of various tools. He was affiliated with no organization and followed no leader. He was an autonomous warrior, his only goals being to fight the Evil God and the continued improvement of his skills. That was Adlet's background.

Those who lived by the sword would normally be affiliated with an order of knights or a mercenary band, as fighting with those groups could earn money and prestige. But Adlet had no interest in either of those things—all he cared about was fighting and bringing down the Evil God. There were very few completely unconnected warriors like him, even across the entire continent.

After completing his long training, Adlet had descended the mountain and attempted to enter the martial tournament in Piena to make sure that he was indeed the strongest man in the world, he told her.

The girl who smelled of apples listened to Adlet's story enthusiastically. He didn't know exactly what she found so fascinating, though. "So that's why I came to show the Spirit of Fate that I'm the strongest man on earth. Sorry, it's not very interesting," he said, finishing.

The fruit-scented girl applauded by way of reply. Adlet had felt embarrassed at first, but gradually, he'd gotten acclimated to talking to her. Besides, it really was nice to have a cute girl listen to him.

"No, it was interesting," she insisted. "I really am glad I made the effort to come down here to meet you. Now I kind of feel like I've heard the phrase 'the strongest man in the world' enough for a lifetime."

"Oh?" Adlet had a habit of describing himself as "the strongest man in the world." Whenever he talked about himself, he always added that line. "Well, it's an undeniable fact that I'm the strongest man in the world, so I'm gonna be proactive about saying it out loud."

"But can you really claim to be the strongest so easily? You still haven't beaten Nashetania, have you?" the girl asked with an edge of challenge.

But Adlet paid that no mind. "I hear she's pretty strong. But I'm stronger."

"There are lots of other strong people out there."

"Of course. But I'm convinced there's nobody out there stronger than me."

"What basis do you have for that conviction?"

"I know I'm the strongest man in the world. That's all."

"That's all?" she pressed.

"I know it. The Spirit of Fate knows it, too. Now all I have to do is show it to the Evil God and everyone else in the world."

"You really do have amazing self-confidence."

"It's not confidence. It's unmistakable fact."

The girl smiled, not quite sure how to reply.

Well, I'm not surprised she's confused, Adlet thought. This was her first time meeting the strongest man in the world, after all. "By the way, can I ask you something?"

"Of course. What is it?" she replied.

"I'd like to get out of here. Do you have any good ideas?"

"You want to escape? Why?"

What an unflappable girl, thought Adlet. He'd been expecting a slightly different reaction from her. Adlet told her about how the high chancellor of Piena had been wailing about putting him to death. The prison sentence had been inevitable, but the death penalty would pose a bit of a problem.

The girl put her hand to her jaw and deliberated. "I believe you'll be all right. The high chancellor is angry, but I doubt he can put you to death since there were no serious casualties."

"Oh, well, that's good." Adlet was relieved. Escaping from prison in his condition would have been a bit rough. "What happened with the tournament after I was taken away? Was it called off?"

"No. It is as if your incident had never happened. Yesterday they had a rematch, and the mercenary Quato won the semifinals by a narrow margin. Nashetania scored an overwhelming victory in the final match." Adlet had the feeling she'd just invoked the princess's name without using her title, but that was probably his imagination.

"That's surprising," he said. "So the mercenary won, huh? The old man was a little better, though."

"It seems you injured Batoal's shoulder with that throw."

"I tried to hold back, but I guess it wasn't enough. I feel kinda bad about that."

After that, Adlet and the girl's conversation turned to more trivial things, like how seeing the magnificence of Piena's capital had left him awestruck and about his troubles on account of how expensive every-thing was there. The girl was friendly and easy to talk to, and they became absorbed in the conversation.

"Oh!" A serious expression suddenly overcame his visitor, as if her memory had just been jogged. "I forgot. I came to tell you about some-thing. This isn't the time for chat."

"What is it? Sounds like it's nothing good."

The girl held her breath, speaking in a whisper. "Do you know about the Brave-killer?"

"What're you talking about?"

"Have you heard of the knight of the Land of Golden Fruit, Matra Wichita?"

"Yeah, I know the name." There were a lot of rumors going around about who would be chosen to be the Braves of the Six Flowers, and that name had come up many times. They said he was a prodigious young knight and the greatest archer in the world.

"And do you know Houdelka of the Land of Silver Sand? And Athlay, the Saint of Ice?"

Adlet nodded. Both were the names of famous warriors. "Did some-thing happen?"

"They were killed. And we don't know who did it."

"Fiends?"

"Probably."

The creatures known as fiends, minions of the Evil God, prepared for the revival of their lord by secretly readying themselves to attack the Braves of the Six Flowers. They infiltrated the continent, carrying out all kinds of plots—and now it seemed one of them was going around elimi-nating anyone likely to be chosen as a Brave.

"They're not the kind of people who'd be taken out that easily by some fiend," mused Adlet. "How the hell would they—?"

"I don't know."

"What a pain in the ass."

"Adlet, I think it would be best for you to stay here," she said. "It will be dangerous no matter where you go, but here, you will be heavily guarded."

.   "That's true. Then I'll stay put until I'm all healed up."

As she looked out the window restlessly, it seemed the girl had finished delivering her warning. "I'm sorry. If I don't go now, they'll be angry with me. Well, they will be angry regardless, but it will be even worse if I stay any longer."

"I don't mind. Go on."

The maiden bobbed her head and was about to leave when Adlet stopped her. "If you do meet the princess, tell her…" He paused. "She's sure to be chosen as one of the Braves of the Six Flowers. Tell her I'm looking forward to the day we fight together."

"…Huh?" The girl's mouth hung open. And then, for some reason, she giggled.

"What?"

"No, sorry. I'll tell her. If I get the chance to see her." She walked to the door, turning back for a moment to stick out her tongue. "Adlet, you're quite the fool, aren't you?"

Adlet wanted to ask what the girl was talking about, but she was already gone. He wondered what that might have been about, but having no clue, he decided to forget it. He lay down on the bed and gazed up at the ceiling, thinking about this killer who was after the Braves.

"A Brave-killer, huh? Once I'm chosen, I guess I'll end up fighting whoever that is, too." The cheerful, happy-go-lucky expression disappeared from his face. Now, a quiet anger lurked in his eyes.

Just as his guest had predicted, for Adlet's sentence, they settled on an indefinite imprisonment. *Well, that's that,* he thought, not bothering to object. Alone in his jail cell, the warrior waited for his wounds to heal.

A few days later, Adlet discovered a gift in his cell—a sword small enough to hide in his bed. He figured this meant that when the time came, he should use it to protect himself. He didn't know if the girl had arranged it or if he had some other fan.

A month passed, then two. He continued training in his cell so as not to get out of shape. This Brave-killer he'd heard about didn't turn up.

After three months, his wounds were completely healed. Right around the time Adlet was starting to consider breaking out, something strange happened. One night, the fierce pounding of his heart woke him. His entire body felt hot, and his chest seethed with indescribable excitement. The feeling passed after about ten seconds, and then a faintly glowing crest appeared on Adlet's right hand. The Evil God had awakened, and Adlet had been chosen to be one of the Braves of the Six Flowers.

"Huh," Adlet muttered, looking at the crest. "That was surprisingly simple." He had imagined that his entire body would be enveloped in light or that the Spirit of Fate would appear and order him to defeat the Evil God or something. Feeling a little underwhelmed, Adlet stared at his hand. After a moment, he realized this wasn't the time. "Hey! Somebody come over here!" Adlet banged on the iron bars of his cell as he called the guards. Once they knew he had been selected as one of the Braves of the Six Flowers, they couldn't keep him locked up. But if the guards didn't come, he wasn't going to get anywhere. "Isn't anyone there? I was chosen as one of the Braves of the Six Flowers!"

The interior of his cell was strangely silent. He couldn't detect the presence of any guards at all. *Oh, well*, he thought, *I guess I'll bust out*, and that was when a sudden commotion sounded from the foot of the stairs.

"Why have you come to a place like this? What on earth are you here for?!"

"Batoal! I'm in a hurry! Please, don't get in my way!"

Both voices were familiar. One of them belonged to the girl who smelled of apples. Adlet figured the other one was the old knight he'd fought in the coliseum. He could also hear the thumping of many footsteps coming from behind the two.

"Adlet! Were you chosen?" the girl cried, running up to Adlet's cell. She wasn't wearing the maid uniform from before. She was clad in magnificent white armor, a slim sword belted at her waist. On her head, she wore a helmet in the shape of rabbit's ears. Adlet had heard somewhere that wearing helmets with animal motifs was a tradition of Piena's royal family.

The moment he saw her, Adlet understood who she really was and also what a fool he'd been. *Most people would've figured that out*, he thought with a wry smile.

Standing before the cell, the girl said, "It's been quite some time since we last saw each other. Allow me to reintroduce myself. I am Nashetania Rouie Piena Augustra, the crown princess of Piena and the current Saint of Blades."

The apple-scented girl—Nashetania—lifted up her breastplate and showed him the Crest of the Six Flowers near her collarbone. "I have now been selected as one of the Braves of the Six Flowers. I'm very pleased to meet you."

"I'm Adlet Mayer, the strongest man in the world. Pleased to meet you, too." Adlet showed her the crest on his right hand.

"Princess! What are you doing?! You don't have the time to be talking to someone like him!" The old knight ran up to the two of them, but then Adlet showed him, too, the Crest of the Six Flowers on his right hand. The knight's eyes widened, and he fell silent.

"We must go now. Our time is limited." Nashetania unlocked the door of Adlet's cell, and he stepped out. Ignoring the old knight's cries as he tried to stop them, the pair broke into a run.

"Did you get us horses?" asked Adlet.

"They're over this way!"

The two of them leaped out a window and landed on the grass. There, a woman who looked to be Nashetania's maid was awkwardly leading two horses toward them.

"You're all prepared, huh?" Adlet observed.

"Yes," replied Nashetania. "Let us be off!"

Together, they straddled their horses and set off at a gallop. The old knight and the soldiers shouted after them, clamoring about a departure ceremony, an audience with the king, and other trivial matters. Looking at Nashetania's profile as she rode beside him, Adlet smiled. It looked like he was going to get along with this girl. Apparently, she was thinking the same thing, as she turned to him and grinned.

One thousand years ago, a woman known as the Saint of the Single Flower defeated the Evil God and sealed it away on the westernmost edge of the continent, a land called the Balca Peninsula. Presently, the area fell under the territory of the Land of Iron Mountains, Gwenvaella. The peninsula was shaped sort of like a flask, with the narrow end attached to the continent. The plan was for the Braves of the Six Flowers to gather at the base of that peninsula. Every warrior who demonstrated his or her power before the Spirit of Fate at a temple surely knew that. No matter from where in the world each of the six Braves hailed, if they waited at that point, they would inevitably meet the others.

After the Evil God awakened, it would take a while for the creature to regain its full strength. Before the Evil God's powers were replenished, the six Braves would have to make it to the very tip of the Balca Peninsula to seal the beast away once more. It would take the Evil God at least thirty days from the time of its awakening to reach its peak strength. Though that seemed like more than enough time, in actuality, it was not. Over ten thousand fiends lay in wait on that peninsula for the Braves of the Six Flowers. Only six warriors would step into that realm. It was bound to be a long and difficult battle. During the past two conflicts, over half of the six Braves had sacrificed their lives. But those who feared death would not be chosen to begin with.

The Balca Peninsula was rarely called by its formal name. This expansive swath of earth, eagerly awaiting the revival of the Evil God, resounded with the wailing of fiends. That was why the place was called the Howling Vilelands.

After leaving the royal capital of Piena, the two Braves first stopped by Adlet's hideout. There, the eager warrior equipped himself. He stuffed a variety of secret tools into the pouches at his waist and packed explosives, poisons, and concealable weapons into the large iron box that he carried on his back. This vast array of instruments would be invaluable in defeating the Evil God. Without them, Adlet would have been unable to declare himself the strongest man in the world. The iron box was sturdy and heavy. A regular person would become short of breath just bearing it on their back. But for Adlet, it was no great burden.

After that, the companions galloped for a whole day out of the Land of Bountiful Fields, Piena. Now, they were in the Land of Golden Fruit, Fandaen.

"They won't chase us any farther, will they?"

"I'm sure they've given up by now, Nashetania." Looking over their shoulders, they were of course referencing the crowd from the royal palace in Piena that had been chasing after Nashetania. "Don't you think that was a little cold of you, though? They're your vassals, aren't they?"

"They are, but dealing with them is still trying."

Adlet was purposely not addressing his partner as a princess. It was his intention to treat her entirely like a comrade on equal footing, and Nashetania seemed fine with that.

As they proceeded down the road, the two of them slowed their pace a bit in order to give their exhausted horses a break. Orchards surrounded them as far as the eye could see. The Land of Golden Fruit, as indicated by its name, was a country that grew delicious fruit.

"It's so pretty," remarked Nashetania. "This is the first time I've ever seen so many cultivated fruit trees."

"Really?" said Adlet.

She seemed to be enjoying herself as she took in the scenery. Adlet thought the trees were nothing special, but he supposed it must have been an unusual sight for her. A horse cart stacked with lemons passed by them, heading in the opposite direction.

"Pardon me," called out Nashetania. "May I have one?"

What're you doing? Adlet wondered.

Without even waiting for the coachman to reply, Nashetania grabbed a lemon. She crushed it in her hand and drank the juice with relish. "That was delicious!" She wiped her mouth and tossed the squeezed remains of the lemon into the cart. It seemed this princess was a little strange—though this was not news to Adlet. "It's so peaceful here, isn't it?" she commented, licking the juice off her hand. "I thought the Evil God's awakening would be so much more serious."

"This is how it is. The last time the Evil God awoke, and the time before that, the world was at peace. You only see disturbances once you're close to the Howling Vilelands," said Adlet. "It only stops being peaceful if we lose."

"Indeed. Let's do our best."

Next, it was a cart stacked with carrots that came down the road toward them. Nashetania hopped off her horse again and took one without asking. *There's no way she's gonna eat it raw*, thought Adlet, but in fact, she did. Nashetania summoned a narrow blade out of thin air. The blade moved too fast for the eye to catch, cleanly peeling the carrot in only moments.

"Is that the power of the Spirit of Blades?" asked Adlet.

"That it is. Fantastic, right? Since I'm a Saint." Nashetania puffed out her chest as she chomped on the carrot. "And I can do this, too," she said, raising her index finger. A blade sprouted from the ground, one over five meters in length. It was slender and frighteningly sharp. If it pierced either human or fiend, its victim would be done for. "And even this." She directed her index finger toward Adlet, summoning blades about thirty centimeters long around the digit. One after another, they shot at Adlet's face.

"What're you doing?! You idiot!"

"This is easy enough for you to dodge, isn't it?" Nashetania cackled as she continued peppering him with projectiles.

Though he dodged them easily, he was privately amazed by the power of the Saint of Blades.

Saint was a general term for warriors who controlled supernatural powers. There were fewer than eighty of them in the world, and all of them were, without exception, women. They said that within the body of each Saint resided a Spirit that governed the providence of all things. By borrowing the abilities of the Spirit within, a Saint could wield powers beyond human capacity. Among the many Spirits, the one that inhabited Nashetania's body was the Spirit of Blades. Each Spirit had only one Saint. No one else besides Nashetania could currently utilize the power of the Spirit of Blades. If she were to die or relinquish her power, someone else would be chosen as the Saint of Blades. In addition to Nashetania and her power of blades, there were also the Saint of Fire, the Saint of Ice, the Saint of Mountains, and others with a variety of powers. A few of these people were bound to be chosen as Braves of the Six Flowers. The Saint of the Single Flower, the one who had defeated the Evil God in the past, had hosted the Spirit of Fate.

"Cut that out!" Adlet grabbed one of the projectiles and threw it back at Nashetania. It hit her helmet and fell to the ground.

"I'm sorry. I got carried away."

"No kidding."

"Are you angry?"

"I am angry. Absolutely furious," he said, and Nashetania suddenly wilted. With a sad look on her face, she bit into her raw carrot. *I'm not that mad*, Adlet thought, now regretting what he'd said.

"I apologize." Sounding depressed and completely different from before, Nashetania said, "I'm a bit strange. I'm always making my father and the maids cross with me."

"Hey, I'm not that mad."

"Maybe I'll just be an annoyance no matter where I go."

She's kind of hard to categorize, thought Adlet. She had dressed up in a maid's uniform and visited him at the jail, fooled around on the road here, but then immediately gotten upset just because he was a little angry at her. It was uncomfortable. How should he deal with this? Grasping his horse's reins, Adlet looked down. Still unable to come up with something to say, he rode along with her in silence. *I'm the strongest man in the world, so why am I worrying over something so trivial?* Adlet wondered, and he was about to say something to Nashetania when he noticed her glancing at him from the corner of her eye.

"Did you seriously think I was upset?" she asked.

"…Hey."

Nashetania put a hand to her mouth, a teasing smile on her face. He'd forgotten…she really loved mischief.

"*Ah-ha-ha-ha-ha!* You really are fun, Adlet."

"Damn it. My concern was wasted on you."

"I wouldn't get upset over something like that. Relax."

Adlet looked away and slapped his horse's rear, galloping away to leave Nashetania behind.

"Please don't be angry!" she pleaded. "I just got carried away."

"No kidding."

"Don't misunderstand. I'm usually more restrained. This is just so nice, I cannot help but enjoy myself a little."

"We're heading out to go fight the Evil God right now. Do you get that?"

"I do. It's just for now. I apologize." Nashetania bowed her head, smiling. "This is a first for me. I know there will be fighting, but still, I can't help myself."

"A first? A first what?" he asked.

"First time being with someone like you." Nashetania's expression changed. Her smile turned from puckish to something kind and affectionate. She had a number of different smiles. Adlet suddenly felt shy.

"Being able to speak as equals like this, to talk honestly about what I think and feel—you're the first person I've been able to do that with," she confided.

Adlet went beyond shy to outright embarrassed. He glanced at Nashetania from the corner of his eye. *Maybe she's just amusing herself by embarrassing me,* he considered, but that did not appear to be the case.

"Oh, look—a wagon. I'll go get myself another carrot." Maybe she realized he was feeling self-conscious, or maybe she didn't, but regardless, Nashetania began chomping on another raw carrot. Adlet's shoulders slumped as he watched her.

                               *   *   *

Following that, Nashetania continued to act as she pleased. Before long, the sun set, and night arrived. The two of them tied their horses by the side of the road and began setting up camp. Adlet wondered if Nashetania would be able to handle sleeping outdoors, having been raised in a palace, but she said she had done it many times, so she'd have no problems. Once Adlet was done laying out his bedding, he scanned the area, checking to see if there were any blind spots or cover where an enemy might hide. It was always best to be ready for a surprise attack.

"What's wrong?" Nashetania asked him. Her eyelids were drooping, and she looked quite sleepy and carefree indeed.

"Hey, before we go to sleep, I'd like to ask you something," said Adlet. "What happened with that killer who's after the Braves?"

"Oh yes, I haven't told you about that yet, have I?" Nashetania's expression grew grim. It seemed the news was not good. "I didn't tell you before, but in fact, six months ago, Goldof left on a journey in search of the Brave-killer."

"Goldof…that's a knight of yours, right?" Adlet knew the name. Goldof Auora: captain of the Black Horns knights. A prodigious young fighter and the pride of Piena's royal army. He was the strongest knight in Piena, purported to rival Nashetania in strength.

"Unfortunately, I haven't heard anything heartening. The last communication I had from him was a month and a half ago, and all he said was that he had no leads."

"The killer might've taken him out."

"I think not!" Unusually for her, Nashetania's voice rose. "Goldof is strong. I've never beaten him."

"What about that tournament last year?" he asked. Nashetania had been the victor of the Tournament Before the Divine the previous year. Adlet had heard that she had faced Goldof in the finals, and at the end of a desperate struggle, she had defeated him.

"At the very end, he went easy on me. But there's no helping that… because of my position. But I've never been so frustrated in my life. That's why I made him promise me—he's not allowed to die until I can defeat him in a rematch. That's why Goldof can't die. He wouldn't." Nashetania deliberated for a bit. "...I think."

"Do you have confidence in him or not?"

"I have confidence in him. But he's a little too young. He's still only sixteen."

"That's young, all right. Not like we can talk, though," said Adlet. He was eighteen, and he had heard that Nashetania was the same age. They were rather young to be shouldering the fate of the world.

"But Goldof is strong. He's just a little unreliable in certain ways," she said.

"Well, I hope he's as good as you say. So he hasn't got any leads. Any other news?"

"Yes. The Saint of Sun, Leura, disappeared a month ago."

"Leura? The Saint of Sun?" Adlet paused. That was another familiar name. That Saint was a living legend reported to wield the power of the Spirit of Sun. About forty years ago, during a war, she had displayed the full extent of her power. She had burned down a besieged castle by shining down rays of heat from the sky. Adlet had heard that she'd conquered over ten fortresses, all on her own. Once she was older, she'd taken over the role of the elder who governed the Saints, but by now, she should have retired from that job, too. "She's famous, but she's too old to be fighting, isn't she?"

"Yes, she's over eighty," replied Nashetania. "No matter how powerful she might be, I don't think she's in any state to be joining the battlefield."

"That's weird, though. There should be others the killer would go after instead. Like me, or you, or Goldof. There's even the Saint of Swamps, Chamo. There're tons of powerful people out there."

"I think it's odd, too..." Nashetania furrowed her brows. Sitting here talking wouldn't change anything.

"Well, whatever," said Adlet. "Let's get some sleep. We'll find out about this Brave-killer sooner or later."

"Sooner or later?"

"We'll end up fighting them. No doubt about it."

"Do you think the killer is a fiend? Or could it actually be a human?"

"I don't know."

Nashetania lay down on her bedding. Adlet closed his eyes, holding his knees to his chest. In that position, he could rest his mind and body while still staying alert. The evening went by without event, and so did the next day, and the next. The fact that nothing was happening only made Adlet more uneasy.

The two of them continued their hurried journey for ten days. They swapped their horses out for fresh mounts multiple times, sleeping less than three hours a day as they progressed. At a normal pace, the trip would have taken nearly thirty days. They ended their long travels as they finally crossed the border into the Land of Iron Mountains, Gwenvaella, beyond which the Howling Vilelands lay. The road twisted through the ravine between steep mountains, and the whole area was covered in deep forests.

Gradually, they started hearing more and more rumors about the Evil God. The closer they got to the Howling Vilelands, the grimmer the expressions of the people they encountered became. Once they reached the Land of Iron Mountains, here and there they began seeing families packing up their things to flee.

"Let's hurry," said Nashetania. Her excitement had ebbed now that they were nearing their goal. She may have been innocent, but she wasn't stupid.

"Watch out. Fiends will probably start attacking us soon," Adlet warned her.

"How do you know?"

"The enemy plans to strike before we can all get together. That's what they did with the previous generation of Braves."

"You sure know a lot about this."

"My master pounded into my head everything there is to know about fiends," he explained. "The different types, the environments they live in, their weaknesses, and behavior you can expect to see from them."

"I'll be counting on you, then."

After that, Adlet and Nashetania continued down the road, and Nashetania spoke less and less. Finally, she stopped talking completely.

Unable to take it anymore, Adlet broke the silence. "Nashetania."

She didn't respond. Nashetania was clutching the reins of her horse, a brooding expression on her face.

"Nashetania!"

"Y-yes?!"

"Are you feeling anxious?" he asked.

The Brave's knuckles were white from her grip on her reins. She released them to rub the sweat off on her thighs. It was evident that she'd lost her composure.

"Calm down," he said. "The fight hasn't even started."

"Y-you're right. I wonder why I'm so anxious."

This bothered Adlet. "Have you ever been in a real fight before? Have you ever experienced a serious battle, where people are trying to kill each other?"

"I…" She trailed off.

Guess not, thought Adlet. There was no helping that. She may not have been a model princess, but she was a princess nonetheless.

"Am I really that powerful, Adlet? What if all this time, everyone has been going easy on me?" Nashetania fretted, looking at her palms as they dripped sweat.

"Calm down. Don't think about that."

"We haven't even encountered any fiends yet… I have to calm down…" The way Nashetania was trembling, it was as if her earlier enthusiasm had never existed. Or no, perhaps her cheer thus far had been an attempt to stifle her anxiety. But Nashetania was no coward. Everyone felt nervous before their first real battle. That was always the case, regardless of strength.

"Nashetania," he said. "Smile."

"Huh?"

"Smile. Start with that."

Nashetania stared at her hands, saying, "I can't, Adlet. My hands won't stop shaking. I can't smile." As she spoke, she lifted her head to face her companion. Adlet pressed up his nose with a finger while smooshing both his cheeks. *Hnerk.* Nashetania snorted, then covered her mouth, averting her eyes.

"So you *can* laugh. Have you calmed down?" Adlet asked.

Nashetania considered her palms again and then touched her neck, checking her pulse. "I feel a lot better. Thank you."

Seeing Nashetania's expression, Adlet nodded. She would be okay. While she was still innocent and inexperienced, she was a fine warrior at heart. "That was the first thing my master taught me. To smile."

"You had a good teacher."

Adlet shrugged as if to say, *I dunno about that.*

Now from that point onward, they headed directly for the entrance to the Howling Vilelands. Their primary goal was to unite with the others, but Adlet figured there would be other trials ahead of them first.

It was then that a man carrying a child and a woman with an injured leg came running toward them from farther down the road.

"What's wrong?!" Nashetania dismounted and approached the trio.

The woman clung to Nashetania and began to cry. "We tried to run away! We tried to run, before the…before the fiends came!"

"Please, calm down!" said Nashetania.

The woman began wailing, unable to continue. Nashetania looked at the man.

"The people of our village were planning to escape to the capital together with the soldiers," he explained. "But on the way, we were attacked by fiends, and we…left behind…our friends…and our youngest…"

As Nashetania listened to the man's story, her hands began trembling faintly again. Adlet put a hand on her shoulder and spoke to her quietly. "Stay calm. With your power, you don't have to be afraid of anything." After reassuring her, he hurried his horse, setting out at a gallop. "Nashetania! Follow me!"

"C-coming!"

As Adlet held his horse's reins, he considered the situation. This was just as he had expected. The fiends were aiming to eliminate each of the Braves individually. That was why they were burning villages and attacking people in this area—to lure out the six Braves. Last time, falling for that tactic had cost one of the Braves their life. If victory were their singular focus, then the correct choice would be to ignore this and move on. But in Adlet's mind, that "correct choice" was a load of bull. Why were they going to fight the Evil God? To protect the defenseless.

"There they are!" shouted Adlet.

Ten fiends were attacking a cluster of wagons. The monsters were about ten meters long and shaped like leeches. A single horn and a few tentacles grew from their head segments, and on the end of each tentacle was a very humanlike eyeball.

While fiends were all of the same species, sharing a common ancestor, they varied infinitely in form. Some, like these, resembled leeches. Others looked like gigantic insects, still others looked like birds and beasts, and some even looked human and could speak. The only thing they shared in common was that they all had a horn somewhere on their heads. That was it.

About a dozen soldiers and farmers with their families were under attack. Many were wounded, and a number had already succumbed. Adlet leaped from his horse and rushed the hoard of fiends. "I'll slow them down! You finish them off, Nashetania!" he yelled as she ran behind him. In a flash, Adlet whipped an iron bottle from one of his pouches, removed the cap, and poured the contents into his mouth.

"…!" A few of the fiends spotted Adlet. They raised their heads and spat liquid at him.

Adlet dodged it with a forward roll. As he regained his feet again, he struck the flint in his front teeth. The iron bottle contained a specially mixed, concentrated alcohol. Flames spewed from his mouth into the fiends' faces. The heat was low enough that most could escape unscathed by batting the flames away, but these fiends writhed in pain. It was just as he had guessed: This breed was vulnerable to heat.

Most of Adlet's secret tools were not powerful in and of themselves.

Their true value lay in their versatility, allowing him to take advantage of the fiends' weaknesses in a variety of circumstances.

"I knew you were good!" exclaimed Nashetania as she employed the power of the Spirit of Blades. Blades sprouted from the ground to quickly decapitate three of the creatures.

The remaining seven paid them no mind as they continued attacking the farmers. Adlet immediately withdrew his next tool—this one a small flute. He put it to his lips and blew.

"…?"

No noise. But the fiends that had been assaulting the villagers turned all at once toward Adlet. This flute emitted special sound waves that attracted fiends.

Adlet calmly dodged the charging monsters, and Nashetania did not let that opportunity go to waste. She stabbed another five to death, and Adlet dispatched the two remaining with his sword. Now that it was over, the battle had actually elapsed very quickly. Killing all ten fiends had taken less than a minute.

"Phew." Adlet wasn't tired, but he had broken a sweat. Though this wasn't his first time, real combat still made him anxious. Nashetania was panting. Adlet put a hand on her shoulder and said, "That was perfect. I wouldn't have known it was your first fight."

"I was able to fight more calmly than I had imagined. If this is how it's going to be, I think I can be useful."

"I'll be counting on you."

Nashetania smiled.

After that, the two of them assisted in treating the farmers' wounds. The villagers piled the bodies of their fellows into the carts. It was difficult, seeing these deaths, especially those of parents who left children alone in the world.

"Is everyone here? Was anyone too late getting away?" Adlet asked as he treated one of the villagers.

They all looked down as if struggling to respond, exchanging looks with one another.

"What's wrong?" he prompted.

"Well…" The villagers seemed hesitant to speak.

Adlet quickly picked up on what was going on. "Someone got left behind, huh."

"Th-there was a traveling girl all alone in the village," one of the villagers said, and Adlet immediately mounted his horse.

He was about to hit his horse's flank when Nashetania, looking panicked, asked him, "Adlet, where are you going?"

"They said a girl's still there. I'm gonna go get her."

As he tried to slap his horse, Nashetania grabbed his wrist. "Wait, please. Do you plan to go alone?"

"Yeah. You handle things here." He snapped the reins to signal his mount to move, but this time, Nashetania grabbed its tail. "Why are you stopping me?" he demanded.

"It's too late, Adlet. You won't make it in time."

"…"

"There are only two of us. We cannot save everyone."

He was a little taken aback. Nashetania's attitude struck him as surprisingly cold. "You're right," he said.

"It's a shame, but we should give up on that girl and move on." Nashetania looked down sadly. She likely wanted to help out as much as he did, but she was right to prioritize defeating the Evil God.

"Defeating the Evil God, saving people… It's hard to manage both," said Adlet.

"This is difficult for me, too. But right now, let's think first about joining the other Braves." The princess, having secured her partner's agreement, released his horse's tail.

The instant she did, Adlet whipped the reins. The horse whinnied and broke into a gallop. "Sorry, but I'm going. 'Cause I'm the strongest man in the world!"

"Just what is that supposed to mean?!" she yelled after him.

I'll defeat the Evil God, and I'll save people, too. Being able to pull off both is what makes me the strongest man in the world, Adlet silently answered to himself.

*   *   *

After about half an hour of galloping, the fence that encircled the village came into view. The streets were quiet. Adlet saw no one, be it human, fiend, or animal. The village was completely desolate. Maybe the fiends had yet to come, maybe they had already finished the job and left, or maybe it was a trap.

Adlet dismounted, drew his sword, and proceeded with caution. There was something strange lying by the entrance to the village—the corpse of a fiend that resembled a giant snake. It was big—a far more powerful specimen than the fiends he and Nashetania had killed. Adlet approached the corpse to get a better look. Some extraordinary power had smashed its head in. Closer investigation revealed an iron ball about two centimeters in diameter buried inside the wound.

"A slingshot? No. It couldn't be...a gun?" Adlet tilted his head.

The gun was a weapon that had been developed about thirty years earlier—a miniaturized version of a cannon. While these devices were gradually becoming more common, they couldn't really be called powerful. At most, they could enable a person with no armor to bring down a boar. Adlet had never heard of any gun capable of killing a fiend.

The Brave entered the village. The bodies of fiends were strewn everywhere. Every last one had been brought down by a single shot to either the heart or the head. That was when Adlet finally realized that the female traveler who had been forsaken in the village...hadn't been forsaken at all. She'd stayed behind to battle the fiends here. And a lone warrior on a journey at a time like this, with the Evil God freshly awakened from its slumber, could have only one purpose. Adlet searched for the girl in houses and the center square, finally approaching a charcoal maker's hut near the fringes of the town.

"Oh." He spotted someone. Raising his hand, Adlet was about to call out, but he stopped midmotion, his voice catching somewhere in his throat. The moment he saw the girl, he froze.

She was alone, walking toward the delapidated hut. She was probably about seventeen or eighteen. Her hair was white, and she wore a cloak with a frayed hem. In her arms, she cradled a puppy, affectionately stroking its neck as she walked. Adlet realized at a glance that this was the girl who had defeated the fiends, thanks to the gun peeking out from underneath a gap in her cloak. But Adlet didn't care about that. The girl was carrying a puppy. The mundane sight left Adlet completely unable to move.

"There you are," she said.

A lone dog was chained to a post in front of the hut. It was probably the mother of the one in the girl's arms. She lowered the puppy at her breast to the ground. It leaped toward the other dog, wagging its tail and frolicking about.

The girl pulled a knife from beneath her cloak, severing the mother's collar and freeing her. "Fiends only attack humans. You can be at ease and live here."

The two dogs romped about the girl's knees and then ran off to disappear into the forest. Adlet stood stock-still as he watched the scene.

The girl was striking. Her face looked rather young. Her right eye was covered with a patch, and her left was a clear blue, heavy lidded, and cold. Her leather cloak obscured the leather clothes underneath that clung tightly to her body. A black cloth wound around her head.

This girl was powerful—Adlet could tell that with a glance. She moved with precision, her bearing reminiscent of a honed blade. It told him she was a near-flawless warrior. Just approaching her would be enough to make him feel as if his heart might stop.

But the way she'd petted that puppy confused him. Her hands had cradled the dog, comforting it. They were kind hands. It was as if she'd been teaching it what affection was. The girl stared in silence at the forest into which the two dogs had disappeared. To Adlet, the light in her eyes, her expression, seemed terribly ephemeral. She looked like a flower on the verge of wilting, a star about to sink at any moment. Like something fragile. Adlet didn't get her. She was cold but also warm. Terrifyingly strong yet simultaneously frail. This contradictory first impression was confusing.

"Who's there?" The girl turned toward Adlet.

His heart jumped. His mind went blank, and he had no idea what to say. He could hear his pulse pounding in his ears. It wasn't that he was shocked by her beauty. He wasn't moved by emotion and probably wasn't in love. He just didn't know what to do. All he could manage was panic. "Do you like dogs?" Adlet finally squeezed out the wrong thing to say.

Her mouth agape, the girl stared at Adlet in astonishment. "I like dogs. I hate people, though."

"...Oh. I like both."

"Who are you?" the girl demanded as she pulled her gun from beneath her cloak, pointing it between Adlet's eyes. He felt absolutely no sense of danger. "Have you come to kill me, too?" On the back of her left hand was the Crest of the Six Flowers. Adlet gazed vacantly at the girl's face and her crest. "You don't care if I shoot?" she inquired.

Those words brought Adlet to his senses. Panicking, he raised both hands, showing her he wasn't hostile. "Wait, don't shoot. I'm Adlet Mayer. I'm one of the Braves of the Six Flowers, just like you." When he displayed the symbol on the back of his hand to the girl, she eyed him suspiciously.

"I've heard of you. You're the cowardly warrior from the martial tournament in Piena. They say you're a genuine sleazebag."

Adlet was flustered. "W-wait. Who said that? I'm the strongest man in the world. I am absolutely not a 'cowardly warrior,'" Adlet stammered, attempting to calm his pounding heart.

"You're one of the Braves of the Six Flowers? There's no way I'd believe that," she scoffed.

He could sense no kindness or transient fragility in the way she leveled the muzzle of her gun at him. The girl who stood there was a cold, cautious, natural-born warrior. Her attitude immediately dispersed Adlet's confusion. "The rumors are wrong," he said. "I'll do whatever it takes to win, but I'm not a coward."

"..."

"I'm Adlet, the strongest man in the world. A coward wouldn't be capable of calling himself the strongest in the world. So don't point your gun at me," he said confidently.

But the girl's expression only showed disgust, and she gave no indication that she would lower her weapon. "Where are your allies?"

"Nashetania is nearby. You know her, don't you? She's the princess of Piena and the Saint of Blades."

"Nashetania...I see. So she was chosen as well." She still made no move to lower her weapon—though she should have known that Adlet wasn't her enemy. She stared at him with jaded eyes. At the very least, it wasn't how most people would regard a future comrade-in-arms. "Tell Nashetania and the others you are about to meet..."

"...Tell them what?"

"My name is Fremy Speeddraw. Saint of Gunpowder."

The Saint of Gunpowder. Adlet hadn't heard the title before. It was said that the Spirits dwelled in all things, governing over the providence of all existence. But he had never heard of a Spirit or Saint of Gunpowder. What bothered him more than that, though... Why should there be any need for him to tell the others?

"I will not be accompanying you," she explained. "I will be fighting the Evil God on my own. I won't interfere with your business, so don't get involved with mine."

"What are you talking about?" asked Adlet.

"Is there something wrong with your hearing? I'm saying that I'll be operating separately from your group. Do not get involved with me in the future."

Adlet was dumbfounded. Wasn't working together what made them the Braves of the Six Flowers? What could one warrior hope to accomplish alone?

"Tell them exactly that. You can manage a basic errand, can't you?" Fremy asked, lowering her gun, then turning and sprinting off. She was quite fast.

"Hey, wait!" Of course, mere words had no effect. Fremy disappeared in a blink. "Damn it!" Adlet scanned the area. His horse was approaching. He drew his knife from the scabbard on his chest and carved into the horse's saddle: *Nashetania. Met another Brave. I'm following her. Don't worry about me—head for our goal.* Then he turned the horse around toward the village entrance and sent it galloping back. "Wait! Where'd you go, Fremy?!" he shouted, but there was no reply. Adlet dashed into the trees.

*   *   *

Running in the forest always left traces—broken twigs, footprints on leaves. If Adlet followed those, pursuing Fremy shouldn't prove too difficult. Adlet climbed the mountain and descended the other side, running all the while. At various points, Fremy's footprints suddenly cut off, as if she was erasing evidence of her passage. Someone used to fleeing would run that way.

"What is up with her?" Adlet muttered as he searched the area with his telescope. When he detected the faint moving shape of a person, he ran off in that direction.

He considered giving up on tracking her and going back the way he had come. He was worried about leaving Nashetania behind. But Adlet kept on chasing Fremy. His intuition as a warrior instructed him. Something whispered deep in his heart, telling him he had to follow. He couldn't just leave her alone.

He caught sight of her back as she ran through the forest. Apparently, Adlet was gaining ground. At this rate, he could overtake her. He chased her for about another hour, then finally circled around to cut her off. "Just cut this out," he said.

"I can't believe you caught up to me," said Fremy. The two glared at each other, panting. She drew her gun and pointed it at Adlet. "I told you what you needed to know. Don't follow me anymore."

"What did you say?"

"If you keep following me, I'll shoot."

Simmering anger welled up from the pit of Adlet's stomach. After saying all that crap about him, now she was going to shoot him? "Stop screwing with me! You're being stupid. What are you thinking? You can't defeat the Evil God all on your own!"

"You're in the way. Move."

"And there are fiends, too. All six of us have to work together, or we're done. Are you too stupid to understand that?"

"I can fight alone. I can win alone. If you want proof, I can show you."

"Oh yeah? Just what do you plan on showing Adlet, the strongest man in the world?"

Fremy's fingertip touched the trigger. Adlet threw the iron box off his back and put his hand on the hilt of his sword. He couldn't back down now. The two of them squared off for a while. Neither would initiate a fight now, not even Fremy. It was a test of wills until one stepped aside.

"At the very least, tell me why," said Adlet. "Tell the Braves why you're going it alone."

"I can't."

"Why not?"

Fremy fell silent.

"Say something," he insisted. She didn't respond.

"Just so you know, I'm a stubborn guy," Adlet continued. "I'll follow you until I get an answer. And then once I do, I'll follow you until you tell me to go away. The strongest man in the world is the least likely to know when to give up."

"You're a character. 'Strongest man in the world'—yeah, right," she said.

"Why are you going alone? Why won't you meet up with the other Braves? You're stuck here until you tell me."

Fremy ground her teeth. Her finger trembled on the trigger. Then she lowered her eyes and whispered, "If I meet them, they will most certainly kill me."

Adlet was stunned. What she was saying was unbelievable, but she was serious. "That's ridiculous. We're all Braves of the Six Flowers. Why would we kill an important ally?"

"They won't consider me 'an important ally.'"

"Why not?"

Fremy's visible eye abruptly went cold—and it was nothing like her earlier glaring. She had the look of someone ready to fire. "If I tell you, you'll try to kill me, too."

Adlet weighed the situation. If he pressed her any harder, they'd end up trying to kill each other.

"You can hear why, and then we can try to end each other, or you can not hear why, and we can do the same. Pick one," she said.

"…"

"Or you can say nothing and withdraw."

Adlet returned his sword to its sheath and picked up his iron chest from the ground.

Fremy lowered her gun, looking relieved. "I will fight the Evil God by myself. You do as you please. If possible, I would like to avoid seeing you again." Fremy stashed her gun beneath her cloak and turned her back to him.

Adlet agonized. Was it okay to let her go like this? He decided it wasn't, based on nothing but instinct, and made a fierce leap at the renegade Brave. The moment she turned toward him, he threw a smoke bomb. Under cover of the smoke, he wrenched away her pack.

"What are you doing?!" she demanded.

"You told me to do as I please, so I did."

"Give me back my things." Fremy drew her gun once more.

Adlet clasped the pack he'd snatched from her against his chest. It most likely carried bullets and tools for gun maintenance. It looked like she also had travel rations and a map.

"Is this some kind of joke? Or are you an idiot?" she asked.

"I'm not an idiot, and I'm not fooling around. I've made up my mind. I'm gonna follow you."

"What?"

"Now that that's decided, let's get going." Adlet gave the frozen Fremy a backward glance and started walking.

"Who said you could decide anything? Give me back my pack." Fremy's expression shifted from confusion to anger. Her finger moved to the trigger of her gun.

"Whoa, there," said Adlet. "If you attack me, I'll run away—with all your stuff. Then you'll be the one in trouble."

"Do you want to get shot?"

"Or are you gonna steal it back and then run away? You should have figured out by now that you can't outrun me, though."

"What the hell are you thinking?" Fremy demanded.

Adlet pondered for a moment, and then spoke slowly, warning Fremy, "I don't know everything that's going on with you, but it looks like you're in some kind of trouble. You're heading off all by yourself to the Howling Vilelands, where the Evil God and its fiends are waiting, and you say that if you run into the other Braves, they'll kill you. I think most people would define that as being in trouble."

"So?"

"I'm not the kind of guy who can just abandon one of my own when they need me. The strongest man in the world is kind. So I've decided to help you out."

"Are you *kidding* me? If this is some kind of joke, you can knock it off."

"No complaints. Let's get going." Ignoring Fremy where she stood with her gun trained on him, Adlet began walking again.

"I can't believe it. What? What the hell? What is up with you?" Fremy seemed at her wits' end, but ultimately, she followed him. The two strolled through the forest in silence.

I've been acting on impulse here, just taking things as they come, thought Adlet. *Is this really a good idea?* He had abandoned Nashetania, and he would never know when Fremy might seriously try to kill him. He glanced back at her. The expression on her face was more than confused—she looked scared. *Well, whatever. It'll work out somehow.* "Hey, Fremy." He turned to her as she trudged behind him. "I don't know your situation, but right now, I'm serious about protecting you. You're one of the only five allies I've got."

"Shut up and walk. This is uncomfortable," Fremy spat, averting her gaze.

Meanwhile, Nashetania was battling fiends in the village where Adlet had met Fremy.

"...*Hungry...want...meat...drink...blood!*"

Her opponent was what looked like a gigantic wolf. The fact that it could speak human language, however imperfectly, was proof that it was particularly powerful. A small trickle of blood oozed from Nashetania's cheek. The fiend lifted its front leg, attempting to crush her. A blade shot up from the ground, intercepting its body. *"Hungry...hungry!"* Though impaled, the fiend still writhed.

Nashetania swiped away the blood on her cheek using her slim sword. She then lengthened the blade, thrusting its tip into the fiend's mouth.

The demon squirmed in agony, vomiting. *"Can't...eat Saint's blood... Can't have Saint's blood!"* Fiends ate people, but the bodies of Saints like Nashetania were deadly poison to them.

"This was frightening at first," Nashetania muttered, summoning blades from thin air to chop up the beast. "But I've gotten quite used to fighting fiends now." She divided her victim into three, four parts, and then finally, it stopped moving.

Once the fight was over, Nashetania surveyed the area. It was deathly still—she saw no fiends and no Adlet. Disappointed, Nashetania picked up a saddle that had fallen on the ground and read the words carved into it.

Nashetania. Met another Brave. I'm following her. Don't worry about me and head for our goal.

"What's going on?" Nashetania cocked her head. "If he's following her, does that mean that she's running away from him? Why would she run away? Just who is this other Brave?" She murmured to herself as she scanned the village once more to see if Adlet had left anything else behind.

That was when a black horse galloped into the village bearing a man of large build clad in black armor.

When she saw him, Nashetania cried out, "Goldof!"

The man—Goldof—dismounted at Nashetania's side and put one knee to the ground before removing his helmet and bowing his head. "Your Highness. I apologize for my belatedness. I have hastened to your side."

Goldof Auora. He was said to be the strongest of the knights of Piena. His face was permanently severe, and most would never guess he was younger than Nashetania. His black armor was heavy and durable, and his helmet was designed to resemble the curled horns of a goat. He carried a large iron spear in his right hand, connected to his wrist by a sturdy chain. His imposing appearance suggested he was a veteran of many battles, but something in his expression bespoke a lingering immaturity.

"So you did come after all. I knew you'd be chosen." Nashetania greeted him kindly.

"It is an honor."

"I'm grateful the Spirit of Fate chose you. I have nothing to be afraid of with you by my side." Nashetania spoke with dignity, but there was something awkward about her tone. It lacked the casual ease with which she'd chatted with Adlet.

"I will protect you with my life, Your Highness," pledged Goldof. "It is my intention to slay the Evil God and escort you safely back to the king."

That statement elicited a bit of a frown. "Goldof."

"Yes, Your Highness?"

"From now on, we are equals. Comrades-in-arms. You won't simply be protecting me; we will protect each other."

"But Your Highness…," he protested. "You are a distinguished individual. I cannot allow the worst to happen to you."

"…I see. I understand. Fine." Nashetania gave him a small nod. "In any case, we have a problem. A fellow Brave who was with me until just a while ago disappeared somewhere." Nashetania showed him the saddle.

Goldof read the text and tilted his head. "I don't understand."

"Neither do I."

"Who was this companion of yours who wrote it?" he asked.

"Adlet Mayer. You know him, don't you?"

When Goldof heard that name, his expression changed. He must also have heard what had happened during the holy tournament.

"Don't give me that look," said Nashetania. "He's a reliable man."

"Even though he abandoned you to go who knows where?" Goldof's eyes were sharp, as if he was wary of the absent Adlet.

"That's why we're going to look for him now. I wonder which way he went," she mulled.

Goldof reexamined the writing on the saddle. His expression said he was not only thinking about where Adlet had gone but considering the matter further. "He must have started toward the Howling Vilelands already. If we continue on, I believe we will encounter him."

"Perhaps that's our only option, but I am worried. I hope he's all right," said Nashetania. Goldof did not reply, simply offering up the horse upon which he had arrived. Nashetania refused, saddling and mounting the horse Adlet had been riding. As they galloped down the road out of town, she said, "Goldof. Adlet is a good person. He's quite odd, and I'm sure you'll find him confusing at first, but I think once you talk together a bit, you can be friends."

"Yes, Your Highness."

"It's a big world out here. I think it's a good thing I came out on this journey. I never would have met as curious a person as Adlet if I had stayed at the palace."

"Is that so?"

"And also...he's so much fun to tease," added Nashetania, sticking out her tongue with a grin.

But Goldof seemed to have mixed feelings. He angled his face downward so as to hide his expression. "Pardon me, Princess, but..."

"What is it?"

"About this Adlet, do you, um..." He started saying something, then faltered. Still looking down, he fell into a long silence.

"What's wrong? I don't really know what you're implying. Perhaps you have changed, too, during the time we've been apart."

"Perhaps that is so. I apologize. Please forget about it," he said.

Nashetania cocked her head, then clapped her hands together and cried, "Oh yes. What about that killer who's been going after Braves? Have you found any leads?"

Goldof shook his head as he rode. "I am ashamed to say that, as of yet, I have failed to dispose of the killer. But I do know her name, appearance, and abilities."

"So you *do* have a lead. And this information is trustworthy?"

"Yes, Your Highness. I obtained this report from someone I believe to be trustworthy who personally fought the killer," he said.

"So who is this assassin?" asked Nashetania.

Goldof's voice grew tense. "The Saint of Gunpowder—a silver-haired girl who wields a gun. Her name is Fremy."

Chapter 2

The
Six Braves
Convene

Adlet and Fremy advanced toward the Howling Vilelands. They walked in silence along a mountain path, where all that grew was grass that cropped up sparsely between the rocks and pebbles. According to the map, once they crossed over two more mountains, they would finally be able to see their destination. It had been six hours since they first met, and the sun was high.

"It's kinda hot, huh?" Adlet remarked to Fremy, who walked ahead of him.

She didn't reply.

"I wonder if it's supposed to be especially hot around here. Do you know anything about it, Fremy?"

Unsurprisingly, no response.

"I've never heard of the Saint of Gunpowder. What kind of stuff can you do?"

"..."

"Well, since you're the Saint of Gunpowder, do you have any explosives? I'd be grateful if you could share some with me."

"..."

"I didn't know there was a gun that could kill fiends. Who made it?"

Adlet made numerous attempts to talk to her in an effort to improve relations between them, even just a little bit. But each time, all he got in return was stonelike silence. He was beginning to feel annoyed. His initial impression of her lonely and ephemeral air was entirely gone. All he could see was a selfish, rude, incomprehensible woman. "Say something. Just what the hell do you take me for?"

"A brazen, thoughtless, unmanageable idiot."

"*Oh,* so you'll answer *that* question, huh?!" Adlet lost all desire to talk to her. He decided to walk mutely.

He wondered what Nashetania was up to. He hoped she was also heading toward the Howling Vilelands. If she was looking for him, she would be late joining the rest of the group. He was also worried about having left her alone.

"If you're worried about Nashetania, why don't you go back?" suggested Fremy, as if she had read his mind.

"Nah, I'm not worried about her. At least, not as much as I am about you."

"*Hmph,*" Fremy snorted bitterly. "I didn't think Nashetania would be chosen. Between you and her, the Braves don't look all that promising this time around."

"You're wrong," said Adlet. "Nashetania is immature and inexperienced, but she's a fine warrior."

"You're sure arrogant enough—*you* calling *her* immature and inexperienced."

"I'm the strongest man in the world. From my point of view, everyone else is inexperienced."

"You're ridiculous," she spat, and they both went silent again.

They crossed over one mountain, and once they finished scaling the next, the Howling Vilelands would be within view. As they approached the summit, suddenly Fremy said, "Can I ask you something?" Adlet was surprised to hear her speak out of the blue. "I have a request," she continued.

"What is it?"

"Eventually, we'll end up trying to kill each other. No matter what you may think now, it *will* happen."

"No, it won't," Adlet insisted.

But Fremy shook her head. "Please. When the time comes, go easy on me. Even if you end up taking me down, don't finish me off."

"What kind of request is that? I'd rather hear you ask to fight together."

"I figured you would be willing to listen to a small request like this one."

"…"

"I can't afford to die. Not until I defeat the Evil God with my own two hands." That was all Fremy said before she stopped talking. Adlet couldn't say anything else after that, either.

I can't afford to die. She had uttered those words determinedly. But behind them, Adlet had also sensed indescribable sadness. He thought of Nashetania. Being with her cheered him up—but being with Fremy was emotionally painful, like something was pressing on his chest.

"That's the Howling Vilelands," said Adlet.

The two of them arrived at the summit of the mountain; before them lay a sprawling landscape. Woodlands extended from the foot of the mountain to the sea, and a thin, twisting road pierced through the center of the forest. Beyond it lay the black sea. Projecting out into the sea was the Balca Peninsula, otherwise known as the Howling Vilelands, the territory where the fiends and the Evil God lurked.

Adlet pointed at the root of the peninsula and said, "We're meeting up there, where the continent and the peninsula converge."

"*You* are," Fremy replied.

They couldn't see the full expansion of the region very well from their position. The land was covered in rugged hills dotted sparsely with forests and brush. Strangely, the entire peninsula was stained pitch-black.

"Wow, that color," said Adlet. "So that's the Evil God's poison, huh?"

The Howling Vilelands were filled with a unique toxin that the Evil God exuded from its body. It had no effect on any living thing other than humans, but if a human touched it, death was certain in about a day. There was only one way to neutralize the poison: to be chosen as one of the

Braves of the Six Flowers and receive the divine protection of the Spirit of Fate. As long as the Evil God's poison was present, only the six Braves were capable of approaching. If it weren't for that, there would be no need for the six of them to attack alone.

"So what will you do?" asked Fremy. "I don't want to encounter the other Braves."

Adlet pointed at the foot of the mountain and said, "I'm a little curious about that fort." There was a small stronghold there. It appeared partially destroyed, and there was smoke rising from it.

The two of them descended the mountain and arrived at the fort. It was damaged, but it seemed there were still people inside. Fremy pulled her hood over her head, hid the crest on her left hand, and stayed alert to her surroundings. Adlet found a soldier sitting in the archer's tower.

"If there are any Braves in there, I'm running," said Fremy.

"I understand." Adlet nodded, then called out to the soldier on watch duty. "Excuse me! Are any Braves of the Six Flowers in here?"

The soldier replied, "No, they came two days ago, but they've already set off! Who are you?"

Adlet exchanged looks with Fremy. It seemed okay for now to go in. "Adlet Mayer. I'm one of the Braves of the Six Flowers. This girl is…well, don't worry about it."

Although he looked puzzled, the soldier descended from the watch-tower and opened the gate. Adlet and Fremy entered the fort, and Adlet showed the soldier the crest that proved he was one of the six Braves.

"I am very glad to see you, Sir Brave," the soldier said. "There is something we absolutely must let you know. Could you please come this way?"

"What is it?" asked Adlet.

"It's very important. The success of your upcoming battle depends on it."

Adlet glanced at Fremy. It seemed she also intended to hear what the soldier had to say.

"Please come with me," invited the soldier. "Oh, I have yet to introduce myself. My name is Loren, private first class of the army of Gwenvaella. I am presently commanding officer at this fort."

"Commanding officer? You?" Adlet asked without thinking. From the soldier's manner, Adlet could tell he was quite capable. But he was of low rank, and his equipment was meager, too.

"Everyone is dead—the general, the captains," he explained. "The lower-ranking troops and I are all that remain. But there is something we must protect, down to the very last man."

Adlet and Fremy followed Private Loren into the fort. The smell of death hung heavy inside. Human corpses and the bodies of a few fiends littered the ground. The damage was graver than it had seemed from outside.

"This way." Private Loren beckoned. In the center of the floor, there stood a heavy iron door, which the soldier opened to reveal a basement. Apparently, the fort had been built in order to protect this. He led them into the basement. In this small room deep in the ground, there were five soldiers. And standing by itself in the center of the room was an altar of a shape Adlet had never seen before.

"Is this what you were protecting?" Adlet asked, pointing to the altar.

But Private Loren shook his head. "This is a replica of what we're here to protect. Please take a look at this map." A map of the Howling Vilelands and its environs sat on a table in front of the altar. "The king of Gwenvaella set up a certain mechanism to help the six Braves in preparation for the revival of the Evil God. That is what we are protecting." The soldier put his finger on the continent side of the map. "Presently, a swarm of fiends is advancing deeper into the continent, targeting the Braves of the Six Flowers. I believe you may have already encountered some. However, the moment they find out that the Braves have entered the Howling Vilelands, they will turn around and head back. Their goal is to exterminate the Braves of the Six Flowers. Nothing else matters to them."

"I see," said Adlet.

"And so, in the utmost secrecy, the king of Gwenvaella has constructed a mechanism to fence off the peninsula after the Braves of the

Six Flowers have entered the Howling Vilelands," the soldier said, pointing to the border between the Howling Vilelands and the continent. "With the help of three Saints—Fog, Illusion, and Salt—the king has readied a powerful barrier in order to prevent fiends from leaving or entering this forest. It is called the Phantasmal Barrier." There was a large circle drawn on the map near the entrance to the Howling Vilelands, indicating the range of the barrier.

Fiends were incapable of crossing the sea. The coast of the Howling Vilelands was incredibly rocky, so even if anyone attempted to set sail, they would have no place to dock a boat. Some fiends could fly, but they were few in number. Sealing off this circle would confine the majority of fiends within the area.

"It's an amazing plan," said Adlet. "So what's this barrier like?"

"It prevents entry and exit," explained Private Loren. "That is all the barrier is intended to do. When it is activated, the entire area within it will be enveloped in fog. Anyone trying to escape the fog will lose their sense of direction, and before they realize what they're doing, they will find themselves right back inside. Conversely, anyone trying to enter will end up exiting the way they came."

"I had no idea. This is quite something," said Adlet, and he glanced at Fremy. From the look on her face, she hadn't known about it, either.

"The barrier hasn't been deployed yet," the soldier said. "Once we have confirmed that all six Braves have entered the Howling Vilelands, we will activate it."

"How do you do that?" asked Adlet.

Private Loren pointed to a spot a short distance from the fort.

"Here, there is a temple built for the purpose of activating the barrier. The temple is surrounded by fortifications constructed by the Saint of Salt that protect it from fiends, so you don't have to worry about it being destroyed."

Hearing the soldier's description, Adlet was impressed. It was a superb plan.

Next, Private Loren indicated an area on the map near the Howling

Vilelands. "One of the Braves of the Six Flowers, Lady Mora, the Saint of Mountains, is waiting here. She visited this fort two days ago. We told her about the barrier then and discussed things."

One of the six Braves was waiting for them. When Fremy heard that, her expression grew somewhat grim.

"So?"

"The plan is that once all six Braves have gathered at that point, Lady Mora will send up a flare to signal us. When we see that flare, we will head to the temple and activate the barrier. If we are attacked by fiends and annihilated before the six Braves convene, then we will send up a flare instead."

"What for?"

"In that case, please send one of the Braves to the temple to complete our mission. After conferring with Lady Mora, we have concluded that is the best plan."

Adlet fell silent. From what Private Loren described, the person who activated the barrier would be unable to leave it. In other words, one of the six Braves would be isolated from the true battle. But Adlet felt there was value in activating this bafflement, even if it meant losing one of the Braves.

"Inside the temple, there is an altar just like this one. Please look," Private Loren prompted.

Adlet stood in front of the altar replica. It was a plain affair. There were a pedestal and a single decorative sword. To the left, there was a slate, and on the right, there was a book written in hieroglyphs.

"Activating the barrier is easy," said the soldier. "You just thrust the sword into the pedestal, put your hand on the slate, and say, *Fog, rise*."

"Roger," said Adlet. "I'll remember that. But activating the barrier is your job."

"I understand. We will carry out this mission, even if it means our lives."

Adlet extended his hand to Private Loren. The soldier smiled and accepted his handshake. The two grasped hands tightly.

*   *   *

Adlet and Fremy left the fort and headed toward the Howling Vilelands. It would take about three hours to reach the point where they were supposed to gather, and where Mora, the Saint of Mountains, was waiting.

"Well, we're in a pickle," said Adlet. Fremy had been silent ever since she'd heard their discussion at the fort about the barrier. "He said Mora is waiting at the entrance to the Howling Vilelands, and Nashetania may well be meeting up with her right now, too. It looks like it'll be difficult to enter the Howling Vilelands without being noticed by them."

"Don't talk to me. I'm thinking."

Adlet shrugged. "Hey, then why don't we just get together with the rest of the Braves for now? We can think about what we're gonna do after that."

"If that was supposed to be a joke, I'm not laughing. If we meet the other Braves, we'll end up trying to kill one another."

Adlet didn't believe things would come to that. They were a team, and there were only six of them. Whatever had happened in the past, they were supposed to forget all that for the time being and work together. Adlet planned to acknowledge every Brave as a comrade, no matter how villainous they might be, for the sake of defeating the Evil God.

"Of course, I don't intend to go down so easily," Fremy added.

"Don't worry. If you do end up fighting, I'll protect you." He meant it as a joke. He figured she'd say something like *Stop screwing with me* and reject his remark anyway.

But Fremy reacted a little unexpectedly. "Adlet, you..." He got the feeling this was the first time she had used his name. "You're a kind person, aren't you?"

Hearing that embarrassed him. Adlet blushed a little. *So she's finally stopped being so surly*, he thought, but then Fremy shot him a look that sent a chill running down his spine.

"Don't show me that kindness. It makes me want to kill you."

He was about to ask what she was talking about, but before the words could come out of his mouth, he shoved her away. He had sensed a murderous aura behind them. There was now a white blade sticking out from where Fremy had been. When Adlet turned, he saw Nashetania in the forest.

"Adlet, get away from her, please!" cried the princess.

Fremy rose to her feet, drawing her gun and firing in one smooth motion. Blades erupted from the ground to block her bullets, and then a tall knight in black armor emerged from the forest to charge Fremy. Adlet blocked his path, knocking aside the knight's spear with his sword.

"Wait! Stop! Don't attack her!" Adlet yelled.

But neither Nashetania nor the knight was listening. "She told you to move! Are you deaf?!" shouted the knight.

"What the hell are you guys doing?!" Adlet screamed back.

Nashetania pressed her attack on Fremy, who kept her gun trained on Nashetania while dodging the blades at her feet. Adlet blocked the knight, who was trying to attack Fremy from behind.

"Why are you so surprised? I told you if we met, we'd end up trying to kill one another," Fremy said scornfully.

Adlet had known that. But he'd also thought they would have a little more room for discussion.

"You're in the way, Adlet." The tall knight swung the handle of his spear around.

Why does he know my name? Adlet wondered, but he didn't have the time to dwell on it. He blocked the handle of the spear with his sword but was knocked back, sword and all. Even in midair, though, he managed to throw some sand into the knight's eyes. Fremy did not let the opportunity go to waste. She pointed the muzzle of her gun at the tall knight, but Adlet used his sword to flick a pebble at his companion, hitting her wrist.

The four of them moved in a dizzying round robin. Nashetania and the knight targeted Fremy, and Fremy mercilessly struck back. Adlet desperately tried to intercede and bring the fighting to a halt.

"Adlet! Why are you trying to stop us?" Nashetania yelled, clearly growing impatient.

Adlet yelled back at her even louder. "Everyone, stop! She's not our enemy! She's one of the Braves of the Six Flowers!"

"Huh? What did you just say?" asked Nashetania.

Fremy and Nashetania froze. The knight stood protectively in front of Nashetania. Adlet forced himself between the three of them. "Look at her left hand," he said. "She's one of the Braves. She's not our enemy."

Nashetania and the tall knight looked at Fremy. When they noticed the crest on her left hand, they gasped but did not lower their weapons. "J-just what is going on here, Goldof?" Nashetania demanded of the tall knight.

"I do not know. All I know for certain is that Fremy is our enemy," Goldof replied, pointing his spearhead at Fremy.

"Hey, you big lug. Are you the one who put this into her head? What the hell is this about?" Adlet accused.

Goldof just glared at the young man without replying to the questions. "So you're Adlet, huh? Just what were you doing, going off who-knows-where and abandoning the princess?"

"Answer my damn question. You're really pissing me off." Adlet and Goldof stared daggers at each other. Nashetania, standing behind Goldof, attempted to pacify him.

In an effort to mediate, Adlet spoke especially quietly and slowly. "First, listen. Nashetania, why are you attacking Fremy? She's one of us."

"No, she is *not*," insisted Nashetania. "Adlet, please get away from her."

"Please answer my question. I don't know what's going on right now."

"Adlet, you may not believe this, but…she's the one who's been killing potential Braves."

Adlet looked at Fremy. She was undaunted, her gun raised as she glared at the other woman.

"She's the killer? What are you talking about?" asked Adlet.

"Goldof is the one who informed me," Nashetania said. "It's trustworthy." Goldof gave a distinct nod.

"…Fremy." Adlet looked at his companion one more time. *It has to be a lie*, he thought.

But Fremy replied as if she had expected all of this. "It's true."

"Wh-what?" stuttered Adlet.

"I told you—I told you that if I explained why, we'd end up trying to kill each other." Fremy swiveled her gun from Nashetania toward Adlet.

"It can't be true," he said.

"It is. Matra Wichita, Houdelka Holly, Athlay Aran. I killed a number of others as well…those who seemed like they might be chosen as one of the six. Goldof and Nashetania over there were on my list of potential targets, too. I hadn't even considered you, though."

Adlet remembered what Nashetania had told him before. "What about Leura? Did you kill the Saint of Sun, too?"

Fremy looked vaguely confused. "The Saint of Sun, Leura? I don't know anything about that. Though she was on my list."

"That doesn't matter," said Nashetania. "Adlet, she's dangerous. Come over here, please."

But Adlet didn't take his eyes off Fremy. "What for? Why did you kill these potential Braves?"

"Isn't it obvious?" Fremy asked. "For the sake of the Evil God's resurrection. If I succeeded in slaying all the strongest warriors, then the chosen Braves would be nothing but weaklings."

Adlet was speechless.

His voice swollen with rage, Goldof broke the silence. "Now you know. This woman—Fremy is our enemy." Nashetania and Goldof split off in opposite directions, converging on Fremy from either side.

Adlet was frozen in place. Fremy was a murderer who had killed potential Braves while being at the same time a Brave who bore the Crest of the Six Flowers herself. If both were true, then which identity should he trust? That was when what Fremy had said popped into Adlet's head.

"No!" Adlet stood, shielding his companion.

"Adlet, why?" Nashetania pleaded.

Is this the best idea? Adlet worried. But Fremy had said that she couldn't afford to die until she killed the Evil God. He believed she'd been telling the truth. "Nashetania, Goldof, listen up," he said. "The Braves of the Six Flowers are not chosen purely on the basis of fighting ability. Will is also part of it—their desire to defeat the Evil God. Someone who wants to side with the enemy couldn't have been chosen as one of the Braves of the Six Flowers, no matter how powerful they were."

"But she—" began Nashetania.

"Fremy," said Adlet. "You're not trying to resurrect the Evil God right *now*, correct?" Fremy nodded, and he continued. "You have a reason *now*—a reason to fight the Evil God that you were trying to resurrect."

"Yes," Fremy admitted.

Adlet turned to Nashetania and spread his hands. "Do you get it, Nashetania? She *is* the one who has been killing potential Braves. But now the situation's changed."

"And you believe that?" asked Nashetania warily.

"I trust her. I can tell her desire to defeat the Evil God is real. Even if she was once the enemy of the Braves, right now, I know she's our ally."

"But—"

"If you're going to keep fighting, I'm siding with Fremy," he said.

Nashetania considered this for a moment, and then Goldof spoke. "Pardon me, but I must say this—Princess, is Adlet really someone we can rely on?"

"You've had it out for me this whole time. Just what is your deal?"

"I am here to protect the princess. Anyone who would expose the princess to danger is my enemy."

"Fine. Right now, though, just ask Nashetania to put away her sword."

"Adlet. Don't refer to the princess so informally." Goldof was clearly angry, but Nashetania restrained him.

"You two quarreling isn't going to get us anywhere. I understand, Adlet. If you're going to be so insistent about it, then I have no choice. Goldof, we will do as he says for now." Nashetania sheathed her sword, and Goldof also reluctantly lowered his weapon. Adlet breathed a sigh of relief. "But...please take care," she added. "You're the type who's easily deceived."

"It's okay," replied Adlet. "I'm the strongest man in the world. Nobody's gonna trick me."

"I'm *quite* uneasy about this," said Nashetania.

Adlet looked at Fremy. "You put away your gun now, too. You don't have to worry about getting killed anymore."

"For the time being." Fremy lowered her gun and then holstered it at her waist.

"Fremy," said Nashetania. "Just so you know, I do *not* trust you. I trust Adlet."

"You sure are naive for trusting a guy like that," Fremy replied.

Even after both Nashetania and Fremy had lowered their weapons, there was still an explosive atmosphere between them. And then there was Goldof, his eyes filled with animosity and fixed on Adlet.

Adlet felt intensely anxious. Would the Braves of the Six Flowers actually be capable of facing the Evil God in battle?

The four decided to start by heading together to the point where Mora awaited them. Since Fremy had agreed to go with them, Adlet returned the pack that he had stolen from her. They began making their way along the forest path. Nashetania and Goldof walked close together, and Adlet was a little farther away. Fremy maintained an even larger distance between herself and the others. Their positions indicated their relative affinities for one another.

"Hey, Fremy," Adlet prompted.

"What?"

"I saved your butt, so maybe you could give me a thank-you?"

"There's no reason for me to do that," Fremy said coldly. Adlet shrugged.

Then Nashetania whispered to him so as not to be overheard. "Adlet."

"What is it?" he asked, but the only reply she gave him was a cold look. "I'm sorry for abandoning you," he said. "But I had no choice. It's her fault for running away." Nashetania's eyes grew even colder as she glared at him. Adlet cringed.

"It seems you've gotten quite close to her in just a day," she commented.

"What's that supposed to mean?"

Nashetania put a hand to her mouth and smiled at him mischievously. What made it different this time was the genuine spite lurking in her eyes. "I was wondering why you would defend her. But now I see. So *that's* how things are, hmm? Indeed, she is *quite* a beautiful woman, after all. I really am envious."

"Hey…"

"Yes, yes, I understand very well indeed. Men are *so* very fond of women of that ilk, the type to inspire their *protective instincts.*"

"Listen, Nashetania…"

"Yes, yes, I hope you two get along *quite* splendidly. *Hmph.*" After heaping sarcasm on Adlet, Nashetania moved away from him.

"…Are you seriously a princess?" he wondered.

"I am often asked that, but yes, I am," said Nashetania, and then she turned the other way.

What the hell? Adlet couldn't help but silently wonder.

A heavy silence hung over the four of them. Fremy continued to completely ignore the rest. Goldof was eyeing Adlet as if quite grumpy about the other man talking to Nashetania. Just thinking about the atmosphere being like this the whole way until they met Mora put a cloud over Adlet's head. And for that matter, why was this Goldof guy scowling at him? He decided to try initiating a conversation.

"Hey. With all that kerfuffle, I wasn't able to introduce myself properly, but it was good to meet you. I'm the strongest man in the world, Adlet Mayer."

"Okay." There was clear disgust in Goldof's tone.

"I hear you were chasing after the Brave-killer…after Fremy."

"That's right."

"I get that you're not really happy about this, but just bear with it for now. At the very least, until we know more about what's going on," said Adlet.

"What are you talking about?" scoffed Goldof. "All I do is follow the princess's orders."

That's odd, thought Adlet. *It seems he's not angry about Fremy. So then, why does he hate me?* "I'm sorry about what I did at the tournament," Adlet said. "I injured your commanding officer. I've been wanting to apologize for that."

"It's not really something you need to apologize for."

It sounds like that's not the reason, either. So then, why? As Adlet mused, Goldof spoke to him—at a whisper, so as not to let Nashetania hear.

"Adlet...how did you butter up the princess?" he asked.

With that one line, it all made sense. Adlet looked at Nashetania and back at Goldof. *Well, then.* "What? You're worried about me being close to the princess?"

"I—I'm not worried about that...," he stammered.

"Relax, it's not what you think. If you worry yourself over stupid stuff like that, she's just gonna make fun of you."

Goldof choked. "What are you talking about? Don't be stupid."

Now this was an easy guy to understand. Goldof apparently just didn't like that Adlet was friends with Nashetania. He didn't look like it, but he was still just around sixteen and merely a kid on the inside. "Do your best and protect the princess," said Adlet. "I talked about a lot of stuff with her on the road. She really seems to rely on you. You're the only one who can protect her."

"Of course. Just me."

Spouting such blatant flattery set Adlet's teeth on edge, but Goldof's bad mood had apparently abated somewhat. His predictability would save Adlet trouble. Goldof was nothing like Fremy and Nashetania.

"There're no enemies coming to us, though, huh?" Goldof muttered.

Yeah, he's right, thought Adlet. It was too peaceful. Why were they able to continue this silly conversation even as they were coming upon the Howling Vilelands, where the demons lurked? Adlet was finding the peace more and more ominous.

That was when Fremy, who'd been silent the whole time, spoke. "This is strange." When the three of them turned, Fremy was facing back, looking up at the sky. "There have been flying fiends circling in the sky behind us for a while now."

Adlet pulled a spyglass from his chest pocket and looked in the direction Fremy had indicated. She was right—a few birdlike creatures were circling in the air.

"There aren't many of them. It can't be anything much," said Nashetania.

"Isn't that direction…?" Adlet eyeballed the distance of the demons and compared his visual measurements to his mental map. "This is bad. That's where the temple of the Phantasmal Barrier is."

Tension simmered among them. According to what Private Loren had said, the barrier was made so that fiends couldn't come near it, but even so, the situation was cause for concern. Adlet turned to Fremy. "Can you hit them from here?"

"It would be difficult. We have to get closer," she replied.

"They just dropped something," Goldof muttered. When Adlet looked, it seemed as if the fiends were spitting something from their mouths. Moments later, there was a thunderous roar and rising smoke.

"Adlet, what on earth was that?" asked Nashetania.

"Bombs. The fiends are dropping bombs on the temple," he said.

"Bombs? That's ridiculous!"

Adlet was surprised, too. Some fiends possessed intelligence, but he couldn't imagine they had the skill or raw materials necessary to make explosives.

Nashetania looked at Fremy and said, "You're the Saint of Gunpowder, aren't you? This isn't *your* doing, is it?"

"I don't know anything about it," Fremy insisted.

"Let's just go!" said Adlet.

The four of them ran back the way they'd come. If they ran as fast as they could, it would take about fifteen minutes to get there. But after about five minutes at a sprint, they encountered a line of fiends standing across the path, blocking their way. They'd seen no sign of any fiends when passing through the area earlier. These were clearly there for the express purpose of holding them up.

Nashetania yelled, "Let's break right through! Goldof!"

In response, Goldof crouched and then rushed at one of the fiends like a giant bullet. He thrust his spear out in a twisting motion, his entire body weight behind it. His target was a fiend that looked like a bear with the head of an insect. Even though his foe was nearly ten times his body mass, Goldof blasted the creature backward. He then tried to break through the opening he'd created, but a tiger-fiend that had been standing beside the bear-fiend screamed. It was difficult to make out what it said, but the creature was definitely speaking human language.

"*They...come. Sur...round...them!*"

The row of fiends attacked their closest target, Goldof, all at once.

He's too impatient, thought Adlet. *It's like he's begging them to overwhelm him.* These monsters were a cut above those they had destroyed earlier. They understood human speech and had the intellect necessary for a certain degree of strategy. They were mature fiends, those that had lived a number of years.

Goldof scattered the demons attacking him from either side. Nashetania defended his back and finished off the ones that fell. Adlet and Fremy were also surrounded. Adlet tossed the iron box off his back and engaged. The battle turned chaotic. At this rate, it would be impossible to break through the ring of enemies and escape toward their goal.

"Adlet, please head for the temple. We'll take over here!" Nashetania shouted as she blocked a wolf-fiend's attacks.

"Yeah, I got you," said Adlet. "Breaking through this kind of tough situation is just the job for me! Hey, Fremy, Goldof—watch this. *I'm* the strongest man in the world!"

"Stop bragging and just go!" ordered Nashetania.

He hadn't been merely fooling around, though—during his speech, he'd come up with a way to break through the line. "Nashetania, Goldof, Fremy!" he yelled. "Attack the fiends on the temple side as hard as you can!"

Nashetania and Goldof nodded. Fremy was expressionless, but she did seem to basically agree. Goldof sent one fiend flying with a thrust of his spear. Nashetania stabbed the one behind it with one of her blades, and Fremy's bullet tore through another that had been in front of Adlet.

"Perfect!" Adlet ran over the flat of Nashetania's summoned blade. When one final fiend attacked him, he used a poison blow dart to force it to withdraw. Adlet broke through the circle and pushed forward toward the temple.

"We're counting on you!" cried Nashetania.

"I'm on it!" Adlet called back. Without being told, Nashetania blocked any creatures that attempted pursuit. None were chasing him. It seemed as though his path was clear of ambush as well.

He ran at full speed for about ten minutes. The sounds of battle grew distant, and finally, the forest opened up so Adlet could see the temple. "This is it," he said, stopping to get a good look. The fiends that had been bombing it were already gone, but the smell of gunpowder remained thick in the air.

The temple was smaller than he had expected—about the size of an average house. But its stone walls were surprisingly sturdy. The entire building was surrounded by about twenty white pillars—probably the Saint of Salt's barricade to keep out fiends. Outside the ring of pillars, he could see footprints left by a great variety of demons, but not a single one within the ring. Apparently, the fiends were unable to pass between them.

Portions of the salt pillars were missing due to the bombing, and there were scorch marks on the temple, too. The building, though, was still firmly intact. *So no damage, huh?* thought Adlet. That was when he saw a woman lying on the ground beside one of the salt pillars.

"Hey, what's wrong?!" Adlet ran up to her. The woman was dressed in the garb of a priestess. Part of her back was terribly burned. "Hold on, I'll treat your wounds!" he said, and he lifted the woman into a sitting position. "Don't worry, they aren't deep!" He searched through the pouches at his waist for medicine.

"*Hur...ry...*," the woman said, pointing to the temple.

"Never mind that now! Don't move."

"*Hurry...now...you won't make it...please...it's all...*"

Adlet ground his teeth. As much as he might have wanted to treat her, he didn't have the medicine. *I should have brought my iron box*, he thought. Then he would have bandages and medicated gauze for burns.

"*I'll be okay…I am…a Saint, after all…*," she said.

"Don't you die on me!" he replied as he gently laid the woman on the ground, then passed through the pillars of salt to stand in front of the temple.

The doors were sealed with a sturdy lock. Adlet thrust his sword into the keyhole and twisted it forcefully, but the lock didn't budge. "Damn it, I didn't hear anything about the doors being locked! Do you have the key?!" he yelled to the woman, but she shook her head.

Adlet pulled some explosives from a pouch, affixed them to the lock with adhesive, and lit it. The lock blew off the door with a powerful bang, and two soldiers emerged from within. The soldiers both wore full body armor with spikes protruding. They charged Adlet.

"The hell are you guys doing?!" he wailed.

The soldiers went straight for him, but they weren't that fast. Adlet didn't even have to use his secret tools—he just whacked them on their heads with the hilt of his sword to take them down. But when their helmets fell off, he saw that the armor was empty.

"What the hell?" Adlet was about to ask the woman in priestess attire what was going on when she erupted into shrill laughter.

"*Hee-kee-kee-kee-kee-kee-kee!*" Prostrate on the earth, she contorted and cackled. Her body bent limply, a single horn grew from her forehead, and she transformed into a creature resembling a skinny, ugly monkey. Adlet knew—this was a transforming fiend. Adlet's master had told him that although very few fiends could disguise themselves as humans and animals, they did exist.

"You bastard!" Adlet cried. The transforming fiend immediately fled. Adlet was about to run after it, but he abruptly stopped himself. *Right now, I should prioritize checking the temple*, he realized, and he turned back toward the building. That was when it happened.

"…Huh?" Terror ran through him. The air around him suddenly

got colder, as if his entire body had been plunged into water. Mist slowly began rising from the ground—from his feet to his chest, from his chest to his head, and then, in a heartbeat, filling the whole area.

Adlet remembered what Private Loren had said. *When the barrier is activated, the entire area within it will be enveloped in fog.* His body began trembling. It sensed the crisis before his mind did. *Once the barrier is activated, you can no longer get inside.* Adlet entered the temple. He looked at the altar positioned in the central area of the tiny room. *And those inside can't escape, either. This affects both humans and fiends alike.* The barrier was activated by putting a hand on the slate imbued with divine power and thrusting the decorative sword into the pedestal. That was what Private Loren had told him.

And now Adlet saw…the sword was already in the pedestal.

"I didn't move it," he murmured. "Who did it?! Who activated the barrier?!" Adlet yelled, running out of the temple to scan the area. He blew his flute, the one that attracted fiends, and did a sweep with his telescope.

"Adlet!" came a voice. It wasn't long before Nashetania ran up to him, her face pale. Goldof and Fremy arrived soon after. "What happened?! Why has the barrier been activated?!" shouted Nashetania.

This was the first time Adlet had ever heard Nashetania lose her composure. Overcome by shock, Adlet replied, "No…it wasn't me. Someone activated the barrier and then disappeared instantly afterward."

"That can't be," she said.

"I'm not making it up," he insisted. "They disappeared. It was only an instant, and then they were gone."

Nashetania's lips were trembling. Goldof's eyes were wide. Even Fremy had lost the ability to speak. It couldn't be… Were they trapped here?

"Let's just go inside!" suggested Adlet. The four of them rushed into the temple.

As she gazed at the pedestal impaled with the decorative sword, the look on Nashetania's face said she had no idea what was going on. She put her hand on the sword, checked the slate and the pedestal, and then squeezed out, "The barrier has been activated. I can't believe this. Who did it?"

"I don't know. Sorry, but I have no idea what happened." Adlet shook his head.

"Well, let us deactivate it, then. Pardon," said Goldof as he approached the altar. He pulled the sword from the pedestal—but they could see no changes in the fog blanketing the area. "Will that not work? Your Highness, do you know how we might nullify the barrier?"

"No, I don't know, either," she replied. "There must be a way…"

That was where Adlet cut in. "Give me that for a second."

"Do you know something about this?" asked Nashetania.

"The previous generation of Braves made something like this before. Back then, I think they canceled out the barrier like this." Adlet ran his hand along the blade of the sword. Blood dripped down it and wet the pedestal. "Barrier, nullify!" he declared, but still, nothing happened.

Next, Nashetania grabbed the sword and yelled random lines one after another. "Nullify the barrier! Cancel it, you! You stop now! Stop the fog! I will be this barrier's master!" But still, the barrier did not lift. Finally, she became impatient and began bashing the pedestal and the slate with the hilt of the slim sword. The sword chipped, and the slate broke.

"Calm down, Nashetania. There's no point in randomly whacking at it," Fremy said coldly behind them. "Private Loren, who was at the fort, should be around here somewhere. Since there was that explosion earlier, he should be on the move."

"You're right. I—I'm sorry." Nashetania seemed ashamed.

"Goldof, you protect the temple. You, too, Fremy," ordered Adlet, and he and Nashetania left the temple to search for Private Loren.

They must have scouted for about thirty minutes. Adlet and Nashetania returned to the temple with nothing to show for their efforts. Had Private Loren and his men not come this way? Or had the fiends already killed them?

"What do we do?" asked Adlet. "Mora was ahead of us. At this rate, she'll end up all on her own."

"And more importantly, we cannot escape from here," replied Nashetania.

The four looked at one another as they tried to think of a way to break out, but none came up with any good ideas.

"What're you all fussing about?" That was when they heard a voice coming from outside the temple. A girl stood in front of the broken doors. She looked to be about thirteen or fourteen years old and quite strange, wearing a frilly, check-patterned dress and a jester's hat. In one hand, she held a green foxtail. A pouch and a water bottle hung diagonally across her chest. She looked like a child who'd gone on a picnic and gotten lost. "Oh, you're that big guy from before," she said when she saw Goldof. "Did you find that Brave-killer? And you, you're the princess of Piena, aren't you? So you were chosen as one of the six?" This time she was addressing Nashetania. Maybe she just didn't understand the situation—there was absolutely zero anxiety in her tone.

"Who're you?" Adlet asked.

The girl grinned. "Nice to meet you, weird belt guy. Chamo Rosso, Saint of Swamps. Chamo got chosen as one of the Braves of the Six Flowers." The girl—Chamo Rosso—lifted the hem of her skirt. The Crest of the Six Flowers marked her skinny thigh.

"The Saint of Swamps is a kid?" Adlet muttered.

Chamo Rosso, the Saint of Swamps.

Anyone who lived in the world of warriors would know that name. Adlet had heard her power far surpassed Nashetania's. She was said to be not only the most powerful person alive in the present day, but the strongest ever, aside from the Saint of the Single Flower. Adlet didn't really know exactly what kind of power she wielded, but he had never imagined she would be so young.

"Who're you?" Chamo asked Adlet.

"Me? I'm Adlet Mayer, the strongest man in the world. I was chosen as one of the Braves of the Six Flowers, just like you."

"'The strongest in the world'? Isn't that supposed to be Chamo?" she asked.

"Yeah," said Adlet, "I hear people generally call you that, but in actuality, you're not. I'm the strongest in the world."

"What are you talking about?" Chamo tilted her head.

Adlet's manner was jocular as he said, "I gotta apologize to you—I'm stealing your title of strongest in the world. Well, second in the world is still pretty amazing, so just be satisfied with that."

"...*Hweh*." Chamo made a weird sound, crossed her arms, and reflected. She pondered for a while and then clapped her hands. "Oh, Chamo gets it. This guy is brain-dead, isn't he?"

"He's a little strange, but he's reliable. Don't worry," Nashetania reassured, cutting in from the side.

That was when Adlet noticed how Fremy, who was behind them, was acting. Though she'd been expressionless this whole time, now she was suddenly pale. Her lips were trembling very slightly.

Chamo fixed her eyes on Fremy and said, "Long time, no see, Fremy. Why're you here?"

Adlet was about to ask, *Do you know her?* But Fremy was just cringing in terror.

"Well, Chamo can deal with you later. What the heck happened here?" Chamo made the foxtail in her hand sway as she gave an uncanny smile.

Adlet and Nashetania took turns filling her in on the details of what had happened up to this point. Chamo had not stopped by Private Loren's fort, but she seemed to know a little about the Phantasmal Barrier, though she said she didn't know how to nullify it.

As they spoke, Adlet occasionally looked over to check Fremy. She said nothing as she stood at the edge of the temple. Chamo made no move to approach Fremy, either. "*Hmm*, oh," said Chamo. "This is a bit of a problem."

What about this is just "a bit of a problem"? wondered Adlet.

"Well, whatever. For now, Chamo will just kill Fremy," she said, as if this were the obvious course of action. Reflexively, Fremy drew her gun.

"Wait!" Adlet immediately stepped between the two of them.

Chamo gave Adlet a puzzled look. "Why are you getting in the way?"

"No, what are *you* thinking?" he demanded. "I just explained this to you. Fremy is one of us."

"What a funny thing to say. You know she's the killer who's been after the Braves? She's the one who activated the barrier, too." Chamo touched the foxtail to her mouth.

Nashetania grabbed Chamo by the wrist. "Wait, please, Chamo. When the barrier was activated, Fremy was with us. She couldn't have activated the barrier."

"Oh, really? It doesn't matter anyway, so let go," Chamo replied.

"I won't."

Eyes brimming with quiet anger, Chamo glared at Nashetania. "Why're you ordering me around? Are you someone important? Are you some princess or something...?"

"Yes, in fact, I am."

"...Oh yeah, you are. What to do, then?" Chamo smiled wryly and shrugged.

"Chamo, did something happen between you and Fremy?" asked Adlet.

The one to reply was not the little girl, but Goldof, who had been watching in silence. "Chamo once fought with Fremy."

"What do you mean?" asked Adlet.

Chamo took over from Goldof. "It was about six months ago, maybe. She was trying to gun down Chamo. It was a close call, but Chamo's pet stopped Fremy at the last minute. She said she was Fremy, the Saint of Gunpowder. There was more fighting afterward, but she ran away. You know, it was the first time Chamo ever failed to finish off a target after deciding to kill them. It was so infuriating." Adlet could sense the bloodlust emanating from her body. "This whole time, Chamo's been thinking, *Fremy needs to die.* So, now she will, right?"

Adlet shook his head. Nashetania did not release Chamo's wrist, either. An air of unrest hung over them.

"Chamo, please hold on," said Nashetania. "First, we need to find a way to resolve this barrier problem."

"You and the big guy can do something about that, Princess," said Chamo. "While you're busy with that, Chamo will deal with Fremy."

"Nashetania is right," said Adlet. "There're five people here, so that means that someone named Mora, who got here ahead of us, is all on her own out there. We need to find a way to dispel the barrier first, for her sake, too."

As Adlet and Nashetania continued trying to convince Chamo to stop, a comment came from the temple entrance. "If you're concerned about me, you needn't be."

All present turned in the direction of the voice. A tall woman stood there. She looked to be in her late twenties and wore a serious expression, with powerful eyes. Long black hair flowed down her back, and she wore blue priestess robes. The large iron gauntlets on both her hands seemed to double as both weapon and armor. Just seeing her standing there, Adlet could tell she was strong. That was the kind of woman she was.

"What a long-awaited reunion, Princess Nashetania, Chamo," the woman said. "And that gentleman over there is Sir Goldof, I presume?" The woman walked to the center of the temple. "I am Mora Chester, Saint of Mountains. I serve as the elder of the All Heavens Temple. It's good to see you all."

Nashetania had continued holding Chamo's wrist, even after Mora's entrance. Mora stepped between the two of them, forcing Nashetania to let go. "It looks like you have some quarrel," said Mora. "Chamo, try not to act too selfishly."

"Auntie Mora, this wasn't Chamo's fault," protested Chamo.

"Oh? Well, you can say your piece later. For now, just settle down." Mora mediated between the two, and Chamo reluctantly stepped down.

Adlet was privately relieved to see such a reliable-looking person arrive on the scene. This meant that they had all six Braves now.

"Let's tackle the subject at hand. Why has the barrier been activated?" asked Mora.

"I think we've probably fallen into a trap set by our enemies," replied Nashetania.

"Most likely," Mora agreed. "The fiends have a knack for using our own weapons against us."

"Come on, it's no big deal," said Adlet. "Once we find a way to nullify the barrier, problem solved."

"Yes, that is indeed true. Now, boy, do you…" Then Mora looked around the area as if she had just noticed something. She considered the faces of each of the other five present in turn and said, "By the way, it seems we have an outsider in our midst. Who is it?"

Everyone aside from Mora looked confused. "Wait, what do you mean?" asked Adlet.

"What do *you* mean? We have one person too many," she replied.

What are you talking about? thought Adlet, when another voice came from the temple entrance.

"*Meow?* Looks like we've got quite the crowd here. Does this mean we've got a full set?" A strange man entered the temple. His eyes were hidden by disheveled hair, and he looked a little dirty. Adlet couldn't quite tell how old he was. He wore shabby hempen pants with a shirt and soft leather shoes. Except for the pair of hatchet-like swords belted at his waist, his dress was utterly commonplace. There was also a cat's tail attached to his rear—perhaps as a joke. The man looked around the temple with a mocking smile on his face. "*Meow-hee-hee*, there's a lotta pretty ladies in this set o' Braves. Suddenly, I'm actually getting into this."

"Who are you?" Nashetania asked.

Mora replied in the man's place. "Let me introduce you—though I only met him just yesterday. This is Hans Humpty, another Brave of the Six Flowers."

What? Adlet was befuddled. *We already have all the Braves right here.*

"It seems that we have an outsider tagging along. Who of the seven here is not a Brave?" asked Mora.

Adlet was entirely unable to reply. All he understood was that this was a preposterously abnormal situation. Nashetania and Goldof were both standing there, stunned. Even expressionless Fremy and unflappable Chamo were caught off-balance.

"All of you, show your crests," said Adlet as he thrust out his right hand marked with the Crest of the Six Flowers. Fremy showed everyone the back of her left hand. Nashetania pulled down her breastplate to reveal the crest near her collarbone. Chamo rolled up her skirt to show the crest on her thigh.

"Wh-what are you doing?" Mora sounded confused.

"Goldof, what about you?" asked Adlet. "I haven't seen yours."

Goldof removed the pauldron from his right shoulder and rolled up his sleeve. There indeed, on his shoulder, was the Crest of the Six Flowers.

Seeing the five crests exposed, Mora and Hans quickly caught on. Both of their faces froze.

"Mora, Hans, please show us your crests, too," said Nashetania.

"H-hey, just what the *meow* is goin' on?" Hans took off his jacket to reveal his full upper body. The Crest of the Six Flowers was indeed there on the left side of his chest, over his heart.

"Mora, your crest," said Nashetania.

"Impossible," Mora refuted. "What is this? Just what on earth is going on?"

All eyes gathered on Mora. She unbuttoned her priestess robes, turned her back to them, and pulled the cloth off one shoulder. In the center of her back, between her shoulder blades, was what was clearly the Crest of the Six Flowers.

"There are…seven?" Nashetania murmured in shock.

Bewildered, Mora cried, "Check more closely! This is impossible! There can*not* be seven Braves!"

The seven of them checked one another's crests. There were multiple rounds of inspection to see if there was any variance in size or shape or difference in the faintly shining pink coloration. But every one of the crests was absolutely identical. All seven were speechless. None of them could understand what was going on.

"Is it possible for seven Braves to be chosen?" Adlet murmured.

"Boy," replied Mora, "long ago, the Saint of the Single Flower divided her power into six and left it for future generations. Each Brave inherits one of those fragments of her power. That is why there can be only six Braves."

"So in other words, what?" he asked.

"There are six Braves. Any more or any less would not be within the realm of possibility," she replied.

"But there are seven, right here." This time, it was Fremy who spoke.

"Yes, we have seven. What is the meaning of this?" Mora asked. But no one could answer.

After a pause, suddenly the temple echoed with laughter. *"Meow-ha-ha-ha!"* The source was the strange man who had appeared last in the temple, Hans.

"What's so funny?" asked Adlet.

"Listen. It's not that hard to figure meowt. Basically, it means one of us is a fake. Get it?" Hans declared without hesitation.

"Come on, why would there be a fake here?" Adlet asked.

"Because one of us is the enemy. You understand?" replied Hans.

Adlet was silent. That wasn't necessarily the case.

"Is it possible…that the Spirit of Fate thought six would not be enough, and so an extra was made…?" Nashetania posited, not sounding very confident.

"If the Spirit did that, then wouldn't we have been told?" countered Hans. "Not that I know if the Spirit o' Fate can even talk." Adlet knew that Hans's explanation was the most rational one. "There's a fake among us, and they're not sayin' who they are," Hans continued. "If the fake ain't our enemy, then who are they? If you can think of any other reasons there'd be an extra, I'm *all* ears." As Hans spoke, he looked over each of their faces. There was cold sweat breaking out on his, too.

Everyone scrutinized everyone else. Like Adlet and Hans, every one of their faces revealed confusion and fear. There was an enemy among them, but they couldn't tell who it was just by looking.

I could burst out laughing, reveled the traitor. Making a concerted effort to act confused, the impostor gloried in the reactions of the six Braves.

The plan had succeeded. Everything was proceeding perfectly, just as expected. The mole had obtained a fake crest and infiltrated the Braves of the Six Flowers. The Braves had been lured into the barrier and then sealed up inside. Every scheme had played out according to plan. It had all been so very easy, it was actually scary.

Now, all that remained was to lay low while picking off the six Braves, one by one. That promised to be a very easy job.

The first target—Adlet Mayer. He would be the first to die.

Chapter 3

A Trap
and
a Rout

An hour had passed since the seven Braves had first gathered in the temple, and Adlet was running through the forest. If his mental map was accurate, then the edge of the Phantasmal Barrier was close by.

"So what's this Phantasmal Barrier thing? I'll be laughin' if we can get meowt of this thing, all easy-like." Hans, whom Adlet had only just met, was running alongside him. Adlet eyed the other man suspiciously. Not that Adlet was in any position to talk, but Hans seemed like a pretty fishy guy.

As they ran, Adlet marked trees they passed. After a while, they found trees ahead of them bearing the marks they had just left. Without even realizing, they had gotten turned around.

"The barrier really is up," said Adlet.

"Just like we thought," replied Hans.

The two of them made one more attempt to escape the fog, but the results were the same. They tried drawing a line at their feet as they walked or throwing a string in front of them and then tracing its path, but they still couldn't get out. There was one thing they did manage to figure out, however. They only lost their sense of direction when they attempted to exit the barrier. As long as they stayed inside the field, they would not get lost.

"So we have no choice but to deactivate the barrier, after all." Adlet sighed.

The group had agreed to focus on dealing with the barrier for the time being. That problem was more urgent than figuring out which of them was the impostor. Adlet and Hans were testing the barrier's boundaries while the remaining five searched the temple for a way to take it down.

"I'm gonna go back to the temple," announced Hans. Adlet nodded, and they set off again. "Hey," said Hans as they ran. "So are you the fella who went and barged into the Tournament Before the Divine in Piena?"

"Yeah. You knew about that?"

"Everyone's talkin' ameowt it. *Adlet, the cowardly warrior.* Is it true ya took old man Batoal's granddaughter hostage?"

"Where'd that come from?" Adlet hadn't taken any hostages. They had no reason to be calling him "the cowardly warrior" in the first place. "By the way, Hans, I've never heard your name before. What have you been doing, and where?" he asked. Aside from Hans, the seven people gathered together here were all famous. Nashetania was a well-known personage, of course, and Mora and Chamo, too, and Goldof. Fremy was famous, too, in a way, as the Brave-killer. This Hans guy was the only total unknown.

"Well, tellin' ya would only cause me problems," said Hans.

"What do you mean?"

Hans only smirked in reply.

When Adlet and Hans returned to the temple, the other five awaited them inside. Nashetania, Mora, and Chamo were all gathered around the altar. A little ways away were Goldof and Fremy. Fremy was bound by the wrists. Goldof gripped her chains as he guarded her, observing her every move. Mora carried her pack and gun. Fremy was utterly at their mercy.

Of course Fremy was the first to fall under suspicion. Chamo had insisted that they kill her right away. After discussing it among all six of them, they'd decided that, for the time being, they should keep her restrained. In chains, Fremy gazed at the altar vacantly. There was something resigned about her expression.

"So how'd it go, Mora?" asked Hans. Apparently, Mora was the most knowledgeable among them when it came to the hieroglyphs, the language of Saints, and barriers that amplified Saints' power.

"Well, we have figured out matters, to a certain extent. But before I speak about that, I suggest we introduce ourselves. I still have not matched names to faces."

"*Meow*, you've got a bad memory," Hans chided, laughing.

"As you all introduce yourselves, give us a brief personal history and explain how you came to arrive here," Mora continued.

"Why?" Hans inquired.

"The information may prove useful in exposing the impostor...the seventh," she explained.

They all gathered around the altar. Goldof shoved Fremy's shoulders, pushing her into the circle.

"Now then, who will begin?" asked Mora. At some point, she had assumed the role of their leader, and everyone else had accepted it quite naturally. She was a woman endowed with composure and dignity.

"I'll do it. My name's Adlet Mayer, and I'm the strongest man in the world." Adlet started off the introductions, giving them an abridged history of himself and talking about how he had met Nashetania and then Fremy, and then the sequence of events leading up to his arrival at the temple. Of course, he repeated many times over that he was the strongest man in the world.

Once his story was done, Mora was the first to respond. "Er...Adlet, was it? What a strange man to have been chosen." She shrugged.

"Yer the strongest man in the world? *Meow-ha-ha-ha!* What an idiot. What a complete moron." Hans laughed raucously.

Adlet ignored him. "I was the closest when the barrier was activated. Should I talk about that, too?"

"No, you may tell us about that in detail later," said Mora. "Who's next?"

Beside Adlet, Nashetania raised her hand.

"*Meow*, I wanna hear some details from this bunny girl," said Hans. "And preferably alone..."

"*Hans*, is that your name?" Goldof cut in. "Know your place. This is the crown princess of the royal family of Piena. Under normal circumstances, you would never be permitted to speak to someone of her stature."

"*Meow?* She's a bunny girl and a princess, too? That just makes me even more interested."

"May I speak?" groused Nashetania, looking annoyed.

Her description of the events leading up to her arrival at the temple was not so different from Adlet's. What was news to Adlet was that after the two of them had been separated, she had immediately encountered Goldof. That had been right after Adlet and Fremy left, around the time the two of them had been at the fort speaking with Private Loren about the Phantasmal Barrier.

Next, Goldof told his story. He spoke of tracking the Brave-killer and how, when he had been marked with the Crest of the Six Flowers, he had been alone in the Land of Holy Rivers. Goldof also recounted his reunion with Nashetania. That part Adlet already knew.

Next was Mora. "My name is Mora Chester. I am the Saint of Mountains and the current elder of the All Heavens Temple."

"The All Heavens Temple?" Adlet interjected. He'd heard that name before but didn't know anything about it.

Nashetania filled him in. "The All Heavens Temple is the organization that supervises us Saints."

"Yes," said Mora. "Though we are not terribly active as an organization. We merely observe the Saints to ensure that their powers are not used for evil. In any case, I have memorized the faces, names, and abilities of all seventy-eight Saints."

"When people like Chamo get our power as Saints, we have to go see Auntie Mora," said Chamo.

"However, I knew nothing of Fremy over there," Mora commented. "The Saint of Gunpowder, you say? I have heard naught of such an individual. I would hazard that she is a new Saint."

"Is it possible for there to be a new Saint?" asked Adlet.

"It is not unheard of, though it has not occurred this past century. Let us get back to the topic at hand." Mora continued, "It was about ten years ago that I took over the role of elder of the All Heavens Temple from the previous elder, Leura, Saint of Sun."

Leura. Adlet had heard that name multiple times throughout the course of his journey. She controlled the light and heat of the sun and had the power to burn down whole castles. They said that, though she was old, her powers over the sun had not waned one bit. But still, her body was frail, and she could not move from her easy chair. And then, about a month earlier, she had disappeared.

"I believe I have fulfilled my duties for the past ten years without serious error," continued Mora. "Though keeping Chamo from getting out of control has been a trial."

"I think you've been doing a wonderful job," said Nashetania. "My father said that no Saint could commit evil deeds as long as you're around."

"The king of Piena said that? An honor." Mora nodded in satisfaction. "When the Evil God awoke, I was in the Land of Crimson Peaks. I departed immediately for the Howling Vilelands, and two days ago, I arrived at the place where we would gather. At the fort, Private Loren told me of the Phantasmal Barrier, and on the very same day, I resolved on my course of action. I concealed myself and waited alone, until yesterday, when Hans came wandering by. Not long after that, I saw explosions occurring from the direction of the temple, and I hurried here."

"You didn't know about the Phantasmal Barrier until two days ago? Isn't it your job to govern the Saints?" asked Adlet.

"I knew of its existence, but no more than that," she said. "I first learned how to activate it and the location of this temple two days ago, from Private Loren. Had I known this would happen, I would have had a proper discussion with Uspa of Fog and Adrea of Illusion."

The names probably belonged to the Saints who had created the bafflement. *So, Mora's acquainted with the people who made the barrier. I'll remember that*, thought Adlet.

"Now then—next, Chamo," instructed Mora.

Chamo nodded. "Sooo, Chamo became the Saint of Swamps at around seven years old, which was seven years ago. Chamo's a little too powerful, so Auntie Mora always gets mad. A long time ago, in the martial tournament in the Land of Golden Fruit, a guy died in the first round, and all the other competitors bailed out of the competition."

Adlet knew that story, too. It was a well-known anecdote used to describe how powerful she was.

"So anyway, getting here was nothing special, really," she continued. "When the Evil God woke up, everything was normal at home. Mom and Dad helped pack. Then Chamo got a map and headed out for the Howling Vilelands. Traveling here didn't take long, but Chamo got lost and ended up coming late. While walking along, killing fiends and stuff, Chamo noticed something was going on and went to the temple and saw Fremy there. It was so surprising! And that's about it." Chamo finished her story.

Goldof added some supplemental details for Mora and Hans. He told them that in the past, Chamo had fought with Fremy, and that Fremy was the Brave-killer.

"*Meow*. So she's the Brave-killer. I can't believe it." Hans sounded doubtful.

"She admitted it herself. It's the truth," replied Goldof.

It seemed as though Hans was preoccupied with some thoughts on the matter, but he wasn't sharing.

"We shall ask Fremy to tell her story later. Next, Hans," Mora prompted.

"All righty," Hans began.

Adlet figured he should pay close attention. Hans's entire image—his appearance, his mannerisms, his nonchalant demeanor—made him the most suspicious of all, though Adlet didn't want to judge too quickly.

"My name is Hans Humpty. I'm from...well, it don't meowter. I'm an assassin."

"Assassin?" Nashetania cocked her head.

"Your Highness, an assassin is someone who kills for money. Someone whose occupation is to murder people."

Goldof's explanation surprised Nashetania. It seemed she had never heard of assassins before. "A man like that is one of the Braves of the Six Flowers?" she exclaimed.

"*Meow?* Somethin' wrong with an assassin bein' a Brave?" Hans scoffed at Nashetania's naïveté. "My job history has got nothin' to do with bein' chosen as a Brave. If you can defeat the Evil God, then yer chosen to be a Brave, assassin or not. Ain't that right?"

"Y-yes, but…"

"Princess, the world ain't as righteous as ya think. A lot of notable people from yer kingdom come to meow with requests."

"That can't be!" Nashetania sounded scandalized.

"Well, none of this goin' on about assassins meowters. I'm continuin' my story. *Meow?*"

Adlet nodded. He felt bad for Nashetania, but this assassin business was a separate issue.

"When I was chosen, I was pretty close to the Howlin' Vilelands," Hans continued. "First, I got meowself an audience with the king of this country and negotiated pay for killin' the Evil God. The king's a pretty generous fellow. He offered a big chunka cash in advance. So then I hid the money and came out here to the Howlin' Vilelands, and that's when I ran into Mora."

"You negotiated pay? Before fighting?" asked Adlet.

"I don't kill nothin' unless I'm gettin' paid for it. You folks ain't doin' this for free, are ya?"

Adlet had never even considered getting paid for defeating the Evil God.

"So you didn't know about the barrier?" asked Goldof.

"*Meow?* The king said somethin' about the fort, I guess. Well, I figured that stuff had nothin' to do with me, so I ignored it. I first heard about the barrier from Mora."

That's a little weird, thought Adlet. *It'd be important to know about the barrier, wouldn't it?* He didn't find Hans's explanation for meeting up with Mora without going to the fort convincing. For the time being, though, he decided to keep his doubts to himself and hear Hans out.

"I got nothin' to say about what happened after that. I saw there was an explosion, so I came to the temple," he finished.

Then Chamo asked what Adlet had been wondering this whole time. "Hey, why do you talk like that?"

"*Ma-meow!* So you've been payin' attention," Hans said, stroking his head with a fist just like a cat. Then he did an aerial somersault and said, "My style o' combat is based on cats. I came up with my techniques by imitatin' how they move. I guess you could say that cats were my meowsters. As a sign o' respect, I make a habit of imitatin' them in how I talk, too."

"This set of Braves is a strange lot," Mora grumbled.

"No kidding." Adlet nodded.

"Look who's talkin', Mr. Dumbest-in-the-world," said Hans, laughing.

Now that Hans's story was over, eyes gathered on their final member. Having been chained up by Goldof, Fremy had been listening in silence as the others talked.

"So then…Fremy, is it?" asked Mora. "You won't get away with saying you don't want to speak. If you hold back, know that it will worsen your position."

"How could it get any worse than this?" Fremy spat, and then she fell silent. The silence persisted for short while, but eventually, she slowly began speaking. "I'm the child of a fiend and a human."

All present, aside from Chamo and Goldof, gasped.

"Goldof, remove my eye patch and the cloth from my head," she said.

Goldof complied, exposing Fremy's bright-pink right eye. In the center of her forehead, there was a mark left by the horn that was proof she was a fiend. It had been broken off at the root, though, and all that remained was a scar.

"Oh yeah, your horn's gone. Did you break it off yourself?" asked Chamo.

Fremy did not reply, relating her history instead. "About twenty years ago, a band of fiends left the Howling Vilelands to infiltrate the human realm. They decided to create a pawn to oppose the Braves of the Six Flowers in preparation for the revival of the Evil God. That was me."

"…"

"My father was human. I never knew his face. Once my mother

conceived, she killed him. I was born from a fiend mother and raised as one of them. My mother and the other fiends abducted large numbers of humans and forced them to construct a new temple for the worship of the Spirit of Gunpowder. That was where I got my power as the Saint of Gunpowder."

"So…," commented Mora.

"I lived up to my mother's expectations and became a powerful warrior," Fremy continued. "And then I went around killing powerful humans on my mother's orders. It was for the sake of the revival of the Evil God. I felt no remorse. Though half human, I thought of myself as a full-fledged fiend. I believed the Evil God was a great being that would protect and guide us."

"So then, why are you here? Why have you decided to defeat the Evil God?" asked Mora. The answer to that question was the crux of her story.

"Even if I were to tell you, I doubt you'd believe me."

"If you don't speak, we can neither believe nor disbelieve."

Mora and Fremy glared at each other, and then Chamo cut in. "She doesn't have to say anything. Chamo's gonna kill her anyway. It's all true, right? We know the impostor is Fremy."

"Don't, Chamo. We don't know that," said Adlet.

Chamo gave Adlet an innocent look, but there was muted anger behind her eyes. "What's your name again? You're a pain in the butt. Didn't your mom ever tell you that you don't tell Chamo what to do?"

"Whatever, who cares?" said Adlet.

"You should. You can't talk back to Chamo," she snapped.

"Chamo! Listen to Fremy's story now!" Mora scolded the girl, and Chamo obeyed. Adlet was grateful for Mora's presence. He didn't even want to consider what would be happening if she weren't around.

"Please tell us, Fremy. Why did you end up opposing the Evil God?" asked Nashetania.

But Fremy just gave them all a cold stare. "You heard Chamo. She said I don't have to tell you anything. I don't want to talk about it, either." With that, Fremy shut her mouth entirely. Even when Adlet asked her to speak, she wouldn't meet his eyes.

Ultimately, Mora seemingly grew impatient and changed the subject. "Wasting our time any further on self-introductions is meaningless. The more important matter at hand is how are we to escape from here?"

Adlet wanted to protest and insist that the conversation wasn't over, but he dropped it. Mora's plan was more constructive.

"I have already spoken of this with Goldof and Fremy, but Chamo, Nashetania, and I have investigated the construction of this barrier," Mora explained. Adlet and Hans nodded. While the two of them had been checking out the borders of the barrier, Mora and the others had been deciphering the book on the altar written in hieroglyphs. "Getting to the crux of the matter: There were no methods of deactivating this barrier recorded in the text. There is a possibility that a method exists, but at this point in time, we know it not."

"*Meow*, what a disaster," Hans muttered.

"However, there are still two ways to do it," said Mora. "First, the one who activated the barrier should also be capable of deactivating it. Alternately, if the one who activated it were to die, the fog would be lifted."

"And you're certain of that?" asked Adlet.

"Ninety-nine percent sure. Theoretically speaking, a barrier that can't be deactivated even by the person who initiated it simply cannot exist. A barrier that remains operational even after the activator is dead would also be impossible."

"I see." Adlet remembered what had happened when the barrier had first been activated. The moment the doors opened, the armored soldiers had attacked him, and then the fiend behind him had let loose that shrill laugh. Someone had activated the barrier during that interval and then run away. But who on earth had done it, and how? Grasping desperately for clues or ideas, Adlet threw questions at Mora. "Is the person who activated the barrier still here inside it?"

"Yes," she answered. "Whether human or fiend, we are all completely unable to escape the fog. That holds true even for the one who activated it."

"Would it be possible to activate the barrier from outside the temple?"

"No."

"Can the barrier be activated only by a human?"

Mora reflected for a moment before replying. "Yes. A fiend should not be able to operate a barrier created by a Saint."

"In other words...this means there's a human allied with the Evil God," reasoned Adlet.

Mora shook her head firmly. "I cannot imagine someone like that could exist. If the Evil God were to be completely revived, it could well signal the extinction of the human race. No human would do that, whatever their reasons might be."

"There's one here among us, at the very least," said Adlet.

"That's why Chamo's been saying it's Fremy. Why can't you guys get that?" Chamo whined, exasperated.

"We don't know that for sure. I believe Fremy is one of us," said Adlet.

"But I cannot imagine any other human would ally with the Evil God." Mora tilted her head.

"They exist," Adlet insisted. "Fiends abduct groups of people and threaten them into cooperating. Not everyone can refuse them under threat of force. Make no mistake, there are humans who will follow fiends' orders."

"I understand, Adlet. Then this means we cannot let our guard down," said Mora.

That was when Fremy spoke. "You know...," she began. All present turned to her in surprise. "You've explained a lot so far. But is what you say really correct?"

Mora glared at her. "I do not speak based on speculation. All of this is most certainly accurate."

"That's not what I mean. Sorry, but you have no proof that you're actually one of us."

"..."

"I'm not the impostor," said Fremy. "I'm not the seventh. The seventh is one of you. From my perspective, you're just another suspect, Mora. You said if you kill the person who activated the barrier, the barrier will be lifted, and that a fiend can't trigger the barrier...but I have no guarantee that what you say is true."

Mora faltered. Adlet was taken by surprise. Mora's background was so solid, he hadn't suspected her. But Fremy was right—there was no guarantee that Mora's assertions held up.

"Fremy, I think Mora is telling the truth," said Nashetania.

"Yeah, Chamo thinks so, too," agreed the young Saint.

"Oh? But you can't forget that one among us is the enemy," countered Fremy. "One of us is lying."

"You're the most suspicious among us right now, Fremy," said Nashetania.

"I'm not the seventh. That's all I can say right now."

"Then who do you believe is the seventh?" Goldof asked. Fremy didn't reply.

Gradually, the terrifying fact that an impostor stood among them began sinking in. One of them was an enemy; one of them was lying. They had to suspect everything, even the slightest remark. Conversely, if Adlet said something careless, he could become suspect as well. He had to be careful in order not to be deceived, not to be suspected, and not to mistake the truth for a lie.

That was when Chamo cut into the conversation. "Come on, this is getting to be way too much trouble. We just need to kill Fremy and get it over with, right?"

"That again?" Adlet was starting to get seriously pissed at Chamo, even if she was just a kid.

"It's like Chamo keeps saying over and over," she stressed, "there's no one it could be but Fremy. She was obviously the one who turned on the barrier, too. Could you break her neck for us, big guy?"

Goldof shook his head. "Chamo, when the barrier was activated, Fremy was right there beside the princess and me. Even if she is the impostor, she couldn't have triggered the barrier."

"Oh. Then let's torture the answers out of her. It'll be new territory, but Chamo will try hard," said the girl, and she put her foxtail to her lips.

Chills instantly shot down Adlet's spine. He didn't know what she would use that foxtail for, but he knew it would be absolutely terrifying. "Wait! Stop!" Adlet yelled, putting his hand on the sword at his waist.

"T-torture? You can't do that! Goldof, stop Chamo!" Nashetania ordered.

Goldof seemed hesitant. "Your Highness, I believe that we have no other choice. It is for your protection. Adlet, escort Her Highness outside."

"Goldof! How can you say that?!" Nashetania sounded extremely distressed.

Chamo slowly closed on Fremy. Mora seemed torn on the matter as well, but she made no move to stop the younger Saint. Nashetania could do nothing but panic.

The moment Adlet thought he would have no choice but to fight, an unexpected voice called for restraint.

"Don't bother. I don't reckon Fremy's the seventh." It was Hans.

Chamo, surprised, moved the foxtail away from her lips. "What're you talking about, catboy?"

"I'm just sayin', Fremy is *too* suspicious."

"That's not a reason," said Chamo.

"*Meow.* Then I'll explain it proper. If Fremy's the seventh, then why is Adlet alive?"

"?" Chamo looked doubtful.

"If Fremy's our impostor, it's weird for her not to have killed Adlet by now. And the princess was with 'em, too—Fremy coulda killed 'em both at the same time. From what we've heard, I think she woulda had any number of meowportunities."

"Well…" Chamo hesitated.

"All seven of us gatherin' here would be the worst possible situation Fremy could be in," continued Hans. "Once all the Braves come together in one spot, it's clear that there's a fake. And hearin' her name and seein' her face, we already know she's the Brave-killer. She would expect to be tortured and killed, ya know?"

"Yeah," agreed Chamo.

"She'd want to avoid all of us gettin' together, whatever it took. But she just casually followed along with you folks, just like Adlet wanted her to. If Fremy were the seventh, what'd be the point in that?"

"You have a point," said Mora. "That's rather too many inconsistencies in her behavior for her to be our enemy."

"Yes...maybe you're right." Nashetania concurred.

Adlet was relieved to have received such unexpected aid.

"But that does not change the fact that Fremy is the most suspicious among us," said Mora.

"Well, that's true," agreed Hans. "But if she was plannin' to trick us, I think she woulda done somethin' of a better job."

Chamo gazed sadly at her foxtail. "Hey, so is Chamo not allowed to torture her?"

"*Meow*. Not yet."

"This is the first time ever that so many people have talked back to Chamo." Chamo sank into despondency. They had, for the time being, avoided the immediate crisis.

"So then, what should we do now?" asked Mora, sounding weary now that the fuss over possible torture had died down. This discussion had been going on for quite some time, but they had largely made no progress.

Suddenly, Nashetania hunched over, pressing her forehead.

"Your Highness!" Goldof released Fremy and ran toward Nashetania. Hans immediately grabbed Fremy's chains instead.

"I'm okay... I just felt a little dizzy," said Nashetania as she tried to stand.

"Sit down. Don't push yourself," advised Adlet.

"All right." Still pressing her forehead, Nashetania knelt. Goldof drew close to her, propping her up. She looked pale. She must have been terribly exhausted. She had not displayed such fragility before, not even the first time she'd engaged with fiends. She was an excellent warrior. But she had been raised without wanting for anything, after all, so she was mentally weak. One of her comrades was the enemy, and the situation was too much to bear.

"Well, there's no helping it. We will take a brief break," Mora said, shoulders sagging. Though this was no time to be taking a breather, each of them got some rest.

Adlet decided to leave Nashetania to Goldof. When he stood, Mora beckoned him over. Adlet and Mora moved to a corner of the temple. "What is it, Mora?" he asked.

"Nothing terribly important," she said. "I merely felt that you seemed like the easiest person with whom to speak."

"Of course. 'Cause I'm the strongest man in the world."

"The fact that you're the easiest person to talk to here points to a difficult future." Mora let out a small sigh. "Why are you so sure that Fremy is not the seventh?"

"I've got nothing to back it up," he admitted. "It's just, when we were together, her feelings got through to me."

"It's been half a day at most."

"Yeah, but when something gets through, it gets through."

"Your rationale is quite vague."

"When we first met, I made up my mind to trust her," Adlet said.

Mora gave him a deeply troubled look. "You're too young. There is danger in youth that knows no suspicion."

"Thanks for the advice. But my opinion isn't gonna change."

"I feel a little uneasy about this. You and the other Braves gathered here now are all so young. Chamo and Goldof are still at an age most would call children. Maybe the Spirit of Fate has made an error in judgment."

It was true. Adlet and Nashetania were still eighteen. Fremy and Hans were of unknown age, but they didn't look to be much older or younger than Adlet. "Strength isn't measured in years alone," said Adlet. "Young people have the strength of youth."

"I hope so."

"It'll make you feel better to think like I do. If you're pessimistic, you'll make even winnable battles impossible."

"I see. I suppose being able to think that way is another privilege of youth." Mora smiled.

But Adlet figured that Mora still counted as pretty young by most standards. Setting aside her slightly weird, old-fashioned manner of speech, just how old was she?

"Do not speculate on a woman's age, foolish boy," she said.

Sharp. Adlet smiled wryly.

Then Nashetania stood. The energy had returned to her face, and fighting spirit burned in her eyes. "I've calmed down. I apologize for being such a burden, everyone."

The seven of them, having scattered about in various directions, now gathered once more around the altar. Goldof took over guard duty from Hans and watched Fremy.

"Let us go outside," said Mora. "We must pursue the person who activated the barrier. First, we will search for clues. Adlet, explain the situation when the barrier was activated, in as much detail as possible," she prompted, and the group left the temple.

As Adlet began walking out, Nashetania grabbed his hand. "What's wrong, Nashetania?" he asked.

"Um, please don't think of me as an unreliable person," she said. "I was just a little startled."

"I get it. It's not like you to be timid—it's more like you to get up to some mischief."

Nashetania pumped a fist. "I'll do my best."

"At mischief?"

"To lift the barrier and find the seventh."

The seven of them walked out of the temple. While they stood in front of the door, Adlet told them everything he could remember. First, there was the transforming fiend that had been lying outside the pillars of salt that encircled the temple. It had disguised itself as a woman and urged him to go into the temple, and then it had revealed its true form and run away.

"That fiend must know something. If we can catch it and get it to talk...," mused Goldof.

Chamo scratched her head, looking embarrassed. "Sorry. It's dead. It just happened to run in Chamo's direction."

"Why did you have to do that?" Goldof sounded exasperated.

Mora came to Chamo's rescue. "Even if we had caught it, it would have been impossible to wrest information from it. Fiends are loyal creatures. If ordered not to speak, they never will, even on threat of death."

Adlet continued. He told them how the door had been locked and how he'd blown the lock with explosives.

"That's weird. It was locked? Wouldn't they normally give you the key?" Chamo cocked her head.

Mora pulled the key from her chest pocket. "I have it. I'd wager Private Loren never conceived a scenario such as this."

Adlet continued. He recounted the pair of armored soldiers who'd attacked after he'd blasted the doors. This was the most baffling part. They had attacked Adlet, but he didn't think they had been pawns of the fiends.

"You mean this armor? I've been curious about it..." Nashetania picked up the fallen armor and peered inside. There was no body within—it was empty. "The inner face of this armor is packed with hieroglyphs. It's so difficult, I can't read it," she admitted.

"These are sentries built by the Saint of Seals. They indiscriminately attack anyone who opens the door via illegitimate means," explained Mora.

"This place was pretty heavily protected, huh?" Adlet commented.

"The one who created this barrier, the king of the Land of Iron Mountains, was highly secretive. He forbade not only fiends, but also humans from entering this place. It must have been to prevent it from being used for evil," she replied.

"It's sure being used for evil right now, though," Adlet remarked. Though made with good intentions, had this barrier never been constructed, they wouldn't be trapped within it like this. It made Adlet want to track down the one responsible. He was about to continue when he noticed something odd. Hans was peering into the armor and then scrupulously examining the broken door. His expression was serious. But before Adlet could ask him what was up, Mora prodded him to go on.

"And after that?" she asked.

"Yeah. When I opened the door, the barrier was already activated. I think the fog was generated immediately after the doors were destroyed. When I went inside, the sword was already in the pedestal."

"So the barrier activated the moment before you opened the doors?" asked Mora.

"Yeah, and there was absolutely no sign of anyone inside. Frankly, I was pretty shocked," Adlet finished.

Mora folded her arms and considered the situation. "It does not appear that this was the work of a normal human. Undoubtedly, a Saint is involved."

"A Saint...," repeated Nashetania. "Why would a Saint cooperate with the Evil God?"

"They were probably threatened. Fiends do that sort of thing a lot." Adlet looked at Mora. "You'd know, wouldn't you? You'd know which Saints would be capable of something like this."

"Illusion, perhaps?" she suggested. "No, impossible. To conceal their presence from you entirely and then escape... I cannot think of any so easily."

"*Meow.* Adlet." Suddenly, Hans called out to him loudly. "Are ya sure yer not rememberin' somethin' wrong?"

"What's wrong?" Adlet asked. "I don't think so."

"I see. I'll ask one more time. Are ya sure yer not rememberin' somethin' wrong?"

Adlet was confused.

"If yer gonna make any corrections, do it now," Hans continued. "If ya try to take it back afterward, things ain't gonna go easy."

"All right. What's your point?" Adlet demanded.

"When ya went in there, the sword was 'already in the pedestal.' You sure o' that?"

"Yeah."

"I'll ask ya one last time. Yer absolutely sure?"

"You just don't let go. I'm sure! Why won't you believe me?"

Then Hans quietly put a hand to the sword at his waist. Adlet thought he might draw it, but he only rested his hand there. "I'm an assassin. Sneakin' in and runnin' out is somethin' of a specialty of mine."

"Oh? It seems you'll be quite useful," said Mora.

"In my line o' work, there's no one we fear more than the great Saint of Seals," Hans continued. "Ya see, the Saint of Seals has made these meowsterious doors all over the place. She's made doors with locks that won't open, doors that won't close once opened, and doors that drop down iron bars once ya open 'em. How many times have those things given me trouble? Anyways, I know quite a bit about her doors."

"...And?" Adlet demanded again.

"This door's pretty well-made." Hans elaborated. "Instead of bein' extra sturdy, it's made so that once ya open it, it can never be closed again."

"Wait, what does that mean?"

"I'm the one askin' questions, Adlet. It sounds funny, don't it? The door was closed when ya came, and the barrier activated the moment ya broke the door. So then, how did the one who turned on the barrier get inside?"

"What do you mean?" Adlet was confused. There should have been any number of ways to get inside.

"Listen, Adlet. There's no way someone coulda entered the temple before ya broke that door. Nobody coulda done it!"

"Wait! That couldn't be!" Adlet went into the temple. He looked for a ventilation window, but there was none. The windows letting in light were iron barred and covered in thick glass. He searched the stone walls, but there was no trace anywhere that they had been broken and then repaired. Dumbfounded, he looked around the temple. He'd considered how the culprit might have escaped after activating the barrier—but he couldn't understand how they'd gotten in in the first place.

"Adlet, if ya don't start thinkin' hard, yer gonna die," said Hans. "How could the person who activated the barrier have gotten into an impenetrable temple? *Meow?*"

"I..."

"Once the door is opened, it won't close again, and that door is the only way in. How could anyone get inside like that? Even if there was a fiend with special meowers, fiends can't come close. Ya'd hafta get into it with human skill alone."

"..."

"I'll tell ya somethin' else while I'm at it," Hans continued. "We call this sorta situation, where no one can get in or out, a 'locked-room meowstery.'"

A locked-room mystery. The unfamiliar term spun around in Adlet's head. He couldn't think of a single solution to this riddle. "Maybe they dug a hole," he suggested. "Removed the flagstones and dug a hole into the temple, and then activated the barrier. And then when I blew up the door, they escaped and immediately refilled it."

"Meow? In an instant? How?"

"There might be a Saint with powers that could do that. Like the Saint of Earth or something." Adlet searched for any sign that there might have been a hole dug inside.

But then Chamo said, "That's not right."

"Why not?" asked Adlet.

"When you and Hans went off to the border of the barrier, Auntie Mora said someone might be hidden around here. So Chamo searched all over the ground and the forest with the power of the swamp. There wasn't any trace of a hole. Chamo has the power to find things in the ground, too."

The power of swamp and the ability to probe underground. *What on earth is she?* Adlet wondered.

"Adlet, I saw Chamo searching through the earth, too. They could not have dug a hole," testified Goldof, and Nashetania nodded. Adlet had to believe them.

"There is one more thing I should add. The Saint of Earth has no such ability. Even with Chamo's power, digging a hole and escaping in a single instant would be impossible," Mora said.

Now that everyone had shot down his suggestion, Adlet was forced to discard the possibility that someone had tunneled their way out. "Then it doesn't have to be a hole. They could have used some kind of Saint's power," he said, turning to Mora. "Mora, there must be someone. There must be a Saint with the power to open the door and get into the temple."

"Sorry, but there is not," Mora replied. "The Saint of Seals's power is unbreakable. This door can be opened by force, but once opened, it's most certainly impossible to close."

"That couldn't be. If there's no Saint with the power, then...nobody could get inside." Adlet thought about it. "Then there's a Saint we don't know about yet. A Saint raised by fiends, like Fremy."

"No. My mother told me that I was the only child of a fiend and a human," Fremy said dispassionately.

When Adlet looked over, he saw that Hans had quietly drawn his sword and Chamo was putting her foxtail to her lips.

"Stop it, Hans, Chamo. Let's talk for a little while longer. It's much too early to cast judgment." Mora restrained the pair, but she, too, regarded Adlet suspiciously.

"Huh? Um...I don't quite understand what you all mean." Nashetania sounded confused. "Everyone...what are you talking about? Goldof? Hans? Mora? Adlet?" Nashetania was the only one in the dark as the tension among the Braves slowly mounted.

"Allow me to explain, Princess," said Goldof. "Right now, Adlet is suspect."

"That's right. And these suspicions are soundin' pretty decisive," added Hans.

"Why? That's not possible! *Adlet* could never be the one!" Nashetania cried angrily. As she did, her voice sounded distant.

"Well, ya know—nobody coulda gotten into the temple before Adlet opened the door. If he was the only one to go in, then who turned on the barrier?"

"It wasn't Adlet. That's a lie!" insisted Nashetania.

Hans's shoulders shook in laughter. "Yer a wicked man, Adlet. Ya need to work hard to clear your name, ya know?"

"I'm shocked. Suddenly, our positions are reversed," said Fremy.

Goldof, still restraining her, also glared at Adlet cautiously.

"Not so long ago he was coming to your defense, Fremy. You're not going to offer similar support?" Mora attempted to incite her to action.

"I can't save him," Fremy replied coldly. "Nor do I have any intention to."

"...The door," Adlet squeezed out. "The culprit opened the door and then went inside. And then they removed the door by the hinges, since it could no longer close, made a new door, and sealed the temple, hiding inside. When I got here, they activated the barrier and then, when the doors opened, sneaked away without me noticing! That would make it possible!"

The explanation was a reach at best. When Hans heard it, he started laughing. It was a mocking chuckle, as if he were saying, *That's all you got?* "This door was made by the old Saint of Seals," he said. "The current Saint doesn't have much experience. She wouldn't be capable of makin' such a fine door."

"So what? So then, the previous Saint made it." Adlet's voice was shrill. He couldn't hide his agitation.

"The old Saint of Seals died four years ago. No one else but her would've been able to install that door." Hans rejected even his most desperate answer.

Without thinking, Adlet shrieked, "You're the seventh, Hans!" That was the only possibility now. The story about the door and the Saint was all a lie. It couldn't be anything else.

"Unfortunately, Adlet," said Mora, "everything Hans says is true."

Adlet couldn't think of a response.

Trembling, Nashetania said, "It—it's not true, right, Adlet? This is...this is just absurd." She was the only one left who believed in his innocence.

Why is this happening to me? Adlet wondered. It was a trap. He'd fallen into a trap. The seventh hadn't just imprisoned them all within the barrier. This was a setup to make the Braves kill one another.

"Now then, what should we do?" asked Mora. "For starters, everyone, tell us your thoughts."

"Thoughts about what?!" Adlet wailed, but Mora offered no reply. She didn't have to. She was asking whether Adlet was the impostor or not…and whether he should live or die.

"Of course, I think Adlet did it. We should kill him now," said Hans.

"I'm against it! Kill Adlet? That's absolutely out of the question!" Nashetania cried.

"*Hmm*, Chamo still isn't sure about Fremy," said Chamo. "That whole explanation just didn't click. Well, for now, why don't we just try torturing Adlet?" She giggled. Was she serious, or was that supposed to be a joke?

"I believe Hans's logic is correct. But we should wait and see just a bit longer before we kill him," said Mora.

Then five sets of eyes turned toward Goldof and Fremy, whom the former held in chains. Fremy spoke first. "I have no opinion. You all just do what you want."

"Fremy." Adlet ground his teeth. Couldn't she have helped him out just a little bit—just a tiny, little bit?

"I see. Then, Goldof?" asked Mora.

Goldof closed his eyes and pondered for a while. His grip on Fremy's bonds slackened.

"Goldof," said Nashetania. "You understand, don't you? There's no way Adlet is our enemy."

Goldof opened his eyes and said quietly, "This is what I think." As he spoke, he pulled out the spear slung over his back and instantly closed the distance between himself and Adlet.

"Goldof!" Nashetania yelled.

Adlet jumped to one side in an attempt to escape. He was just a moment too late and barely dodged the spear while Goldof's large frame still knocked him backward. He slammed into the wall of the temple. While this was going on, Hans was drawing his sword, preparing to leap at Adlet.

In that moment, Adlet's mind was blank. So what was it that made him act? Was it his warrior instincts? A subconscious reflex? Or was it fate? Adlet's hand simply moved. The item he pulled from his pouch was one of the finest among his many secret tools. It looked like nothing but a bit of metal wrapped in paper. But when he squeezed it, a special chemical came in contact with the fragment of rare metal within the paper, causing a chemical reaction.

"Wha—!"

An intense light burst forth, many times brighter than staring straight at the sun. Hans and Goldof were powerful opponents—a smoke bomb probably wouldn't have worked on them. But they wouldn't be able to respond right away to a new kind of attack. Everyone covered their eyes, cringing.

In that moment, Adlet's brain whirled furiously, searching for a way to escape this crowd of six. Was the plan he hit upon the correct choice or not? He didn't have the option of stopping to consider it. Adlet ran to Fremy, whose wrists were still bound by chains, even now that Goldof had moved away from her.

Adlet would do whatever it took to win, use everything available to him. He could never be choosy about his methods. Adlet had declared himself to be the strongest man in the world, and that was what he believed. Whether those convictions were correct or not was another matter—they only underpinned his actions.

By the time the others' vision had cleared, Adlet had Fremy slung over his shoulder. There was a needle dipped in sleeping serum poking out of her shoulder. Adlet's sword was pressed against Fremy's neck. "Nobody move. If you move, I'll cut her," he said. The tip of his sword cut a few millimeters deep into the skin of her neck. The five surrounding Adlet all froze.

This was the only way.

Adlet had only two sleeping needles, and none of his other tools could have created such a certain opening for him.

"It can't be... This is just..." Nashetania's sword slipped from her hand, and she slumped to the floor.

"The secret is out now, I see," said Mora.

"M-meow. I didn't really expect this," gasped Hans.

Adlet glared at the five Braves around him. The immediate problem was Hans, who blocked the temple entrance. "Get out of the way."

"Tellin' me to move is not gonna make me move. I might if you tell me not to, though."

"Then don't. Stay right there," said Adlet.

"What should I do, I wonder?" Hans was quietly looking for an opportunity to separate Adlet's head from his shoulders. But the world's strongest man would not give him the opening.

"Let Chamo do it," said Chamo, twitching her foxtail.

But Mora stopped her. "Wait. Your power would swallow up Fremy as well. We cannot have that."

"Then what do we do?" Chamo asked.

Growing impatient, Adlet yelled, "Who said you could chat?! Make a decision, Hans! Are you gonna move or not?!"

"*M-meow!* I get it. I'll move, so don't yell at me!" Hans snapped, taking one step away from the door.

Adlet immediately set off his second flash grenade. Everyone else was blinded again. But of course, it wouldn't be as effective the second time around. Still carrying Fremy, Adlet ran out the door. That was when he felt something slam into him from behind. Hans had thrown his sword, burying it in Adlet's back. "*Ngh!*" This time he threw a smoke bomb to slow down Hans and the others as they chased him. Making use of every single secret tool in his arsenal, Adlet fled. He passed through the pillars of salt and into the forest. He ran and ran from the sound of his pursuers' footsteps, close on his trail. The pain in his back was intense, but he couldn't pull out the sword. If he did, blood would spurt from the wound, and he would very quickly be unable to move. Adlet had no choice but to get away with the sword still in his back.

"Damn it…" He'd thought it would be enough to just get out of there. But of course, it wasn't. After *that*, none of them would believe he was innocent. But there had been no other way to survive.

How long have I been running? The fog was dyed a thin red that was eventually supplanted by dusk. The sun was setting. Suddenly, Adlet realized he couldn't hear the footsteps behind him anymore. He stopped where he was, slung Fremy off his back, and sank to the ground. Once he was down, he couldn't move another step. Oxygen wasn't reaching his brain, and his thoughts wouldn't settle. He had to remove the sword and stop the bleeding before Fremy woke, prick her with another sleeping needle, and ready himself for his pursuers to catch up with him. But his body wouldn't move anymore. He collapsed on the ground. His consciousness grew dim.

"...Hey." Adlet's lips barely moved. He was calling out to himself—trying to tell himself that if he passed out, it would all be over. But his consciousness was sinking into darkness as if it were dragging him down. *What are you doing, Adlet Mayer? You're the strongest man in the world, aren't you? There's no way you can die here*, he silently muttered to himself, and he reached around to his back. His hand tried to extract the blade and then fell limp.

Then he stopped moving.

Hans was sweeping the dark forest, searching for Adlet.

"Hans! We have searched enough for now! The sun has set!" Mora's voice echoed through the darkness that had enveloped the Phantasmal Barrier.

Hans stopped and replied, "*Meow?* How can you be so calm about this?"

"'Twould be dangerous to continue any farther. We have no idea what kind of tricks Adlet has up his sleeve. The darkness is his domain."

"You think I'd let a guy like that beat me? Besides, he's gonna kill Fremy."

"Hans, show me your crest. My own is on my back, so I cannot see it myself," said Mora.

"Why?" Hans pulled up his shirt to show her the crest on his chest.

"Fremy is not dead. If she has not yet perished, that means that Adlet has judged her to be of value as a hostage."

"Meow can you tell that?"

"Look at your own crest."

Hans looked down at his chest. It was just as it had been before, faintly glowing.

"I did not have the time to explain earlier," said Mora, "but there are six petals, are there not? When one of the six Braves falls, one of those petals disappears. This signals to you whether your comrades are alive or dead."

"I didn't know that," remarked Hans.

"Goldof, Chamo, and the princess have returned to the temple. Let us return as well."

"…" Though Hans's expression said he wasn't convinced, he followed Mora back.

When they returned to the temple, the other three were waiting.

"No go," said Chamo. "We totally lost sight of him. He's super fast."

"To move with such speed, even when stabbed in the back… We cannot underestimate him." Mora sighed. "We have little choice. We will begin our search anew on the morrow. Let's pray that Fremy remains alive until then," she said, and she leaned against the wall and closed her eyes. The others, too, each rested in their preferred ways.

Nashetania was the only one among the group who was curled up, holding her head. "Adlet, why? Why would you do something like that?"

The seventh had been surprised by Adlet's speed, quick wit, and luck. Escape had seemed impossible, surrounded like that. Perhaps it had been a mistake to judge Adlet as one rung below the rest.

But that would not pose too much of a problem. Whatever the case, Adlet was cornered. The impostor would just have to wait until Adlet fell at the hands of his own allies. The seventh would simply watch him struggle in vain for a while. There was no need to rush things.

Around the time the other five gave up pursuit and headed back to the temple, Adlet was lying on the ground, unconscious. In the darkness, he dreamed—an old, wistful dream of his youth.

Adlet raised a stick over his head with a yell. He was trying to hit the boy who stood before him with a little wooden stick wrapped in cotton. But the boy easily dodged his playmate's attack, striking Adlet's shoulder with his own stick instead. Adlet let out a cry and dropped his childish weapon.

"*Ah-ha-ha!* I kicked your butt again!" The boy laughed. His name was Rainer, and he was Adlet's friend, three years his elder.

They lived in a tiny, ordinary village deep in the mountains of the Land of White Lakes, Warlow. There were about fifty people there who made their living by herding sheep, farming grain, and picking mountain mushrooms. The name of the village was Hasna.

In a corner of a pasture where sheep grazed, Adlet and Rainer practiced sword fighting. They were the only two boys in the village. Whenever they could get a spare moment, they would swing sticks wrapped in cotton at each other. The rumors that the Evil God would soon be revived had spread as far as this remote area. Warlow, Land of White Lakes, was not that far from the Howling Vilelands. The fiends of the Howling Vilelands might well invade this far inland. Such thoughts prompted the boys to organize a defense corps of two.

"Adlet, you've gotta get better at this. At this rate, forget fiends. You can't even beat my mom." Rainer pulled his utterly bruised friend up off the ground.

"Then maybe your mom should join the defense corps," Adlet muttered as he rubbed his battered body.

"What're you talking about? The defense corps is you and me," said Rainer.

The truth was, Adlet was not enthusiastic about playing defense corps. The fiends weren't going to come this far anyway, and the Braves of the Six Flowers would defeat the Evil God. Even if fiends did come, the people should just turn tail and run. That was what Adlet thought. But Rainer was his only friend in the world, so Adlet couldn't turn him down.

"Rainer! Where are you? I know you're just playing with Addy!" a voice called from far away. Rainer had been skipping out on his work in the fields, so his mom was coming to get him. The boy stuck out his tongue and ran off in the opposite direction.

It had been quite the rough day for Adlet. Not only had he been dragged into playing defense corps, but then he had to pacify his friend's livid mother.

"Oh, welcome home. Rainer really beat you good, didn't he?" When Adlet returned to his stone cottage, he was welcomed by the smell of mushroom stew and a woman in her midtwenties. Her name was Schetra, and she was Adlet's guardian.

"Schetra, tell Rainer to give me a break from all the practice fights," said Adlet.

"Tell him that yourself. Besides, he's not trying to be mean."

"I'm sick of it. I don't have to be a fighter. I hate fighting," complained Adlet, depositing a cloth bundle on the table. A pleasant smell wafted from within it.

"Those are meadowcap mushrooms, aren't they?" asked Schetra. "Perfect. I was just looking for some ingredients to add flavor."

After Rainer ran away, Adlet had gone into the forest to look for mushrooms. He'd acquired a number of rare specimens that day. Finding delicious mushrooms was Adlet's hobby, and it was what he was best at. Schetra cut up the meadow morsels and put them in the stew, producing a fragrant smell reminiscent of chargrilled meat.

Three years earlier, Adlet had lost his parents to the plague, and Schetra had lost her shepherd husband the same way. Schetra had taken Adlet in, and the two of them had been living together ever since. Adlet's guardian tended to the sheep and cut their wool, while the boy used their milk to make cheese. The pair sold both to the other villagers to support themselves.

That was Adlet Mayer's memory of being ten years old. He had been content then. After he'd lost his parents, Schetra had kindly embraced him. She'd brought the smiles back to his face. Adlet loved the smell of earth and sheep steeped into Schetra's body. Rainer was a pain in the butt, but he was a good friend. Adlet was sick of playing defense corps, but he understood quite well that Rainer felt strongly for Adlet and the rest of the village, in his own way. And the other villagers were good people. They bought Adlet's clumsily made cheese and told him it was good, despite the fact that it would have tasted better if Schetra had made it.

Adlet had been a truly ordinary boy then. He had never considered that he could become one of the Braves of the Six Flowers. He'd never even wanted to, not once. What he'd been good at was finding mushrooms. His goal for the future had been learning to make better cheese.

Young Adlet had believed that those days would go on forever.

It was a dream. A dream of things past.

"......Why have you come here?"

The setting of the dream had changed. There was a house in a forest, a modified cave in the thickly overgrown trees—not very homey. An old man sat cross-legged within.

"Atreau Spiker. I heard you could teach me to become a warrior." Adlet looked like death. His clothes were tattered, and his body was rail-thin. Both his hands were covered in blood, and his eyes were those of a man who'd died with lingering resentment.

"Leave this mountain. If you wish to be strong, join the knights. If you be a commoner, join a mercenary band." The old man—Atreau—refused in a quiet but resonant voice.

"That wouldn't be enough. That would make me strong. But it wouldn't make me the strongest in the world."

"The strongest in the world?" Atreau's eyebrows wavered, their long hair obscuring his expression.

"I can't become the strongest in the world through normal training," continued Adlet. "I need to walk a different path. I will become the strongest man in the world. I'll become the strongest and destroy the fiends."

"Why do you want to be a warrior?" the old man asked.

"To take back what was stolen from me," Adlet replied. "I can't get it back unless I become stronger than anyone. Stronger than everyone."

"Give up," said Atreau coldly. "What is gone cannot be retrieved. Give it up and live on."

"I can't!" Adlet yelled. "I have to get it back! If I don't, then what have I survived for?! If I can't defeat the Evil God, if I can't fight fiends, my life isn't worth living at all!"

Atreau looked into Adlet's eyes for a while, thinking.

"Do you think I'm stupid?" asked Adlet. "You think there's no way I can become the strongest in the world, don't you?" There were tears in his eyes. "I don't care if you think I'm stupid. I don't care if you laugh at me. I'll keep on believing I can become the strongest man in the world. I'll keep on yelling that I'll be the strongest man in the world. How could I become stronger if I didn't?!"

Atreau gazed up at the heavens contemplatively. Then he slowly stood and kicked Adlet hard in the gut. It knocked the wind out of him, acid welling up from his empty stomach. Atreau kicked Adlet's sides and his back over and over. He stepped on the boy's face and ground it into the cavern floor. And then Atreau said, "Smile."

"...Huh? Sm...ile?" Though he tried to reply, the words wouldn't come out. He hurt so much he felt he would die.

"If you want to be a warrior, then smile." Atreau kicked Adlet's back. "When sorrow inspires the urge to die. When agony makes it necessary to throw everything away and flee. When you drown in despair and can see no light. One who can smile even then will become strong."

Adlet's trembling lips twisted. His cheeks spasmed, and though his expression didn't look much like he was smiling, he was.

After that, Atreau continued beating him. He kicked Adlet's face until blood spurted from his nose. He punched Adlet's stomach until blood mixed with vomit. But even then, Atreau did not stop. To smile, even when spewing red-tinted bile, with his nose dripping blood, and tears streaking down his face. That was the first technique of battle that Atreau taught Adlet.

Adlet opened his eyes. It had been a vague, incoherent dream. "*Ugh.*"

He was in the forest, surprised to be still alive. "...?" He thought he'd collapsed facedown, but now he was lying faceup with a tree root as his pillow. When he touched his back, the sword that should have been there was not. His wound had been treated, sewn up, and wrapped in bandages. Who had treated him? Had Nashetania found him?

Then he heard a voice.

"You're awake." He could just barely see Fremy's blurry shape within the dark fog. "They missed your vitals. If you rest, you should be able to move around again soon."

"You treated my wound?" Adlet asked, sitting up.

"Yes."

"Why?" Fremy should also have believed that Adlet was the seventh. They had gotten off to a rocky start when they first met, too. He couldn't understand why she would save him.

"I'm ninety-nine percent certain that you're the seventh," said Fremy. "But not completely. This is for the sake of that one percent chance."

"Well, you're right. I am a real Brave. I came here to fight the Evil God."

"Oh? I don't believe you," Fremy said, looking away.

Silence fell upon them. The nighttime forest was quiet. Adlet figured the other five would have given up searching now that it was dark. There was no sign that they were still chasing him. So what should he do at this point? He had to prove his innocence, no matter what. But how? "This is gonna sound pathetic," said Adlet, "but I have no idea how the impostor got into the temple."

"Of course. Because you're the impostor."

"Was it really true, what Hans said? Was there really no way to open that door?"

"I'm not as informed as he is, but I do know a bit about the doors created by the Saint of Seals. I don't think what Hans said was wrong," she said.

"..."

"Besides, Mora shot down your ideas, too. There's no way anyone could have gotten into that temple."

If that was the case, then Adlet really was stuck. If it was, in fact, possible to get in the temple, that would mean that Hans, Mora, and Fremy were all lying. But only one among the seven of them was the enemy. Six really were Braves. It would be unthinkable for any of the real Braves to be conspiring with the enemy of their own free will. That meant that if multiple Braves were telling the same story, it had to be the truth.

"The impostor might be Mora," suggested Adlet. She'd said there was no one who could have broken into that locked temple. But if her testimony had been a lie, then what? What if she was an accomplice to the Saint who'd broken in?

"That may be possible," Fremy conceded. "But you can't prove it. You would have to capture the person who broke into the temple and demonstrate their powers to all of us."

"Well, maybe there's some unknown Saint, one that even she doesn't know about. She didn't know about you, so you can't say for sure that there aren't any as-yet-unknown Saints."

"That amounts to the same thing. You can't prove this Saint did it unless you catch her."

Anyway, that just meant he had to catch the person who'd activated the barrier. "Let me sort this out," he said. "First, we have two or more enemies. One of these two is among the seven Braves who have gathered here. The other is the one who broke into the temple and activated the barrier." That much was certain. It wasn't possible for any of them other than Adlet to have activated the barrier. When it had been turned on, Fremy, Nashetania, and Goldof had been fighting fiends. Mora and Hans had been on their way to the temple. The only one whose position at the time was unknown was Chamo, but Mora had testified that Chamo could not break into the temple with her powers.

"We've been calling the one who infiltrated our group, the one who bears a crest, the seventh," Adlet continued. "Let's call the one who activated the barrier the eighth. Of course, they're working with the fiends. The fiends dropped bombs on the temple in order to lure the Braves of the Six Flowers to the temple and attacked us to separate me from the rest of you. This was most likely a carefully prepared plan."

"That still leaves us with a question," said Fremy. "What is the seventh here for? If the plan was to lock us in, it could have been accomplished without the seventh's presence."

"Don't be stupid," said Adlet. "If the seventh wasn't among us, framing *me* as the seventh wouldn't be possible. The plan wasn't to lock us up. The plan was to set me up and get me killed."

"I didn't think of that. Because I thought you were the seventh." Fremy was going along with the conversation, but she didn't seem to trust him at all. Adlet had thought he could persuade Fremy to side with him, but it seemed that would be impossible.

"Anyway, we can put off dealing with the seventh," he said. "Our number one priority is finding the eighth."

"*Can* you? On your own, I mean."

Adlet was forced into silence. He'd be looking for an unknown enemy with unknown powers, all while shaking the other five Braves. Of course, this eighth person wouldn't just be strolling the woods. They'd be desperately hiding to avoid capture. Could it even be done? It seemed completely impossible to him. But the more convinced he became that it was impossible, the bigger the smile on his face grew. His lips relaxed, and his spirit was invigorated.

"You're a strange man. What are you smiling about?" asked Fremy.

"I'm smiling because, as usual, I'm the strongest man in the world." Adlet clenched a fist. "I'm in a lousy situation, but it doesn't even come close to breaking my spirit." To smile at despair: That was the first thing Adlet's master, Atreau, had taught him. "I'm looking forward to tomorrow. Tomorrow's the day I ruin my enemy's plot. I'll prove both my innocence and the fact that I'm the strongest man in the world at the same time. I can't wait for sunrise."

Adlet kept smiling. He had no idea who the eighth really was. It didn't seem likely that he could continue to evade the other Braves, either. But if he stopped smiling, it would all be over.

"You're deluded."

"No. I'm determined." As Adlet smiled, he thought about the eighth:

who it might be and what kind of powers they might have. He searched his memories to see if, perhaps, he had overlooked some clue, anything out of the ordinary. After he'd been thinking for a while, Fremy suddenly spoke.

"Why did you want to be one of the Braves of the Six Flowers?"

For some reason, this was new and surprising to him. Fremy had seemed uninterested in the other Braves all this time. This was the first time she'd shown interest in another person. "Why are you asking me that?" asked Adlet.

"Because you're ordinary."

"..."

"Hans is a genius. Goldof, too. But you're not. You're just an ordinary person with a lot of strange weapons."

"You're saying I'm weak? Me, the strongest man in the world?"

"That's not what I'm saying. I'm asking how an unremarkable person like yourself could become such a powerful fighter. That's what I want to know."

Adlet didn't reply. Hans and Goldof were geniuses, and Adlet was ordinary. He couldn't deny that. He couldn't touch either of them when it came to pure swordplay or martial arts. "It's thanks to my master," said Adlet. "I hesitate to say this, but he was a little crazy. He was obsessed with killing fiends. He spent all his time by himself, deep in the mountains, devising new weapons and then coming up with ways to use them. He didn't do anything else. You wouldn't even think he was human."

"..."

"He hammered the skills into me. I trained every day until I puked and couldn't move anymore, and when that was over, I was confined to my desk to study. I learned about making his tools and poisons, refining gunpowder, and even cutting-edge science."

"Science? Even that?" asked Fremy.

"I'm grateful to him. He made me the warrior I am. Learning a normal style of combat wouldn't have made me the strongest man in the world."

"I know that man," she said, and Adlet looked at her. "Atreau Spiker,"

Fremy continued. "He was one of my targets. He was quite old, so he was low on my priority list, though."

"Yeah, that's the guy," said Adlet.

"I heard all his disciples ran away. They couldn't handle his severe training."

"Your information was wrong. There was one who didn't run away: me."

"How were you able to put up with it?"

Adlet didn't reply.

"Something happened, didn't it?" pressed Fremy. "There was a reason you wanted to be one of the Braves of the Six Flowers."

Adlet suddenly remembered his conversation with Nashetania in the prison. She'd asked him all sorts of things, but Adlet hadn't told her everything. The subject was heavy for him and not something he could talk about easily. Some things were like that. "When I was a kid, a fiend came to my village." And yet, why did it feel so natural to talk about his past now? "I couldn't believe it. I'd thought that fiends were creatures from some faraway land. My best friend tried to hit it with a stick. I was crying when I stopped him."

"What was this fiend like?" asked Fremy.

"It was shaped like a human. Its body was patterned with green- and skin-colored mottles. At the time, it seemed like it towered to the heavens, but I think it probably wasn't actually that big. About the same size as Goldof."

"It had three wings, didn't it? Three crow-like wings on its back."

That was exactly right. "You know it?" he asked.

"Continue your story."

"It didn't attack us or eat us. It just approached us with a smile and patted my head. It was kind. Unbelievably kind. The fiend called the adults of the village to convene together and told us kids to go to sleep. Of course, there was no way I could fall asleep. I trembled all night in my guardian's arms."

"And then?" prompted Fremy.

"The next morning, the fiend was gone. No one had been killed. No one was even injured. I was relieved. And then the village elder told us that the entire village would move to the Howling Vilelands and that from that point on we would be ruled by the Evil God."

"…"

"Every single adult in the village said the human world was going to end and there was no way the Braves of the Six Flowers could win. But they all believed that if we joined the Evil God right away, our lives would be spared. After speaking with that fiend for just one night, it was like they were all completely different people. I didn't know what to do. All I could do was quiver in my boots. The only ones who opposed this plan were my guardian and my best friend. But the fiend had also said one more thing—to prove our loyalty to the Evil God, the villagers should go carve out the hearts of anyone who objected and bring those hearts to it."

"That seems like something it'd say," Fremy remarked.

So Fremy did know the creature, after all. "What was that fiend?" asked Adlet.

"It's one of the three commanders that govern all fiends. It was also the one that came up with the idea of making a human/fiend child and ordered my mother to bear me."

"…"

"Continue," she said.

"Neither my guardian nor my best friend hated the villagers for it, no matter what. The fault lay with that fiend, not the people of the village. My best friend told me not to hate them. My guardian told me that things would surely go back to how they'd been before, that one day we could live together peacefully. *Pick us some mushrooms again. Let's make the defense corps again*, they said."

"What happened to them?" asked Fremy.

"My best friend died defending me. My guardian died so I could escape. I was the only one who survived," Adlet said, and his story ended there. "What was I talking about again? Oh yeah, the reason I became a warrior." He closed his eyes, and as he imagined their faces in his mind, he said, "When I told my master about this, he said that it was because of my guardian and my friend that I was able to become strong. That I became so capable because I believed in what they said; that one day, things would be sure to go back to how they were before and we could live together peacefully. He said people can't become strong for the sake of revenge. They get stronger when they have something to believe in."

"…"

"Is that enough for you?" asked Adlet. The story had ended up longer than he'd expected. But the night was long. They had plenty of time to talk.

"I envy you," said Fremy.

Adlet doubted his ears. "What did you just say?"

"I said I envy you."

Forgetting the pain in his back, Adlet stood. His hand reached for the sword at his waist. "What did you say? You couldn't have said that you *envy* me, right?"

"I do envy you. I don't even have anything to believe in."

"…" Adlet's hand moved away from his sword. He sat down again.

"I was abandoned by those closest to me," said Fremy.

"What do you mean?"

"I mean the fiend who gave birth to me and raised me. The fiend who gave me my gun, gave me my powers as the Saint of Gunpowder, gave me happiness. It abandoned me."

Adlet didn't urge her to continue. He just let her talk.

"As I told you before, I was raised among fiends," she said. "Not peons like those we killed today. Proper fiends with intelligence, courage, and loyalty to the Evil God. I loved them all. I believed they all loved me."

"…"

"I killed a lot of people on my mother's orders. I had no doubts. On the contrary, I felt like I had to work harder, kill even more. I wasn't a full demon, and I had dirty human blood. But I believed that even a half demon could be recognized as a full fiend if I could kill lots of humans," said Fremy, and her expression looked younger than it ever had. "But I also understood that merely killing weaklings would not count as service toward the Evil God. I had to kill one of the strongest six warriors in the world, break one of the links in the chain. Nashetania and Mora were very heavily guarded. I was unable to approach them. So I decided to challenge Chamo. I believed that if I could defeat Chamo, I would be recognized as a full-fledged fiend."

"Then you lost," said Adlet.

"I regret it. I should have gone for Nashetania or Mora instead of challenging *that*. It was all I could do to escape. And I made another mistake... When she provoked me, I told her my name."

Adlet couldn't imagine what the battle had been like.

"I barely survived," she continued, "and when I came back...my mother tried to kill me, as did the other fiends I had thought of as family. They were done with me. Maybe I should have died then. But I managed to get away." Fremy stroked her forehead. There was the proof she was a fiend, the scar left by her horn. "What I cannot forgive is not that they tried to kill me. It's that they pretended to love me. If they had just treated me as their puppet, then the betrayal would not have hurt. If they had always intended to betray me, then they should have raised me as a slave born to fight humans. My mother...my mother..." Fremy was clenching her fists. "My mother pretended to love me."

"Revenge, huh?"

"It's not enough to just kill her. I have to destroy what my mother has devoted her life to. I won't be satisfied until I destroy the Evil God. Once I do, I'll tell her... *Regret what you've done. This is what it's wrought.*"

When Adlet had first met Fremy, something in him had resisted the idea of leaving her alone. Now he finally understood why. She was just like him. Her pain was the same as his—the pain of being betrayed by the people she trusted, of losing her place in life. Pain that made her burn with hatred. *Revenge is meaningless. Revenge is a mistake. Revenge gives birth to nothing.* There were a lot of people who said things like that, but they didn't understand. Revenge was not something you did because it was meaningful or right or because you could get something out of it. You sought revenge because it was all you had.

"Back then, I was content," Fremy continued, as if talking to herself.

"I had my mother and my friends. We played together, and we fought together. I had a dog. I wonder what's happened to it now. Are they still feeding it? Or have they already gotten rid of it, maybe?"

"Hey, Fremy," he said.

"What?"

"Well, um…hang in there." Adlet sincerely wanted to support her. He thought she might appreciate a little encouragement.

But what he got in return was an even colder gaze, one heavy with suspicion. "Adlet—why don't you suspect me?" she asked.

"Huh?"

"How can you believe that story was true? You can't imagine that I just made it up?"

"What are you talking about, Fremy?"

"If you're really a Brave, I should be your number one suspect. From your point of view, I have to be the most suspicious."

"Yeah, maybe so, but…" Adlet trailed off.

"If you were a real Brave, the first thing you would do is try to look for proof that I am the seventh. But you don't. That alone is enough reason to suspect you."

Adlet thought her logic was strange. But from her perspective, it wasn't an irrational argument. "I…" He searched for the answer. Several came to mind, but none quite fit. He had a hard time putting his feelings into words. He remembered when he first met Fremy. It felt like a very long time ago, but in actuality, it had been just that morning. He made a desperate attempt to express how he'd felt at that moment. "I don't want to believe that you're my enemy."

"I can't understand that," said Fremy. "Whether you're a real Brave or the seventh."

"D-don't get me wrong, Fremy. It's not like I like you or anything."

"I wasn't talking about that. Don't be gross," Fremy spat. "I can't understand it. I just can't understand you at all," she said, and then she abruptly stood. "I'm going back to the temple. The other five will probably be there."

"You're going?" he asked.

"Of course." Fremy's outline disappeared into the darkness.

Adlet had thought that by talking about their pasts, they had come to understand each other a little. But maybe that, too, had only been momentary delusion. Adlet called into the darkness, "Won't you come with me?"

Fremy stopped and thought for a moment. "We may have talked a lot, but ultimately, that still doesn't change the fact that you're the most suspicious of all of us."

"I see."

"But I would be willing to hear you out, just once." From the darkness, Fremy threw something at him. It was a tiny firecracker of rounded gunpowder. "That was made with my power...the power of the Spirit of Gunpowder. When you strike it on the ground, it explodes. If you set it off, I will know where it happened."

"So you're saying I can use this to summon you?" asked Adlet.

"Don't get the wrong idea. I don't trust you. The next time we meet might be when I kill you."

"..."

"To use it or not is up to you," said Fremy, and she disappeared into the darkness.

Adlet stared into the night as he thought. After having spoken with Fremy, he was certain of one thing: She was absolutely not his enemy. It wasn't logic that inspired this certainty, but his heart. He wanted to protect her—from the Evil God, and also from the seventh. "I'll protect you, Fremy. And not just you—I'll protect Nashetania and the others. I'll protect everyone." He got no reply.

Adlet lay down and gazed at the dark, fog-covered sky. As he did, his thoughts returned to the past. Five years ago, during his time training with Atreau, slowly edging closer and closer to becoming the strongest man in the world, Adlet had, just once, returned to his home village. The entire area had been nothing but a burned field. Nothing remained. Not the places he'd played with his friend or the house where he'd lived with

Schetra—nothing. The scorched remnants of his village told him that what was gone would not return.

Adlet believed that he'd grown stronger not for the sake of revenge. He didn't fight out of hatred. He had become a warrior because he didn't want to lose everything again.

But despite those feelings, the ones he wanted to protect weren't cooperating.

Chapter 4

Counter-
offensive

Meanwhile, the seventh was privately thinking that killing Adlet personally wouldn't be the best strategy. The impostor wanted to leave the task to one of the other Braves of the Six Flowers, if possible. Then if things went well, they would be able to blame everything on the one who'd done the deed. Even if the impostor wasn't able to pull that off, Adlet's death would still tear a wide rift in the bonds of trust between the six Braves. The seventh just had to stay vigilant and use that failure of trust to lead the group to an irreparable falling-out.

The seventh didn't know what was going to happen. The important thing was to be flexible—to observe the situation closely and use whatever was at hand without getting too attached to any single idea. And most of all, avoiding suspicion was crucial. If the seventh could manage that, victory was assured.

Now then, who would kill Adlet...?

When Fremy returned to the temple, Chamo, Nashetania, and Hans were already asleep. Mora and Goldof were standing watch outside.

"So you live. What happened to Adlet?" asked Mora.

"I lost him," said Fremy. "He was wounded, and while I would have liked to capture him, I didn't have my gun."

"I see," Mora replied. "You should sleep. You can talk more about it tomorrow morning."

When Fremy walked into the temple, Goldof called out to her. "I'm sorry for suspecting you," he said.

"It doesn't matter. Any normal person would have," she replied.

Eventually, dawn broke. Fremy told the other five about what had happened after Adlet carried her away. And then she told them about herself, and in particular, her reason for fighting the Evil God.

"Fiends are such heartless creatures." Mora knit her brows.

"What an awful story," said Chamo. "If it's true."

"Chamo, you still suspect Fremy? The truth has already become clear—Fremy is an indispensable member of our team," Mora chided her, but Chamo just giggled.

"*Meow-hee-hee*," chuckled Hans. "I'm feelin' a little uneasy 'bout this, though. Should we really think she's one of us?"

"Hans, you too? How can you say that?" puzzled Mora.

"Didja actually fight with Adlet?" Hans asked Fremy. "That sword I threw at him sank in pretty deep, ya know?"

"It missed his vitals," Fremy replied. "Your arm isn't as good as your mouth."

"Adlet really seemed to take a likin' to ya. When everyone was suspicious of ya, he protected ya. When Chamo said she was gonna torture ya, he got mad and stopped her. It's no surprise yer feelin' attracted to him."

"You're so obnoxious."

"*Meow-hee-hee*, the heart of a woman is an eternal meowstery. Yer mouth and yer heart aren't singin' the same tune."

"Hans, be silent for one moment," ordered Mora. Hans made an exaggerated display of his shock and then shut his mouth. "I have doubts as well," she continued. "What did you think of Adlet, Fremy? What was your impression when you found out he was the seventh?"

"I thought, *Ah, I knew it*," said Fremy.

"How so?" asked Mora.

"He was trying to get on my good side, showing this forced concern in an attempt to win my trust. Now that I know why, it all makes sense."

"*Meow-ha-ha,* what a terrifyin' woman. Poor Adlet's love is unrequited!" Fremy glared at Hans.

"We should be talking about Adlet. How do we capture him?" asked Goldof.

Hans looked at the iron box in the corner of the temple and said, "Most of his weapons are in there. He can't fight without 'em. If we wait here, I think he'll be comin' round to get 'em."

"Not necessarily," Fremy countered. "He still has a certain number of weapons hidden on his person."

"Not enough to fight all of us," Hans replied.

"That doesn't mean we can go without a plan," said Goldof. "We should make our move. We have only a finite amount of time. We should split up and track him down."

"Goldof is right," said Mora. "We'll split into groups of two. First, Fremy—you will come with me to search for Adlet." Fremy nodded. "Princess, you go with Goldof," Mora continued. "Do not be gentle with Adlet. Goldof, take care of the princess." Goldof nodded. Nashetania gave him an uneasy look. "Chamo and Hans, you stay here and lay an ambush for him. Keep your wits about you."

"*Meow?* I'll have only half the motivation if I'm not with a pretty lady. Can't I switch places with Goldof?" Everyone ignored Hans's complaint.

"No objections?" verified Mora. "Then let's go."

That was when Chamo said, "No. Chamo doesn't wanna wait."

"All right, then Fremy can stay here, and you come with me, Chamo," said Mora.

"Walking all over the place doesn't sound fun, either. Chamo's just gonna go play somewhere until the barrier is down."

"May I scold you a little, Chamo?" A blue vein popped out on Mora's forehead.

Hans smiled and said, "It's fine. I can deal with a guy like that by myself."

"What reliable allies you are," said Mora. "Well, so be it. Chamo, do avoid getting lost and don't stray too far."

Nashetania and Goldof headed out westward. Mora and Fremy were setting off in the opposite direction when Hans called out to one of his companions. "Hey, Fremy."

"What?" she replied.

"Can you really fight the fiends?"

"What do you mean?"

"If yer beloved mama was standin' right in fronta ya, sayin', *I'm sorry, forgive me, I've always regretted it, let's live together again*, could ya kill her?"

"I could. Because I would know she was lying," said Fremy.

"No, ya couldn't."

Fremy shot Hans an angry glare.

"I'm an assassin," said Hans. "I've taken on a lot of jobs. Husbands betrayed by their wives. Children abandoned by their parents. They all came to me and said, *Kill them for me.* But ya know, not a single one of 'em was happy to see me do it. At the last moment, most of 'em would be like, *No, don't kill them, after all.*"

"So what?" Fremy demanded.

"Well, I guess it don't really matter."

"Let's go, Fremy," said Mora, and the two women turned away from Hans and ran into the woods.

After Nashetania and Goldof left the temple, they ran for a while, until Nashetania suddenly stopped. She turned to look behind them and scanned the area multiple times.

"What is it?" Goldof, who had been following her, was confused by her behavior.

"Goldof, I know this is sudden, and this is going to sound strange, but do you trust me?" Nashetania looked Goldof straight in the eye.

"Of course. Whom could I trust but you?" he replied.

But his response made Nashetania frown. "You don't understand what I mean. What I mean to ask is, will you support my ideas without questioning them?"

"Your Highness, just what are you thinking?"

Nashetania kept her eyes locked on Goldof's. "Adlet isn't the seventh. And now I will prove it."

"Your Highness!" Goldof cried.

"Just this time. Say you will with no complaints. I can tell—Adlet has fallen into a trap, and he's waiting for my help!"

"I cannot acquiesce. Even if it's you, Your Highness. Anything but that."

"I'm not saying this with no plan in mind," Nashetania persisted. "There's something that has been bothering me. I still have no proof, and I may just be wrong. But it might be the clue that leads us to the truth."

"Whom do you suspect?" asked Goldof.

Nashetania replied quietly, "Hans."

Meanwhile, Adlet was also making his move. He ran soundlessly across tree branches so as not to leave any footprints. Occasionally, he would stop and listen to the sounds around him, check that no one was approaching, and then continue. He was heading toward the temple. If he could find proof there that the eighth really existed, he could clear the suspicions against him for the time being. It would be more efficient than running around the forest and searching for the eighth at random.

What are the others doing? As Adlet jumped from one tree to the next, he reflected. Most likely, the six of them had split into groups of two or three to look for him. That would be the logical decision if they wanted to avoid surprise attacks from him. Things might get nasty if they were in groups of two. That would mean one of them was alone with the seventh, who could kill their companion and then pin it on Adlet. That could be the seventh's next plan. Adlet had to hurry before such underhanded tactics were put into action.

But would surveying the temple be doable? There would be at least two standing guard. At least if Nashetania or Fremy were among them, there would be a way. Adlet could get one of them to cooperate and have her make sure the temple was empty, or he could negotiate with them directly to get into the temple. Adlet knew full well his plan had holes. It was haphazard and chance-based. But at that point, it was all he had.

"Okay." He had made it to the temple without running into any of his pursuers. It seemed that luck had not forsaken him. He climbed another tree, pulled out his telescope, and surveyed the area. There was no sign of anyone around the temple. Were they lying in wait for him inside? He went around to the back of the temple, approaching it cautiously. He leaped down onto the roof, put his ear to the stone, and listened for any sounds inside. He could hear none. Either the temple was actually empty, or it was a trap to lure him in. And if it was a trap, was it one of the other Braves who had set it for him, or was it the seventh?

Then he felt something that sent shivers down his spine—he could sense bloodlust in the air. His body reacted before his conscious mind.

"Meow-meow!" Adlet rolled to one side just as the sword stabbed into the roof where he'd been. The other man had approached from behind without making the slightest sound. "Hiya," Hans said. "I thought ya'd show up, Adlet."

"Hans. So it's you." Adlet had forgotten—Hans was an assassin. Traps and surprise attacks were his field of expertise. Hans had probably predicted his arrival and concealed himself beforehand somewhere in the forest.

Hans yanked his sword out of the roof, and then, grasping a hatchet-like blade in each hand, he whirled them around, moving only his wrists. It looked like he was playing, yet he revealed no openings. His movements were bizarre. "I thought all ya could meownage was cowardly tricks. Yer better than I thought." It sounded as though Hans was surprised that his ambush had failed.

"Well, damn," said Adlet. "Now that I've run into you, it looks like I've got no choice but to do this." He drew his sword and faced Hans. But that was just bluster. Since negotiation was off the table, Adlet was already considering his only option: flight.

"Come at me like yer gonna kill me. If ya don't, this'll be over real fast." Hans had a broad smile on his face as he swung his sword. It was as if he enjoyed fighting so much he could barely control it.

"You go first," said Adlet. "It'll be a nice learning experience for you."

"*Mya-hee. Mee-hee-hee. Hmya-mya-meow!*" Hans emitted a strange laugh and leaped at him.

Just what I wanted, Adlet thought. He would block Hans's first attack and use the opportunity to throw a smoke bomb in his face.

But an instant before Hans would have struck, the assassin dropped to all fours and came to a halt. Adlet wasn't ready for that. Hans threw a spinning roundhouse kick to smack away the smoke bomb in Adlet's left hand. "That same trick ain't gonna keep workin' again and again." Hans swung his sword, using the momentum of his spin. Adlet jumped backward, barely avoiding it. Hans twisted his body and pounced once more.

The two fell from the roof of the temple. Adlet landed, and when he saw Hans falling headfirst, he thought this would be his chance to run. But Hans landed on his fists, swords still in hand, and smoothly, with the strength of his arms alone, launched himself at Adlet. "Yah!" Twisting through the air, he struck.

It was all Adlet could do to block the blow with the flat of his blade. Hans's full weight behind the attack threw Adlet off-balance. Hans landed on his hands and then, of all things, ran upside down toward Adlet. Then he flipped forward to plant his feet on the ground again, aiming for Adlet's head with both swords.

"*Ngh!*" Though Hans's build wasn't that large, his strike was terrifyingly heavy. Just blocking it made Adlet's shoulders scream. Hans's stream of attacks was continuous—he flipped upside down, rolled forward, cartwheeled to the side, all four of his limbs working freely to harry Adlet. It was as if gravity didn't even exist. *How can a human move like that?* Adlet wondered. He had no idea where the onslaught would come from next. Though it seemed as if Hans was just messing with him, his manner of movement was utterly efficient. He followed Adlet about like a cat playing with a ball, keeping his prey from getting too far.

"*Tsk!*" Adlet tossed a poison needle from his sleeve as he kicked at Hans with a nail hidden in his shoe. But neither hit their mark. There was no way they could. Adlet's weapons were all for catching an opponent off guard. But at the moment, Adlet was the one off-balance.

"*Hnnmya!*" Hans grunted as Adlet's desperate kick connected with his stomach. Hans dropped both his swords. In that brief moment, Adlet tried to throw a smoke bomb.

"*Hnnmya-meow!*" But as the swords flew through the air, Hans caught them between his feet. Then, spinning his body with the strength of his arms, he lunged at Adlet. Adlet somehow managed to block the attack from Hans's feet with a sword, but Hans took advantage of the opportunity to grab his opponent's legs and pull him to the ground.

"Damn it…" Adlet fell on his face. He didn't even have time to cry out. Hans was instantly on his feet, pressing a steel edge against Adlet's neck. Hans had defeated him utterly with little effort. Adlet had been crushed. Dumbfounded, the boy gazed at the blade at his throat. It prevented him from moving at all. If Adlet so much as twitched, he would be unceremoniously decapitated.

"*Meow*, too bad for you, Adlet," Hans said, smiling. "It wasn't a bad plan. Most people wouldn't have thought up turnin' themselves into a fake Brave. If I hadn't been here, ya might've done a better job foolin' everyone."

"Hans, I…"

"Are you gonna say yer not the impostor? That's not gonna work." Hans was smirking. "I was blown away when ya went and took a hostage. I thought ya had more brains than that."

So that had been a poor move, after all. At this point, Adlet was regretting it. But there was no time for that. He had to get himself out of this.

"So why don't ya spit it out?" goaded Hans. "Who's behind this? Why'd ya betray the human race and join up with the Evil God? I won't do ya no wrong if ya come out and tell me all proper-like."

"I won't 'spit it out,' because I'm not the impostor," insisted Adlet.

"Ya don't need to hesitate here. I get it. Ya got yerself a little sob story to explain why, don't ya? Ya need medicine for yer ailin' mama? Yer cute little gal got taken hostage?"

"I have no family. I have no lover. I'll say it as many times as you'd like. I'm not the impostor."

"Well then, there'll be nobody left to grieve when yer dead." Hans's sword nicked Adlet's skin.

As it did, Adlet made his move. He hadn't exhausted all his secret weapons just yet. A single thread was woven through Adlet's sleeve. He grabbed it with his fingers and pulled. Instantly, one of the pouches at his waist exploded with a bang, and yellow smoke enveloped them.

"*Nghmrow!*" With a cry, Hans pressed his hands against his eyes. This wasn't a mere smoke bomb; it was tear gas that worked equally well against fiends and humans alike.

"Shit! You made me use it, you stupid ass! This hurts so—*agh!*" Adlet had taken the hit at point-blank range, so the tear gas had affected him far worse. But still, he had escaped Hans's grasp. Adlet turned from Hans and tried to run away, but with his eyes stinging so badly he couldn't see straight, he ran face first into a pillar of salt.

"*Mya-mya-mya!* Just how stubborn do ya gotta be?!"

"As stubborn as it takes for me to get away, duh!"

As both Braves rubbed their weeping eyes, they fought. Adlet had used his trump card and had only a few of his secret tools left. He knew he couldn't beat Hans. And at the very least, it was highly unlikely he could get away from him in a head-on situation, either. He couldn't flee unless he caught Hans off guard with some kind of inspired plan.

Hans could barely see a thing, but his attacks were still extremely fierce. His swords struck at Adlet's feet, from above, from every direction, as he stuck to Adlet as if they were dancing together.

"Stupid genius," Adlet muttered.

Hans was unmistakably brilliant. His talent was one in a hundred thousand, or maybe one in a million, or perhaps he was the only one of his kind in the world. How could he wield such fighting technique otherwise?

Adlet wasn't like that. He was ordinary. Hopelessly ordinary. But Adlet thought, *Just who decided an ordinary man couldn't become the strongest in the world?*

"I'm not lettin' ya get away meow!" Hans somersaulted forward in the air. Adlet couldn't predict what kind of attack was coming. He doubled his guard against the strike from above by blocking with both sword and scabbard. Hans landed, and with a cartwheel, he struck simultaneously with both swords and a kick. While Adlet was busy blocking the swords, the kick slammed into his stomach.

"Ha! That didn't work at all!" Adlet yelled, even as he felt like he might puke.

The man who'd taught Adlet to fight had never held back. It was by going through hell that Adlet had become strong. He'd trained his body, practiced his sword, and learned all there was to learn about his master's secret tools. But the more he had trained, the more keenly he'd felt that there was an insurmountable wall between the mundane and the genius.

"Over here!" Adlet taunted, and the moment Hans leaped, Adlet threw his final smoke bomb on the ground, dove underneath Hans, and ran.

All of Adlet's training had enabled him to somehow manage to block Hans's attacks—but he couldn't go on the offensive. An ordinary person couldn't surpass a prodigy. However, even if he wasn't as powerful as Hans, he could still win. He could beat a genius, though he lacked innate talent himself. Believing that had allowed Adlet to come this far.

Adlet's breath was ragged. Their fight had dragged on for a long time. Adlet had used up most of the tools on his belt. Hans was barely scraped, while Adlet's body was covered in wounds. Even so, Adlet could see the faintest signs of fatigue in his opponent. Hans's attacks were growing just a little bit less aggressive. Adlet had been waiting for this—the momentary lapse in his assault. Adlet removed one of the belts from which his various pouches hung and threw it away. Confused, Hans stopped. While Hans hesitated, Adlet quickly whipped off the second, third, and then fourth, tossing them all away. The belts fell to the ground between the two warriors.

"…" For the first time, Hans looked leery. He was not so simple a man as to think he was at an advantage because Adlet had thrown away his tools. "Hey…what're ya doin'?"

"Come at me," said Adlet. "I don't need any more tools. I can beat you fair and square."

"This is some kinda ruse."

"Yes, it is," Adlet acknowledged readily. Hans was overwhelmingly his superior when it came to swordplay. It would be crazy for him not to assume it was a trap.

"*Meow…*" Hans groaned. He seemed at a loss as to how to continue. It was curious. Hans had been utterly dominating the match thus far, and now that Adlet had thrown away his tools, he was at an even greater advantage. But despite that, Hans was unable to move.

The truth was, if Hans were to charge him without a single thought, Adlet would have been unable to do a thing. But Adlet was convinced that Hans wouldn't attack. Hans was sharp. And it was that sharpness that immobilized him. Even if Hans realized that the trap was the pretense that there was a trap, he couldn't attack.

"What's wrong, Hans? You scared?" taunted Adlet.

"Yeah, I'm scared," said Hans. "I can't fool ya there."

"You're honest."

"I do kill people, but I don't lie. Lyin' ain't good."

Adlet thought about it. In this situation, defeating Hans wouldn't spell victory. Victory for Adlet was clearing his name and finding the seventh. That was what he was aiming for.

"*Meow.*" Hans eyed Adlet warily—looking for something in the boy's clothes or mouth. To see if there was a weapon he could use among the paraphernalia strewn on the ground. But Hans wasn't paying attention to the one weapon Adlet still carried—his sword. Adlet took advantage of that.

"!"

Adlet grasped the hilt of his sword and twisted. Instantly, there was the sound of a powerful spring, and the blade of his sword shot out in a straight line, piercing the scabbard at Hans's waist.

"*Meow!*" Hans jumped away.

Without a pause, Adlet yelled, "Hans! You get it, don't you? You can tell that miss was deliberate!" As he spoke, he threw away the hilt that remained in his hands. Now he was completely unarmed.

"Why'd ya miss?" asked Hans.

"A man of your caliber should understand that, too." After throwing away the hilt, Adlet then removed his armor and stripped off his clothes. He showed Hans that he was completely unarmed. "Think about it, Hans. If I were the seventh, would I have any reason to deliberately miss? That shot was my only chance to defeat you. Why would I let that opportunity slide by?"

"...Meow."

Adlet would use this desperate situation to win Hans over to his side. A man of Hans's caliber should have understood that Adlet wasn't the seventh. *Please understand*, Adlet prayed.

"Yer not gonna trick me," said Hans.

"If I were the seventh, I would definitely kill you, but not necessarily trick you. It's incredibly unlikely that I'd be able to deceive you, but I could have almost certainly killed you."

"...Ngh."

"I'm one of the Braves, for real," said Adlet. "That's why I couldn't kill you—you're my ally. That's the answer. That's the reason I missed. Let that convince you!"

Still clenching his sword, Hans agonized.

Adlet was sure his argument was logically consistent. He was certain that it could convince Hans. But there was one big hole in his plan. If Hans was the seventh, then Adlet was completely defenseless and standing before the enemy. This was a gamble. Adlet had no choice but to bet on the chance that Hans wasn't the traitor. Adlet prayed. *Please, Hans, let this convince you. And please be one of the real Braves.*

In the end, Hans's body abruptly went slack. "Okay. You've convinced me. Yer a real Brave." Adlet had convinced him. Suddenly, the boy burst out in a cold sweat all over. It had been a risky bet, but he'd won.

What Hans said next, though, chilled his spine. "It's a good thing I was the one who stayed behind here," Hans mused. "Ya could've convinced any of the others."

"Huh?"

"You were close. You were real close." Hans smiled. Adlet ran toward the belts he'd discarded, groping for them. "Too bad I'm the seventh!" Hans cried, moving in the same instant Adlet did. The moment Adlet grabbed one of his belts, Hans sliced Adlet's throat in a horizontal sweep.

The searing impact ran through Adlet's body. He felt the sensation of his own head flying away.

But...Adlet was alive, still grasping for his belt. When he touched his neck, his head was still attached. Not a single layer of skin had been cut.

Hans stood behind him, smiling, as he said, "People can lie with their words. They can deceive with their actions. Ya can't trust their eyes or their voices or the looks on their faces. But right before they're about to kick off, their expressions don't lie. A man's true nature is always there the meowment before he dies." Adlet wasn't really listening to Hans. "If ya were the impostor, ya would've had a look on yer face like, *That's ridiculous.* But the look ya had said, *It's all over.* It looks like yer not the impostor."

"I thought...you'd...cut off...my head...," Adlet barely managed to squeeze out.

"Right? 'Cause I cut ya in a way that made ya think that." Hans smiled and then gathered up Adlet's armor and clothing and threw it at him. "How long are ya gonna stand there like an idiot? Get yer clothes on. I'm not into oglin' naked men."

Adlet composed himself and stood. He put on his clothes and belts and reassembled his sword.

"I'll be countin' on ya from here on out," said Hans. Now that Adlet was all equipped, Hans extended a hand to him. Adlet accepted the handshake. "To be honest, I thought it was a little strange. 'Cause if ya were the seventh, there'd be no reason for ya to try to protect Fremy."

"If you thought so, you should've said that in the first place."

"*Meow-hee-hee,* sorry."

Adlet had taken the first step forward, and it was a big one. He now had a dependable ally—and the one who had suspected him most, too—on his side. Adlet was finally starting to feel hopeful.

Fremy and Mora were at the location where Adlet had spent the night.

"There are various traces of his passage here, but...I cannot determine which way he ran." Mora, who had been crouching as she examined the ground, seemed to have given up as she stood to go.

"The bloodstains and the footprints all cut off partway," commented Fremy.

"I am forced to consider that scoundrel first-rate when it comes to flight."

Fremy looked around. "I wonder if he's still nearby?"

"The possibility is remote. I doubt he would remain here to be found," said Mora.

"He may have purposely made us believe that and then stayed in the area."

Mora folded her arms and pondered for a while.

"What's wrong?" asked Fremy.

"I don't know. What is Adlet's aim?"

"He's just running because he's out of options."

"No. He must still be plotting something. His plans thus far have been meticulous. I cannot imagine that this is the end."

"Whatever the case, we just have to catch up to him. Let's go. We have no choice but to search for him randomly." Fremy turned her back to Mora and began walking.

But Mora called out to her. "No need to rush. Let us talk a spell. We can make our move once we have put our thoughts in order."

"All right," said Fremy.

"First, I would like to ask you something. Did you know about this trap?"

"No."

"You have not heard fiends talk to one another of any of this?" Mora asked.

"Is this an interrogation?"

Mora put her hands on Fremy's shoulders and said, "Wait. Don't misunderstand me. It's no surprise that you are cautious around us, due to what occurred yesterday, but we doubt you no more."

"Oh? What about Hans? And Chamo?" Fremy sounded skeptical.

"Let me amend myself. I doubt you no more. I believe you are our valued comrade."

"I see." The pressure of Mora's gaze caused Fremy to lower her own a few degrees. "Sorry, but I don't know anything. Fiends split off into their own small units, and there's almost no interaction between each cell."

"I thought that they were a more unified lot," said Mora.

"The internal affairs of fiends are complicated. Far more complicated than you think."

"I see."

"Don't *you* have any information?" asked Fremy. "We have a human siding with the Evil God. You had no inkling of anything about that?"

"I did not. I suppose I must be ridiculed for my incompetence." Mora sighed. "Bits of information did reach me. I had heard that some were making deals with fiends and that the monsters had abducted entire villages. But I judged both of these rumors to be false, though I had nothing to substantiate that assumption. Had I fulfilled my duties more thoroughly, I could have prevented this situation." Mora put a hand to her forehead. Her expression revealed regret.

"Don't trouble yourself over it. It's not your responsibility."

"Oh? So you *are* capable of being kind," said Mora smiling. Then she patted Fremy's head. "Adlet did do one good thing. He brought you to us. Though it may only have been a part of his plot, it was good nonetheless."

"Don't treat me like a child."

"From my perspective, you *are* a child."

Fremy shook her head, sweeping aside Mora's hand.

"It matters not that you were the Brave-killer," said Mora. "You were simply following orders. When a soldier kills on the battlefield, they are charged with no crime. Though it seems the princess and Goldof are not convinced, in time they will come to understand."

"…"

"Chamo will warm up to you soon, too. She may be a troublemaker, but she's not a bad child. As for Hans, just leave him be. There is no need for you to build walls around yourself because you were the Brave-killer or the daughter of a fiend."

Fremy was silent for a while, refusing to look at Mora. "We shouldn't be wasting our time chatting. Let's track down Adlet," she said, and she broke into a run.

Mora followed after her. "I know there are some things weighing on your mind when it comes to Adlet, since he was the only one who tried to help you when you were under suspicion." Fremy did not reply. "But you cannot go easy on him," Mora continued. "He is our enemy—and one frighteningly prone to foul play, to boot."

"Relax. I hate him from the bottom of my heart," said Fremy.

"That's the spirit. As soon as we find him, kill him. Be sure to kill him, Fremy." *Be sure to kill him*, Mora emphasized over and over. She repeated it so many times, her persistence began irritating the former Brave-killer.

Nashetania and Goldof were near the border of the barrier, at the end of the road that led to the Howling Vilelands, where the Braves of the Six Flowers were supposed to have gathered. Mora and Hans had been waiting there until the day before.

"Can you hear anything from the direction of the temple?" asked Goldof.

"No, nothing," Nashetania replied. "But never mind that. We have to search for Adlet."

Hidden in the broad thicket by the side of the path was a pit. It looked like Mora and Hans had been hiding there. Her expression grave, Nashetania searched the pit, but she was the only one pursuing the matter with such fervor. Goldof did nothing but stand and scowl.

"It's no good," said Nashetania as she emerged from the pit. "Hans and Mora were most definitely here, but that was all I could find out. Hans must have received some kind of information from the fiends here, but there are no signs that any approached this area." Nashetania scratched her head. "I want to meet with Mora. Though I wonder if she will listen. She believes that Adlet is the seventh. How can I convince her?"

"Your Highness..."

"I'm angry at myself. I am unable to do anything or think of anything, even though they could be killing Adlet right this minute!"

"Your Highness, stop it already, please!" shouted Goldof, unable to stand it any longer.

Nashetania glared at him. "I thought you said you trusted me."

"Adlet is our enemy! You may say what you will, but that will not change!"

"That's enough. If you don't trust me, then I will just have to go after him by myself!" Nashetania said, but she immediately put a hand to her mouth. "I'm sorry, Goldof. That was going too far." Her expression was sorrowful. "I cannot believe this. I never imagined we would have a shouting match like this, not ever."

Goldof also looked pained. The moment Nashetania turned her back to him, the dam broke. "Your Highness, why Adlet?"

"Huh?"

"Why do you trust him and not me, who has served you ever since my youth?"

"What do you mean?" asked Nashetania.

"Pardon my saying so, but this is the first time I've ever seen you like this," he said. "You've been acting wild, when you've always been so much more composed. You're not yourself! Something has changed you!" Nashetania was dumbfounded. "Just what is he to you?!" Goldof demanded. "How can you be so concerned with this—this *outlaw* who barged into the Tournament Before the Divine, this oaf who came from who knows where whom you have known for only a short journey of ten days?!"

Nashetania looked at Goldof, her face overcome with surprise. "No, *you* are not yourself."

"Your Highness, I—"

"What are you talking about, Goldof? The fate of the world hangs in the balance with this battle, and it's only just begun. The life of one of our allies is in danger. How could I act normally?"

"I—I—"

"Adlet is our ally. He is a valuable comrade in our fight as we stand together against the Evil God. What did you think it was besides that?"

"..."

"You're not yourself," said Nashetania. "I apologize, but this is not the time to be making concessions to your jealousy."

"You're right. I should be protecting you. I haven't been myself." Goldof was looking at the ground. He was so humiliated he was trembling.

"Goldof, I noticed your feelings quite some time ago. But now is not the time. It really is *not* the time."

"Yes, Your Highness."

"Let us forget this conversation," she said.

"As you wish."

Nashetania breathed a quiet sigh. "So even you can lose your composure at times. Of course, you're still only sixteen. Still a child. I had thought of you as someone I could rely on, so I had forgotten."

"..."

"We don't understand each other as well as I had thought, I suppose." Nashetania returned to her search, and Goldof stood there, paralyzed. Her manner gave him the impression that there was now a large rift in their master-servant relationship.

"Hey, let's search the whole temple through one more time," proposed Hans.

Adlet and Hans went into the temple together and checked again to see if there were any possible exits or hidden doors. But they couldn't find anything, not even a trace. As they searched, Adlet was a little cautious around Hans. If they couldn't find anything, maybe Hans might decide Adlet was the seventh, after all.

Hans nimbly clung to the ceiling, checking to make sure nothing was strange about any of it. "*Hmmmeow.* There's got to be somethin'," he said. It didn't look like Hans was reconsidering his judgment. He didn't even seem leery of Adlet.

That made Adlet a little suspicious himself—maybe Hans actually was the seventh, and he was just watching to see what Adlet would do.

"What're ya doin'?" asked Hans. "Yer the one in trouble here. Keep lookin'."

"Y-you're right. Sorry." Flustered, Adlet returned to his task of examining the floor. It was a frightening thing, for one among them to be an impostor. It made them unable to trust even those they should trust most. For the time being, Adlet couldn't afford to doubt Hans. He had no choice but to bet that Hans was really one of the Braves of the Six Flowers.

"Nope, no exits here," Hans said as he released his grip on the ceiling and landed on the floor. They had investigated the entire floor and every wall, and all they had learned was that there was no way out. "I've got no idea," said Hans. "If yer not the seventh, that means somebody must have come in here before you did. But there's no way in. What does this mean?"

"It must have been a Saint, after all," said Adlet. "She had the power to create a way out, or the power to pass through walls. Or even a power that would allow her to close a door once it had been opened."

"But Mora said there weren't no Saints like that. So does that mean we should be suspectin' her?" asked Hans.

Mora had asserted that she was informed as to the powers of every single Saint. She had also said that even a Saint would have been unable to enter the temple without leaving a trace of her passage. There was the possibility that she had been lying.

"That'd be premature," said Adlet. "There might be one with abilities that Mora doesn't know about. The eighth could be one of the Saints that Mora knows—she's just hiding some of her abilities."

"True. But then…that means this is a stalemeowt."

"Yeah… Oops, I almost forgot." Adlet opened up the iron box that he'd left in a corner of the temple. Fleeing from the others and fighting with Hans had used up all of Adlet's tools. He had to restock in preparation for the next battle.

"Ya sure have a lot of stuff. Ain't there anythin' we could use? Like some kinda lie detector?" asked Hans as he peered into the iron box.

"All I brought with me are tools to fight fiends. If I'd known this would happen, I would've brought other stuff, too." That was when Adlet found an iron bottle tucked away at the very bottom of his box. He pulled it out and started thinking.

"What's up?" asked Hans. "Figured out who the seventh is?"

"No…not exactly, but…" Adlet thought some more. Then he pulled the stopper from the little spray bottle with red liquid inside. He spritzed some of it on the altar.

"What're ya doin'?"

"Oh, this isn't anything that major, but…"

"What?" Hans examined the little bottle.

Just as Adlet was about to explain, they heard a faint sound from outside the temple. Hans immediately ran outside, and Adlet stowed the bottle away in one of his belt pouches. "Has someone come back?" Adlet poked his face out the broken door, looking around the area.

Hans gave him a wave to signal that there was no trouble. "They might come back soon," he said.

"We should hurry."

The two of them searched the outside of the temple for any indicator that there was a way in. As before, they found nothing—no traces of anything unnatural and no footprints. They didn't even get a faint feeling that something was out of place.

"What're we gonna do meow, though?" asked Hans. "Things ain't gonna be so great once the others come back."

"We could give up searching here and look for the eighth," Adlet suggested.

"Just at random?" Hans replied. "I'd like to find some kinda clue, at least."

Adlet leaned against a pillar of salt, closed his eyes, and reflected. He couldn't find any proof that the eighth even existed, to say nothing of clues as to the conspirator's identity. But the eighth had to exist, because when Adlet had walked into the temple, the barrier had already been up. Someone had initiated it beforehand. When the barrier activated, Fremy, Nashetania, and Goldof had all been together. Hans and Mora had been together. Only one of them had been alone.

"Maybe Chamo?" Adlet speculated. She'd wandered into the temple on her own. No one could prove what she'd been doing or where she'd been before that.

But even if she had no alibi, that didn't change the fact that it would have been impossible for Chamo to enter the temple. Either way, Adlet wouldn't be able to resolve anything without finding a way someone could have broken into the temple.

"By the way," said Hans, "we were all in a rush, so I didn't get the chance to ask ya somethin'…"

"What?"

"How d'ya turn on this barrier? I didn't stop by the fort, so I don't really know."

"So Mora didn't tell you? The barrier…," Adlet began, and then he stopped. Lights flickered on in his head. What Hans had said was important.

"What is it?" asked Hans.

Adlet racked his brain to recall everything from the time he'd entered the fort until the present, including every single word each of them had exchanged. And he was convinced that his flash of insight was on the mark. "Chamo."

"She's the seventh?"

"No. There's something I want to ask her," said Adlet. "Where is she now?"

"Chamo should be playin' around here somewhere. I'm too much of a scaredy-cat to call her, though."

"It wouldn't be good for me to be seen here, I'm sure. You go. Just ask her one thing."

"Ask her what?"

"Well…" Adlet was about to tell him what the question was when he caught sight of a big earthworm right in front of them. It was gliding over the ground with unbelievable speed, heading into the forest. A moment passed, and then a voice called out from the direction that the creature had gone.

"Chamo's right here." The young Saint came over to them, her foxtail swaying in her right hand. "Wasn't this guy the fake, catboy? Why're you guys just chatting casually?"

Hans panicked and stood in front of Adlet. "*Meow.* Don't attack him, Chamo. I've found out he's not the enemy."

"That sounds weird. Why not?"

"Well—"

"If it's gonna be a long story, don't bother." Chamo cut him off. "Chamo doesn't really care, anyway."

Hans was confused. Adlet didn't know what Chamo was thinking, either. Did she even want to find the seventh?

"Being stuck here sucks," said Chamo. "It's boring being alone, and there's nothing to play with. Chamo wants to get out now and go kill fiends."

"I get it," said Adlet. "Me too. So there's something I want to ask you. This is really important so we can find out who's the seventh."

But Chamo just gave him a bored pout. "Chamo's sick of that stuff about who's the fake and who's real or whatever." She raised her foxtail and smiled faintly. As she did, goose bumps raised on Adlet's skin. "It's probably you, Adlet. Then if it's not you, Fremy. Then if it's not her, catboy. If it's not him, then obviously it's the princess and the big guy. Auntie Mora couldn't be the seventh, so Chamo won't kill her."

"Wait, Chamo! What are you talking about?!" Adlet yelled, and as he did, he reflexively drew his sword. Hans, too, arched his back in a catlike fighting stance.

"If you all die, there's no enemy. Just Chamo alone is enough to beat one lame Evil God." Chamo's foxtail moved. She put the tip into her mouth and pushed it to the back of her throat. She made a retching noise and gagged dramatically. Soon Chamo was vomiting loudly, spewing black and brown mixed with dirty green onto the ground. The amount was unnatural—ten times more than the volume of her small frame.

"*Meow—m-meow!*" Hans cried out in fear.

The vomit was taking shape into a gigantic snake, a leech, a frog, and a lizard—the forms of fiends that lived in the water.

"Time to explain. There's a swamp in Chamo's stomach. All the creatures Chamo's ever eaten live together in harmony in a swamp inside," she explained as she wiped the drool off with her sleeve. The fiends rushed Adlet and Hans all at once.

"*Run!*" cried Hans.

"I'm with you there!" agreed Adlet.

The two of them turned without a moment's hesitation. But there were even more fiends waiting for them in the forest. Adlet and Hans ran back the other way, passing through the pillars of salt. But the fiends Chamo had spat up disregarded the barrier, rushing in to attack Adlet and Hans. There were nearly fifty of the regurgitated creatures surrounding the temple.

"We've got no choice!" Adlet yelled. Now they could do nothing but fight. Adlet pulled a bomb from one of his pouches and tossed it into the mouth of a snake-fiend. Hans whirled through the air to cut off the head of an attacking lizard, but in moments, the fiends revived as if the assault had been nothing at all. The two men cooperated to bring down a water spider that sprang at them, but when Adlet and Hans tore off its eight legs, they grew back again instantly.

"What in the heck is this?" groaned Hans. "How can we fight meownsters like these?" Adlet finally understood why Fremy was so terrified of Chamo.

The fiends from Chamo's stomach lined up in a row and then curved into a circle. Now there was nowhere for the pair to run.

"Stop screwing around, Chamo!" yelled Adlet. "Why're you attacking Hans, too?!"

"Why not?" she said. "You can't prove he's not a fake, too."

"You idiot! What are you thinking?!" Adlet was enraged.

But the look on Chamo's face told him she didn't even get why he was so mad. "Here's an idea. Chamo kills you, and then if the barrier goes away, catboy doesn't need to die."

Adlet looked at Hans. Hans smiled wryly and said, "Don't worry. That ain't gonna happen." Hans pointed his sword at Chamo.

"Hans," said Adlet. "If there's no getting out of this, you should escape, at least."

"Screw that. Don't you start tryin' to act the heroic martyr."

The two of them charged at Chamo. She smiled and vomited up even more fiends.

Trapped within a ring of demons, Adlet and Hans fought. Chamo stood between them in the center of the ring, her arms crossed.

Chamo was their only target. There was no point in trying to fight her fiends. But no matter how many times they charged, one monster after another stood in their way. They even blocked Adlet's projectiles with their own bodies.

"Attacking separately isn't gonna work! We've gotta work together!" shouted Adlet.

"*Meow!* I know! You come up with somethin'!"

The two of them split up and then came at her from either side. Adlet drew her attention while Hans circled around behind her. Neither of their attacks connected. Each fiend moved independently. There was no point trying to catch Chamo off guard.

The little Saint giggled. "That's what everyone does. Trying to work together to get Chamo, huh? Nobody's ever been able to do that." There was no anxiety in her voice—she didn't act as though she was in the middle of a fight.

"Can't ya think of anythin', Adlet?!" Hans yelled.

The world's strongest man was unable to reply. A leech-fiend had come up from behind to spray acid at him. Adlet jumped sideways to evade it, but then a lizard-fiend pressed down on him from above. He cut open the lizard's stomach with his sword and tossed the creature behind him.

Adlet was tired. He hadn't yet recovered from his battle with Hans, and it was probably the same for Hans, too. The longer this dragged out, the greater their disadvantage. "Hans! Cover me!" Adlet cried.

As Hans sliced open a frog-fiend's tongue, he replied, "I've got my hands full here! Don't ya get lazy meow!"

"While you're protecting me, I can think!" said Adlet.

Hans made a wide leap to stand beside Adlet, and then, as he'd been told, he fought off Adlet's attackers. The way he moved seemed frantic and reckless. He wouldn't last long.

"How long can you hold out?" Adlet asked him so as not to be overheard.

"Sixty seconds," Hans replied.

"Once those sixty seconds are up, don't think of anything else—just rush Chamo. I'll back you up," said Adlet, and then he fixed his eyes on their target as his thoughts raced.

First, he had to pick out an effective tool. Adlet threw a variety of poisoned needles and checked their effects. The sleeping needle and the paralysis needle didn't work, but the needle that caused pain was effective. Next, he took the bottle of alcohol from its pouch and poured some into his mouth. He clacked the flint in his teeth and sprayed the fiends with flames. All the fiends Chamo controlled were aquatic—so flame worked, after all.

"Whoa, that's surprising. Spitting fire isn't something normal people can do," Chamo said nonchalantly.

You're the last one I wanna hear that from, thought Adlet. And then he pulled one more tool from another pouch—the one he'd used when he and Nashetania had been protecting the villagers, the flute that attracted fiends' attention. Fire, poison needles, and the flute. Would those be enough to stop Chamo? Adlet doubted it. His plan needed one more thing.

But Hans couldn't hold out much longer. They'd have to play it by ear from here. "Hans, go!" Adlet yelled, and he blew the flute. All the fiends twitched in response and turned toward Adlet. While they were distracted, Hans closed most of the distance between himself and Chamo. Adlet blew fire at the fiends that attacked him to keep them at bay. But the flute could serve as a distraction for only a moment. The fiends attacked Hans from both sides, but Hans made no move to evade them. He trusted Adlet, and Adlet did not betray that trust. He pierced the fiends with poison needles thrown so quickly his hands were a blur. The fiends shrieked, their bodies writhing in agony.

"Hope you're ready for this, Chamo!" cried Adlet.

Hans leaped. There was nothing between him and his target. But Adlet still didn't think this would be enough. Fremy had been so terrified of Chamo. It would take more than a simple surprise attack.

Chamo smirked. "Dummies," she said, opening her mouth wide.

As she did, Adlet yelled, "Don't dodge! Block it!"

A large, armful-sized sea roach spewed from Chamo's mouth. It charged Hans like a ball from a cannon. Hans crossed his swords to block the sea roach's attack in midair. It hurled him away easily. But now Adlet moved—he made a beeline toward Hans and Chamo and then jumped, kicking Hans in the back with both feet. The kick offset Hans's backward momentum to send him spinning in the air like a ball.

Adlet yelled, "Finish her, Hans!"

Hans soared toward Chamo. Chamo looked as though she didn't understand what was going on as she stared at the man.

"Got ya meow!" Hans cried as he whirled through the air. He struck Chamo's head with the flat of his blade. Chamo collapsed, and Hans landed with a roll.

Both feet back on the ground, Adlet ran toward Chamo. But there was no need to strike the final blow—she was unconscious. Instantly, her fiends lost form. They returned to their original mud-like state and, in only a few seconds, were sucked back into Chamo's mouth.

"Adlet! Stopper her up!" Hans yelled.

Adlet pulled bandages from one of his pouches and shoved them into the unconscious girl's mouth. "*Mgnh!*" Chamo's eyes opened, and she tried to spit them out.

"*Meow!* Don't let her spit 'em out!"

Adlet grabbed both of Chamo's arms with one hand, and with the other, he stuffed the bandages farther into her mouth. Hans got to his feet and ran toward them to help pin down the squirming Chamo. "Stop strugglin'!" ordered Hans.

"I'm tying her up!" said Adlet.

The two of them discarded their swords and wrestled Chamo. Adlet pulled out another bandage and forcibly tied it around her head as a gag. He then removed his belt, using it to bind her arms behind her back. Even then, Chamo continued struggling for a while, but eventually, she settled down.

Once the fight was over, Adlet was so exhausted he just didn't say anything for a while. Hans was the same. They were tired—just incredibly tired.

"My back hurts," Hans muttered.

The two of them lay collapsed on the ground beside Chamo for a long while.

"So what are we gonna do? What're we gonna do?" they asked each other.

They both looked at Chamo where she lay on the ground. She was glaring at Adlet with the expression of a child who had gotten up to no good, been scolded for it, and was now sulking, as if saying, *You don't have to get so mad at me.*

When she's not fighting, she really is just a kid, thought Adlet. "I don't think Chamo is the seventh," he said.

"Me neither," agreed Hans.

The seventh was most likely an exceedingly well-prepared and cautious person. The way Chamo acted, on the other hand, was incredibly shortsighted and careless. Of course, Adlet couldn't say anything for sure.

"*Meow.* Since we've come to this temple, we've done nothin' but fight our own allies."

"You're right. This seventh is a pain in the butt." Adlet stood. There was no time to waste. The others who were out searching for Adlet would soon be returning to the temple.

"So what was yer question for Chamo?" asked Hans. "I don't think she can reply all tied up, though."

"It's okay. It's just a yes-or-no question." Adlet stood beside Chamo. As she continued glaring at him, he asked, "Just answer this one thing. You can just shake or nod your head. Please." Chamo didn't look happy but seemed willing to reply. "Do you know how to activate the Phantasmal Barrier?" he asked.

Chamo gave him a blank stare. She looked as if she didn't know why he was even asking her that question. She shook her head.

"Did you know how to activate the barrier before you met us in this temple?"

Chamo quietly shook her head again.

About fifteen minutes after their battle with Chamo had ended, Adlet dashed through the misty forest, attempting to keep his footsteps quiet. He was heading eastward from the temple. When he looked up at the sky, he saw the time was past noon. The sun had begun its descent.

"*Ngh.*" With every jump from branch to branch, his back sent a jolt of pain through his body. He was unable to make sound landings or quiet ones. The sword wound from the previous day still hurt. He was out of painkillers, and his battles with Hans and Chamo had made the injury worse. He was wounded and tired, and the pain doubled his exhaustion.

"Keep holding on, Adlet," he told himself.

Hans, his only comrade, wasn't with him. Hans had stayed with Chamo in the temple to keep an eye on her and make sure she didn't get out of control again—and also to protect her from the seventh. The wildly powerful Chamo bound and helpless on the floor was the perfect chance for the seventh. Though it was discouraging not to be able to fight along-side Hans, they had no choice.

Adlet scanned the area, checking to make sure there was no one nearby, and then pulled the firecracker from one of his pouches. It was the firecracker that Fremy had handed him the previous night, the one that would alert her to his position. He deliberated for a moment, then struck the firecracker against the trunk of a tree, making it explode. After that, he concealed himself high in the tree and waited for Fremy.

Adlet had an idea—a clue as to how to break out of the seventh's trap.

Fremy and Mora were on the northern side of the forest, running toward the temple. Fremy said, "I'm sure. That was the sound of Chamo fighting."

Mora replied, "But we cannot hear it now. Either she let him escape, or the battle is over."

"Chamo would never lose. Besides, Hans is there, too."

"But I can hear no signal. What is the meaning of this?" wondered Mora.

The groups hunting Adlet had decided that if they were to discover him or anything else important, they would signal the others with a loud blast from one of Fremy's bombs.

Suddenly, Fremy stopped. She looked around the area, thinking.

"What is it?" asked Mora.

"Mora, you go to the temple. I'm heading the other way."

"What are you talking about?"

"Adlet most likely fought Chamo and ran. If he comes this way, you fight him. If he went in the other direction, I'll find him."

"…All right. You take care." Mora seemed to be implying something in her words. Her eyes were sharp and attentive as they fixed on Fremy.

Once Mora was out of sight, Fremy sprinted straight through the forest.

Adlet was waiting in his tree for Fremy to show up. He had no guarantee that she would be on his side. On the contrary, she might just as readily bring

Mora to murder him. His chances were fifty-fifty or slimmer. If he'd been able to contact Nashetania, he would have preferred to rely on her. But she had Goldof with her, and he probably wouldn't leave her side, no matter what happened. At this point, Adlet had no choice but to count on Fremy.

As he waited, he recalled his discussion with Hans. Before they'd fought Chamo, while still searching the temple, Adlet had proposed summoning Fremy.

Hans's reaction had been a troubled look. "*Meow*, I thought that was a li'l strange. So she did let you go deliberately, after all."

"You could tell?"

"I just had a feelin', like meowbe. Fremy wasn't sayin' nothin', though."

Adlet became somewhat uneasy. That meant any of the others might have caught on to Fremy and Adlet's secret agreement. "Let's call Fremy. She might have found something."

"Forget it. In fact, don't ever call her up, no way. That woman is dangerous."

"What makes you say that?"

"Well, meow that I'm not suspectin' you no more, she's the one most likely to be the seventh."

Adlet shook his head. "Fremy is a real Brave. I just know."

"Then I'm gonna have to disagree."

The two of them stared each other down for a while. It looked as though neither was going to change his mind.

"Let's leave aside if she's the real thing or not for meow and think about this," said Hans. "I reckon that even if Fremy is a real Brave, we should steer clear of her."

"Why?" asked Adlet. "She let me go."

"Yeah, for now. I think she's gunnin' to ultimately kill ya."

"Why do you think that?"

Hans's eyes shone sharply. The flippant attitude he'd displayed thus far disappeared. What Adlet saw there now was a coldhearted and unfeeling assassin. "Fremy lives in darkness," said Hans. "She don't love no one,

and she don't trust no one. All she's got in her life are enemies and people
bound to become her enemies. That's the world she lives in. Ya know?"

"..."

"I live in darkness, too. But where she is, the darkness is even deeper,"
said Hans.

"Is that what you think?"

"Yep. She's a totally different kinda critter—not like you. Yer thinkin'
about trust and friendship and comrades. Don't assume you guys are just
gonna understand each other."

He didn't think Hans's warning was fake. Hans was telling him, in his
own way, that he was concerned on Adlet's behalf. But Adlet didn't agree
that it would be impossible to build trust between himself and Fremy.

"Adlet, Fremy hates you, even after ya tried so hard to stick up for her."

"..."

"Don't get the wrong idea. She's not playin' hard to get or nothin' like
that. She hates you sincerely with all her heart—naw, she loathes ya. At
least, that's what it sounded like from how she was talkin' this mornin'."
Adlet had thought that had been an act.

"Well, forget about Fremy," said Hans. "We've gotta talk about this
locked-room meowstery." On that note, they dropped the subject.

After Chamo's defeat, Adlet had told Hans that he was going to find
Fremy and left the temple. Hans had emphasized over and over that Adlet
should be careful.

The boy thought about Fremy. The previous night, the two of them
had talked about each other's pasts. At the time, he'd felt that they'd made
a connection, however small. He couldn't imagine that feeling was just in
his head. He didn't think she trusted him, but there was no good reason
for her to hate him, either. He didn't know what she was thinking. He
couldn't read her mind. Was ignoring Hans's warning the right decision?
Adlet would know soon.

He spotted Fremy deep in the fog. He could see her blurry outline,
and it seemed as though she was looking for him. He waited for a bit, just

to get a grasp of the situation. There was no sign of anyone else around. He steeled himself and jumped down in front of her.

"I'm impressed you're still alive." That was the first thing Fremy said to him. Her hand was on her gun, finger on the trigger, but she didn't point it at him.

"It was exhausting," he said. "There were a bunch of times I thought I was gonna die. When I went back to the temple, Hans was there, and—"

"Just talk about things relevant to the deactivation of the barrier," Fremy said coldly.

Adlet flinched a little, but on further consideration, her attitude wasn't something to be concerned about. She had always been like this. "I have an idea," he said. "I want your opinion on it and some information."

"That depends on what you have to say," she replied.

"I've figured out part of the seventh's trap."

"I'm listening."

"First of all, we had it all wrong. Or rather, the seventh gave us the wrong idea. It wasn't that someone activated the barrier immediately before I opened the door to the temple. When I opened the door and went inside, the barrier hadn't been activated yet."

"That story doesn't sound very plausible," said Fremy.

"Just listen. We know how the barrier is activated. You thrust the sword into the altar and order the slate to activate it, and it turns on the barrier. Who gave us that information? It was the soldier who was at the fort, Private Loren." His eyes fixed on Fremy, Adlet continued. "But what if Private Loren was working with the seventh? Neither you nor I even knew that the barrier existed until Private Loren told us. And it was just yesterday that Nashetania and Goldof heard about it for the first time. Mora knew, but she said she didn't know how to activate it, and she's the one who told Hans. And just now, I checked with Chamo. She said she found out how to activate it yesterday from me. In other words, none of us would know if Private Loren was lying."

"...Continue."

"This is how the seventh's plan was set up: First, they'd use Private

Loren to tell us a fake way to activate the barrier. Then they'd use fiends to lure all of us inside the barrier. They estimated when I would open the doors to the temple and then used some means to generate fog throughout the forest. That would trick us into thinking that someone had activated the barrier and then fled the scene, when in fact, the barrier wasn't actually active at all. It was just regular mist. And the sword had been stuck in the altar from the beginning."

"…"

He continued. "Then the seventh would approach the altar, looking totally innocent, and activate the barrier for real. Everyone was fiddling with the pedestal in an attempt to deactivate the barrier, right? The seventh used all that as cover to turn it on. After that, it was revealed that there had been no way in or out of the temple until I opened the door. So once they pinned the deed on me, the trap was complete."

"Hans was the one who accused you of doing it," said Fremy. "So does that mean he's the seventh?"

"I don't think so. The seventh most likely planned to make the accusation, but Hans happened to know a lot about the Saint's doors, so they left the talking to him."

"You don't think Hans is the seventh? Why not?"

Adlet supplemented his explanation a bit, adding that he and Hans had mutually recognized that neither of them was the seventh and that they'd fought Chamo afterward. "The important part is that someone guessed when I would enter the temple and then activated the fog. If we can catch the person who caused the fog, then I can prove my innocence."

"I see." Fremy considered this for a while. "I think your idea is great. I'm impressed."

Adlet made a fist and struck his other palm with it.

But then Fremy said, "But it's wrong. Definitely wrong."

"Huh?"

"Because it would be impossible. You couldn't create fog without activating the barrier."

"Couldn't the Saint of Fog do something like that?" he asked.

"You have the wrong idea about the Saints. You think they can use the power of the Spirits to do anything. That's not true. The power Saints wield is limited to certain abilities."

"But there is a Saint who can create fog, isn't there?"

"Yes, the Saint of Fog, one of the Saints who created the barrier. But it's unthinkable that she could have created this mist."

"Why?"

"First of all, when the Saint of Fog uses her power, it's activated directly around her," explained Fremy. "Her radius is about fifty meters. And the fog would take time to spread over the whole forest. I think it would take her at least fifteen minutes, considering the scale. But yesterday, the fog appeared over the whole area all at once."

"Wait. When the barrier was activated, didn't the fog cover the forest instantly?" asked Adlet.

"It did. But that was because they spent a long time building it up. The Saint infused the power of the Spirit of Fog throughout this whole forest over the course of ten years. That's why the barrier was able to generate it immediately." Fremy shook her head. She pointed at Adlet's feet and said, "Try digging there."

Adlet used his sword to dig a little in the ground and found a stake there with text written on it in hieroglyphs.

"That stake is imbued with the power of the Phantasmal Barrier," she said. "There are countless others like that buried all over the forest. Oh, and I forgot to tell you—you can erect only one kind of barrier at a time in any given location. If you were to try to erect two or more, one would be nullified."

"B-but…"

"It wouldn't be possible to create the fog without the power of a barrier, and you can't create two barriers in this forest in order to generate that fog. In other words, your proposal is impossible."

Adlet was speechless. He'd thought it was a brilliant solution, but she'd overturned it so easily. And he didn't think there was any other way. There was no room for rebuttal.

"Do you have any questions?" Fremy emotionlessly asked the stricken Adlet.

"You fools!" Mora's shriek echoed throughout the temple. She punched the floor with a gauntlet-clad fist, and the ground all around shook slightly.

"*M-meow.* Ya don't have to get so hollerin' mad." Hans quickly explained to Mora what had happened.

As Mora listened to his story, her face grew redder, and when he finished, she laid bare her anger. "Chamo was out of line. But, Hans! I'd thought you an utter simpleton, but not to such an absurd degree!"

"Hey meow, that's not a nice thing to say," the assassin protested.

"Why did you allow Adlet to escape? That may have been our best chance—no, our only chance!"

Hans sounded fed up as he said, "Hey, hold yer horses, Mora. I think I can prove he's innocent."

"What are you talking about?" Mora demanded.

"He's quite the guy. He saw through the seventh's ploy."

"I'm listening. Pray that my patience will hold until the end."

Hans told Mora of Adlet's deductions. Mora listened quietly, but once Hans was done talking, she heaved a large sigh. "You have no understanding of the power of the Saints. It would be impossible to create that fog."

"It's more possible than breakin' into the temple."

"No difference. Nobody could have broken into the temple, and generating such mist would be unworkable." Mora explained why it would have been impossible to create the fog—that in order to generate it instantaneously, it would be necessary to create a barrier, and that two barriers could not exist simultaneously.

"*Meow*, you're a stubborn woman. Even after hearin' that, I still figure it could be done."

"Chamo, can you think of anything? A way you could generate fog instantly?" asked Mora.

Hans was still restraining Chamo's arms where she stood. The little Saint shook her head.

"You guys ain't got it right. Just thinkin' for a minute ain't enough to figure it out. The seventh put this plan into motion 'cause they came up with somethin' we totally wouldn't expect."

"Oh, I see. Well then, go ahead and think all you like. I will search for Adlet." Mora was turning away from Hans when she found his knife stuck in the ground at her feet.

"You hold on. I know Adlet ain't the seventh," he said.

"Haven't you been scolded enough?" Mora glared at him.

"If Adlet is the seventh, then why didn't he kill me? Why was he protectin' Fremy? Why didn't he kill Chamo? Ya can't explain that."

As if to express her complete exasperation, Mora sighed. "You fail to grasp why? Allow me to explain in simple terms why Adlet did not kill you."

"..."

"Why did he appear in our midst in the first place?" Mora posed. "If his goal was simply to shut us in, showing himself at this temple wouldn't have been necessary. He could have secretly activated the barrier and then concentrated on evading us. But he deliberately created a fake crest for himself and blended among us. To what end?"

"*Meow*, well—"

"To sow confusion. He raises doubt to incite conflict. *What if Adlet is a real Brave? What if the seventh is someone else?* His trap is one that assaults our hearts. How can you fail to understand that?!" Hans was unable to reply. Chamo, her mouth still gagged, smirked. "And right now, his plan is succeeding," said Mora. "He has wholly deceived you, and it seems the princess also believes that Adlet is not the impostor. Two of our six have already fallen for his tricks."

"But Adlet—"

"Why did he attempt to protect Fremy? To lure her to his side. Why did he not kill you? To beguile you. You believe he could not be the seventh because he didn't kill you? On the contrary, he would most certainly spare you. Have you anything to say to that?!"

"But I saw his face!" protested Hans.

"You believe a man incapable of deception at the moment of his death?

That's nothing more than your pet idea!" Hans faltered. Her voice resolute, Mora said quietly, "We can no longer be picky about our methods."

Adlet asked Fremy question after question, trying to conceive of any possible means by which the barrier could have been activated or if perhaps a Saint could have done it. Adlet didn't know much about Saints' power. To find out more, he had no choice but to grill Fremy.

But Fremy wasn't very responsive, merely repeating again and again that it would have been impossible. "Why don't you just give up?" she suggested stonily, cutting off his string of questions. "It's over. Your suppositions are most likely wrong, and you've run out of places to hide. Even if you were a real Brave, there's no way you can survive now."

Adlet hesitated. Maybe it would be impossible to convince Fremy to cooperate with him, after all. Maybe no matter how much he talked to her, it wasn't going to work out. Maybe it would be better to turn to someone else for help. "I can't. I can't give up. If I die, then the seventh will go for you next. They'll lay the blame on you, and you'll get killed, just like me."

Fremy lowered her gaze in thought. She also had to be keenly aware of how precarious her own situation was. They had been speaking for a long time, and Mora could have been heading their way. Remaining together any longer could prove dangerous. Just as Adlet thought about leaving, Fremy said, "Are you going to go look for Nashetania now?" There was an expression of disgust on her face. She had hit the nail on the head. Now that Fremy was done with him, Nashetania was the only one he could count on. "You rely on Hans, then me, and next, Nashetania," she said. "Strongest man in the world, are you?"

"I'm used to being laughed at."

"Do you have no pride?"

"I do," Adlet said, smiling. The effect was powerful. "The strongest man in the world isn't the one who *looks* strong. The one who looks like the biggest fool is the strongest of them all. I'll keep on struggling as long as I'm capable of it."

"…"

"Don't you worry. Just leave it to me. As long as I'm alive, they shouldn't suspect you. Trust me, Fremy," Adlet said. He turned away from her and began making his way into the forest.

"Wait," she said. Surprised, Adlet turned.

"Trust you?" repeated Fremy. "I can't do that. I can't understand you."

"..."

"How can you keep smiling? How is your spirit not broken? Why are you trying to protect me? I can't understand a single thing going on in your mind."

"Fremy..."

"I know the situation is dangerous. But stay here a little longer. I want to know you better," she admitted quietly. "Maybe I can trust in you."

Meanwhile, Nashetania and Goldof were still on the western edge of the barrier. A few wrapping papers from travel rations littered the ground nearby. Nashetania picked them up, inspected both sides, and tossed them away. Goldof searched the area, too, looking over one tree after another, investigating them for traces of anything unusual. It seemed that by losing his composure and disgracing himself, he had created a rift in his dynamic with his master. The air between them was heavy.

"Let's give up," said Nashetania. "We should find Adlet and protect him." She began walking away. The two of them were far from the temple—too far to hear Adlet and Hans fighting or the two men battling Chamo after that.

"Princess, you still haven't told me," said Goldof. "Why do you suspect Hans?"

Nashetania turned back to him and stopped. "I suppose I'm not certain myself, either, am I? I haven't told you the most important part."

"Let's run as we talk."

The two of them jogged side by side. "There's one thing that bothers me," said Nashetania. "But I may just have been hearing things wrong. If it was a misunderstanding on my part, you're allowed to make fun of me."

"I will not. But please tell me." Goldof nodded, encouraging her to continue.

"Do you remember when we all first introduced ourselves, Hans said, 'Meow? *She's a bunny girl and a princess, too?*'"

"Of course."

"But that's odd," said Nashetania. "When Hans and Mora came into the temple, Hans called me *Princess*, just once."

"Are you sure?"

"You can't remember. But that's understandable. We weren't talking about anything important at the time." Goldof tilted his head. It seemed he couldn't recall, either.

"At first, it just felt a bit off," she said. "It was only long after that I realized how odd it was. And the more I thought back on it, the more it began bothering me."

"So that means…"

"He knew all along that I'm a princess but then pretended not to. Why is that?"

As they ran, Goldof considered the situation. "When Hans and Mora came into the temple, I stayed by your side the whole time. It is possible observing that led him to conclude that you are a princess."

"That's true. But there was one more thing. It was when Hans stopped Fremy from getting tortured."

"What was strange about that?"

"There was something. Something wasn't right." Nashetania smacked her face with her palms. "Why can't I put my finger on it? I'm so close—just a little closer, and I feel like I could figure it out! Are you going to keep being completely useless this whole time, Nashetania?!"

"Anyway, let us hurry," said Goldof. "There will be no more hesitation on my part. I will trust your judgment."

"Thank you. Goldof, will you take a look and see if Adlet is still alive?" Nashetania opened up the breastplate of her armor and showed him the crest near her collarbone.

"Do not worry," he said. "No one is dead yet. Adlet and the rest are all alive."

"I see. Then Adlet is doing his best. I will not fail, either."

The two of them continued running toward the temple.

Maybe I can trust in you. When Adlet heard Fremy say that, hope blossomed inside him. Hans was already on his side, and Nashetania most likely trusted him. If he could get Fremy to side with him, too, he wouldn't have to flee anymore. In a way, that was his ulterior motive.

But then Fremy crushed that feeling of hope as she aimed the muzzle of her gun at him. "I've always been skeptical—why do you keep protecting me? Why haven't you suspected me, even once?"

"**Why are** you pointing your gun at me?" he asked.

"If you try to dodge the question, I'll shoot."

Fremy's behavior confounded him. Her abrupt question, her impatient desire for answers. Fremy had said she didn't understand Adlet, but he didn't understand her, either. Adlet reflected. He decided to be sincere, to abandon any sort of calculated plan to get her on his side or convince her to believe him. "It was just a feeling. I felt that you weren't my enemy. I wanted to protect you. I don't have any reason to give you."

"Did you not hear me? Don't evade the question," she ordered him.

"Fremy…" Staring down the barrel, Adlet searched his heart. He had indeed been trying to protect her. A neutral observer would see the lengths to which he had gone as unnatural, and Fremy would, too. *Why?* Adlet asked himself. As she watched him, her gun trained on his heart, he searched for the reason.

"Answer me," she demanded.

Adlet quietly began to speak. "A long time ago, I tried to turn myself into a weapon. I tried to rid myself of my human heart. I tried to become a creature that existed purely for the purpose of killing the fiends that had stolen everything from me." Fremy didn't ask what he was talking about. She kept silent and listened.

"Because, like you said, and like my master said, I'm just ordinary. I thought that was the only way I could become the strongest man in the world. But it didn't work."

"What didn't work?"

"You can't throw away your heart just because you want to. No matter how many times I thought I had, I found it was still there."

"You're wrong, Adlet," Fremy said icily. "I did get rid of my heart—not my human heart, but my fiend heart. I did it to get revenge on my mother and revenge on the Evil God. I'm alive now because I rid myself of it."

"No, Fremy," he said. "You can't throw away your heart. Even the desire to do so comes from your heart."

She looked at him. He couldn't tell what she was thinking.

"You want to cast it all aside to become stronger?" asked Adlet. "You can't. You can't stop yourself from loving someone, no matter what you do."

"…"

"I care about you," he said. "I always have—well, I guess it's only since yesterday. But I've always cared about you."

Fremy's eyes opened wide, and she stared at Adlet. "Is that what you were thinking? Is that what you were thinking when you were with me?"

"I only just realized now how I feel, though. But I've felt this way since we first met."

"And that's why you tried to protect me?"

"I did worry over it when we met with Nashetania and Goldof and I learned that you were the Brave-killer. But when I saw Nashetania and Goldof suspect you, I thought, *I can't let this happen.* If even your fellow Braves wouldn't trust you, then I'd just have to trust you in their stead. I felt that if no one else in the world would protect you, then I would be the one to do it."

"And after that?" she prompted.

"I felt the same way when we found out there was an impostor among us," said Adlet. "I didn't even consider suspecting you. I guess you obviously find that unnatural. But I couldn't help myself. I'd fallen for you."

"Just what do you find so attractive about me?"

"I don't know. But when I see you suffer, it hurts me, too. I may be the strongest man in the world, but I can't handle that."

"And that's why you decided to protect me," she said. Adlet could see faint hesitation in Fremy's cold expression. Sometimes, she looked like a doll holding a gun, but he was convinced she wasn't a heartless monster. She had a heart. And if that was true, that meant their hearts could connect. He believed they could.

"Sorry, but you can't protect me," said Fremy. "I'm going to die anyway, once I defeat the Evil God."

"Why?!"

"Where should I live once the Evil God has been defeated? I can't go back to the fiends. There's no place for me in the human world. I will have no choice but to die. Dying and taking the Evil God with me is my ideal."

"You can't do that." Adlet shook his head. "Revenge might be everything to you right now. But that's only temporary. Once your vengeance is complete, you have to start over again."

"I can't start over. Humans will never accept me. They will never accept the daughter of a fiend, or the Brave-killer."

"Don't you worry," said Adlet. "I'll figure something out."

"What are you talking about?"

"It's a big world out there. I'll find a place that'll accept you."

"Don't be stupid," said Fremy. "There's no way you could."

"You're the one being stupid. Just who do you think I am? I'm Adlet, the strongest man in the world. You're telling me I couldn't manage to come up with one measly place you can call home?" Adlet understood that what he was saying was stupid. Far from defeating the Evil God, his allies were on the verge of being exterminated themselves. But first, he had to believe. *If you don't believe you can do it, you'll never get anywhere*, Adlet thought. "Do you think I'm just messing with you here? Do you think I'm an idiot? I don't. I'll do it. You can bet on it. ...And that's it. That's how I feel."

Fremy looked down, apparently thinking, for a long time. Adlet remembered what Hans had said. *Fremy lives in darkness. She don't love no one, and she don't trust no one. All she's got in her life are enemies and people bound to become her enemies. That's the world she lives in.*

That's not true, thought Adlet. *She's not like that.*

She's a totally different kinda critter—not like you. Yer thinkin' about trust and friendship and comrades. Don't assume you guys are just gonna understand each other.

Hans. I trust you, but you're wrong about this. She and I can understand each other.

Time passed, and Adlet waited patiently.

"I understand you now," said Fremy. And then Adlet saw—clear intent to kill in Fremy's downcast eyes.

"!" A gunshot rang out. Adlet crouched, just barely dodging the bullet.

"I understand that you are my enemy," said Fremy. Her eyes were filled with endless, deep darkness.

Mora dashed toward Hans. He was still restraining Chamo, leaving him unable to avoid her charge. Mora snatched Chamo away and then removed the restraints from the girl's hands and mouth. Now free, Chamo expelled a deep breath as Mora handed her her foxtail.

"What're ya doin'?! Do you have any idea how dangerous that gal is?!" Hans yelled.

"Listen, Chamo," said Mora. "You keep an eye on him. Do not let him leave this temple."

"Sure. Leave it to Chamo." The little Saint smirked.

Mora grasped her shoulder roughly. "And I do mean *watch* him. I am not telling you to attack him—only move if he moves. If you do a proper job, I won't become even angrier with you."

"Oh...so you are mad, after all." A cold sweat oozed down Chamo's forehead.

"If you get out of hand again, next time you will get more than just a spanking," Mora threatened.

"Okay...," Chamo replied, hands over her bottom.

"Chamo, is Mora so strong she can scare even you?" Hans was surprised.

Chamo replied, "Chamo's a lot more powerful than her, but...Auntie Mora is scary."

Mora sighed deeply. Though she hadn't done anything, a heavy sound echoed from her body. "Spirit of Mountains, give me strength," she murmured, and then she opened her mouth wide and shouted. The sound was like an explosion. **"PRINCESS! GOLDOF! FREMY!"** It was more than just a shout. Her voice echoed manyfold, sounding throughout the entire forest.

"What the heck?!" cried Hans.

"It's her mountain echo power!" explained Chamo. "Auntie Mora is the Saint of Mountains. She can do lots of stuff!" Hans and Chamo were both covering their ears and could barely hear each other talk.

"HANS HAS BEEN BEATEN! HE SURVIVED, BUT HE'S IN CRITICAL CONDITION! THE CULPRIT WAS ADLET! HE IS THE SEVENTH!"

Hans was shocked.

"KILL HIM RIGHT AWAY! DON'T HESITATE!" With that, Mora's echo faded.

"What the hell are ya thinkin'?!" Hans was enraged.

Mora grabbed him by the collar. "Now the princess will steel herself. I know not what is on Fremy's mind, but I doubt most deeply that she would allow Adlet to escape. Now he is without recourse."

"You hag, are you—" Hans was about to say something when a snake-fiend wrapped around his arm.

Chamo spat out a few more fiends to hold him fast. "Auntie Mora, do we really need to half kill him?"

"Don't be foolish. You need only restrain him." Mora adjusted her collar and ran out of the temple.

"Wait! Wait, damn you!" Hans tried to follow, but he was unable to shake off the fiends. "Wait! Are *you* the seventh?"

Mora did not turn back toward Hans's cries. She just dashed straight toward Fremy's location.

*   *   *

Mora's mountain echo had reached every part of the forest. As Fremy loaded her gun, she said coolly, "I see, then."

Adlet shook with rage as he skittered here and there, keeping his body low to the ground. "What the hell are you doing, Mora?!" He looked at his hand. None of the petals of the flower crest were missing, but was Hans going to be okay? Adlet was worried that maybe something really had happened to him and that he was going to die. To make things worse, this meant that Adlet might have lost his final ally. Adlet prayed silently, *Please, Nashetania. Please realize that was a lie.*

Fremy manifested a roughly apple-sized lump of gunpowder in her palm. She tossed it up high in the air and made it explode. Adlet figured she was alerting Mora, Goldof, and Nashetania to her position. If he lingered, he would be surrounded, but if he headed to the temple, he'd run into Mora. What was he to do? Where on earth could he run?

"Your Highness, did you hear what Mora said?"

Nashetania was standing stock-still, stunned. It seemed that Goldof's voice had not reached her ears. Next, they heard the sound of an explosion.

"That must have been Fremy," said Goldof. "I'd wager she's telling us Adlet's position. Let's go."

"..." Nashetania just gazed in the direction of the fog-covered temple. "I'm sorry, Hans. You did nothing wrong."

"Your Highness..."

"What have I been doing here?"

"Come on, let's go." Goldof took Nashetania's hand and pulled.

But she just staggered and made no move to follow. Her eyes were still fixed on a point in space as if she was lost in thought. "Wait a moment," she said.

"What is it? What's on your mind?" Despite Goldof's impatience, he was determinedly loyal as he waited for Nashetania.

Maybe a minute passed, and then she suddenly broke her silence.

"*Ah-ha!*" Nashetania burst into laughter, startling Goldof. "*Ah-ha! Ah-ha-ha, ah-ha-ha-ha!*"

"Your Highness, please calm down! What's wrong?"

Nashetania continued chuckling for a while. When her laughter subsided, she suddenly grew quite calm and said, "I really haven't been myself today. Too much has been going on, and I just don't know about anything anymore. But I have calmed down. I am finally able to think clearly, Goldof."

"Well...as long as you feel stable...," he replied.

"I understand now. This is it." Nashetania looked at him. "This is the first time I have ever experienced this. So this is what true anger feels like."

"Your Highness..."

"Not that I have never been irritated before," she said. "But I have never been angry in earnest. Now, for the first time, I know just what it means to be truly furious." Nashetania smiled, and then she dashed off. The person wearing that smile was different from who she had been before. "I finally understand... So this is what it's like. How do I express these feelings?"

"Your Highness..."

"Adlet...I trusted you... I trusted you." Nashetania's hand trembled as it grasped her sword. "This is lovely, isn't it, Goldof! It's been nothing but new experiences ever since I set out on this journey! And I will continue to encounter so many new things from now on, too!" Nashetania ran straight ahead, not turning back to look at Goldof. "I do so want to know! What will it feel like when I give in to anger and slice my enemy to shreds?"

Goldof was speechless as he watched Nashetania sprinting ahead of him.

Fremy was trying to kill Adlet. Chamo had restrained Hans, and Mora, Nashetania, and Goldof were all rushing toward Adlet's position. As all this was transpiring, the seventh was thinking, *I can't say this is going well.*

Initially, the seventh had expected that eliminating Adlet would be a simple matter. Adlet taking Fremy hostage had come as a shock, and the idea that the boy would be capable of evading the others for a full day thereafter hadn't even been a consideration. Adlet had been nothing but surprises. His self-designated title of "the strongest man in the world" no longer rang entirely false.

But that was nothing more than a minor error in the seventh's calculations. It had always been a matter of time before Adlet was dead. Even if he held out for an extra day or two, it still wouldn't change anything.

What to do after slaying Adlet? Of course, Fremy would be the next to go. That should prove simple enough. Her allies would kill her of their own accord. Things would get a bit more difficult after that. The best course of action would be for the impostor to eliminate any individual with lingering doubts. If it seemed that opinions were divided, then instigating a confrontation in which two killed each other off made the most sense. Improvising as things unfolded rather than clinging to any particular plan was the surest course.

Though the chances were low, there was the possibility that the impostor could become suspect. If that happened, then flight was one option. Two of the six Braves should be slain by that point, though, and that should prove good enough for this battle.

But if Adlet succeeded in stopping all their fighting and urged them to settle everything by talking, what then? That would just change the order of slaughter. The impostor would manipulate the conversation and kill Fremy and could do away with Adlet after that. While that situation could bring about certain difficulties, it probably wouldn't be a big problem.

A famous strategist had once said the outcome of any battle was already 90 percent decided before it even began. The seventh reflected upon the inherent truth of that statement. When Adlet set foot in the temple, when the seventh had set in motion the trap that had generated the fog, all the while evading the notice of the entire group—that was when it had all been decided.

The seventh had just one worry. Once Adlet and Fremy were dead, when all the others realized that neither of the two had been the seventh, what expressions the Braves of the Six Flowers would wear! Would the laughter finally be irrepressible? It had been a desperate struggle to tamp down the snickering thus far.

"Fremy! Go back to the temple! If you go there, you'll know that Mora is lying!" Adlet yelled as he fled through the forest.

Fremy did not reply. She just maintained pursuit, her gun trained on him. It was not so easy for her to attack him—her weapon was such that, once she fired one shot, she had to load another bullet to fire again. It was not possible for her to fire continuously. "So what?" she asked, taking aim at Adlet. "Mora may be lying, but that won't change the fact that you're the impostor."

"Why do you think that? I—" The moment Adlet tried to turn around and contradict her, he was forced to throw himself to the ground. Fremy's bullet passed over his head. Hot, sharp wind scorched his skin. If he took even a single hit, his body would be blown to pieces.

"I missed," said Fremy, and she loaded another bullet. With a normal gun, she would have had to stuff the gunpowder down the muzzle and then pack it in with a stick. But Fremy kept her hand on the grip as she loaded the iron ball. Adlet had no idea how that gun was constructed. "Mora! You're still not here yet?! Adlet is over here!" Fremy called.

How close was Mora? Adlet was running around at random with no idea which way he should go. He was naturally faster than Fremy. If he were to put some distance between them, he could get out of her line of sight.

But the moment she vanished behind him into the fog, he heard her cry, "I won't let you get away!"

This time, she threw a bomb. Adlet leaped onto a tree branch. The explosion flattened the surrounding trees, and a second and third bomb arced toward him from beyond the smoke. He threw knives to intercept them. The wind of the blast and sparks roasted his body.

Running away wasn't working out, either. She had far more firepower than he did, like a cannon-wielding warship fighting a single rowboat. Once again, Adlet was forced to reflect upon the fact that he was powerless. All he had that could be called weapons were his tiny sword, poison needles, throwing knives, smoke bombs, and a few piddling explosives that couldn't compare to Fremy's aresenal.

But even so, Adlet believed that he was the strongest man in the world.

Fremy flung bombs haphazardly, heedless of the damage. Adlet was bound to fail to intercept one of them eventually. He pushed off the tree branch and flew through the air, curling into a ball as he braced for impact.

"*Oh, did I get him?* will not be enough for me," said Fremy. "I'm never satisfied until I can see clearly, with my own eyes, that my enemy is nothing but a lump of meat."

If he fell to Fremy's pursuit, it would be over. Before she could toss another bomb, Adlet threw one of his needles that caused intense pain.

"*Urghk!*" It hit. He was lucky.

With Fremy frozen in her tracks, Adlet would be able to escape. But instead, he chose to stay. If he tried to run while still out of breath, his blood wouldn't reach his brain, and he wasn't going to survive this unless he used his head. What should he do now? Should he try to discover how the fog had been generated? Should he try to help Hans? The answer was neither.

It was Fremy. There was no way Adlet could win unless he could earn her trust. He would not run away. He would face her—he would face her mistrustful heart. "What makes you think I'm the impostor?" he called out.

The smoke was clearing. Adlet could see Fremy in front of him now. She yanked out the poison needle protruding from her right shoulder and threw it away. "Don't you talk to me with that filthy mouth of yours." She sounded furious.

But why was that? He hadn't done anything to enrage her. At the same time, Adlet had thought of this as his chance to get to understand her. If he could discover why she was so livid, he could find a way to change her mind. "Answer my question, Fremy!" He raised his voice intentionally; attempting to pacify her would have the opposite effect.

"Because I can see who you really are. I can see you're really just a cowardly con artist."

"I told you to answer me," he said.

"Because I can see the filthy motives behind the things you say, your clear attempts to string together what you think I want to hear in an attempt to deceive me."

"I was being sincere! You don't see anything!"

Fremy glared at Adlet as she created a gigantic bomb. She clearly intended to blow up him and everything around him, leaving nothing. Adlet restrained the urge to run, instead standing his ground.

"Liars always say the same thing," said Fremy. "*I trust you. I'll protect you. I'm thinking of you.*" That was when Adlet saw the faint tears in her eyes. "No one will ever deceive me again," she continued. "Nobody is going to protect me. I won't even consider such a *convenient* idea. I will fight alone, live alone, and die alone."

"Fremy…"

"I know now! I've felt it keenly on my body, on my skin! I know that if trusting someone is just going to result in betrayal, it's better not to trust anyone!" she yelled, throwing the bomb.

As Adlet watched it coming toward him, he thought about Fremy's past, about the time she'd been betrayed by those she loved. It wasn't that she couldn't trust people—she'd just made the firm decision that she wouldn't, to avoid the possibility of future betrayal. But from another angle, that meant some part of her wanted to trust someone.

Adlet jumped back and threw a bomb at his feet. This one wasn't smoke or tear gas: It was lethal. A backward retreat alone wouldn't be sufficient to evade her explosives. The only way he could possibly avoid it was to blow himself backward riding the blast of an explosion of his own. He barely survived, earning full-body burns in exchange for not being pulverized.

Then Adlet heard a voice behind him. "Fremy! Is he dead yet?"

"Mora!" Adlet and Fremy cried out simultaneously.

Mora charged toward Adlet with violent speed. "Don't use your bombs! Support me with your gun! I'll finish him!"

Fremy tossed aside the bomb she had just manifested and raised her gun. Mora closed on Adlet, focusing into her gauntleted fists her intent to obliterate him.

Adlet stood, turned away from Fremy, and charged straight for Mora. Just before her fist connected, he crouched, and as he did, Fremy fired. He was completely defenseless for that one moment. There was no way he could block Fremy's shot.

"!" But Adlet survived. The bullet made a high-pitched noise as it was repelled. Adlet had not been the one to intercept it. It had been Mora.

"Mora, why did you block it?" asked Fremy.

"Calm down," said Mora. "Look at him."

Adlet was on his hands and knees before Mora. He had thrown away his sword and had extended both his hands, palms up. It was a pose of submission. Fremy lowered her gun.

Her expression utterly scornful, Mora said, "So you have finally surrendered. But it's too late. Do not think you can survive."

"We're down one, too, after all," said Fremy.

"But before you die, you will tell us everything," said Mora. "Confess to us your plan and who is behind it."

Adlet raised his head and asked, "Is Hans all right?" There was just one thing he was afraid of—that maybe Mora and Chamo really had beaten Hans half to death together.

Mora's expression changed very slightly. From her discomposure, Adlet could tell that Hans was safe. "What are you talking about?" she said. "You are the one who hurt him."

"As long as he's safe." Adlet did not alter his submissive pose. Mora's fist was above his head. From that position, she needed only to swing downward to crush his skull.

"Then speak. Tell us the reason you allied yourself with the Evil God and how you obtained your counterfeit crest."

"Unfortunately, I can't tell you that. There's just one thing I can say."

"Then die," said Mora.

The moment she raised her fist, Adlet yelled, "That now, I'm going to prove that Fremy is a real Brave!" Shocked, Mora's hand stopped. And then she looked at Fremy.

Adlet couldn't see behind his back, so he didn't know what kind of expression Fremy had on her face. "Will you listen?" he asked. "Of course, even if you say no, I'm still gonna talk."

Mora did not reply. Instead, Fremy asked, "What is this about?"

So you will listen, thought Adlet, and he continued. "I'll assume one thing—that the one who activated the barrier was one of the seven of us who bear the Crest of the Six Flowers. We have no grounds to say that anyone else entered the temple. I have no time, so I'll leave out the basis for that."

"You are the impostor. That is proof enough," said Mora. He could hear clear agitation in her words. Adlet deliberately ignored her.

"That's no reason to pull out your weapons. Restrain yourself, be quiet, and watch," said Adlet as he began rummaging through a pouch on his belt with his left hand. He pulled out a small iron bottle and set it down in front of him. "This is a special substance that my master created. It's valuable. Use it carefully."

"Your master? You cannot mean…" Mora faltered. Did she know about Atreau? Adlet didn't have the time to ask.

"This chemical is used to uncover traces of fiends. It changes color in reaction to a unique substance secreted by fiends' bodies."

"…?" Mora seemed suspicious.

Without turning around, Adlet said, "Fremy. Give me one of your bullets. Throw it beside me."

An iron ball rolled over to him. Fremy wanted to hear what he had to say. It seemed she had doubts, though small, about Adlet being the impostor.

His face still on the ground, Adlet opened the stopper of the tiny bottle with one hand. He dripped some of the liquid inside on the bullet.

The bullet turned red, and after about thirty seconds, it returned to nor-mal. "Do you think this is a trick?" he asked. "If you do, then you should inspect this carefully. You'll be able to tell that this substance will, unmis-takably, show you where a fiend has been."

"Just what are you thinking, you monster?" Mora groaned.

"I sprinkled some of this substance on the altar used to activate the barrier, and the altar did not change color," he said. "Hans saw it, too. And this drug reacts to Fremy."

"Adlet..." Fremy started to say something and stopped.

"Fremy did not touch the altar once," Adlet finished. "This is proof that she is a real Brave; proof that she did not activate the barrier." Now he had demonstrated beyond a doubt that Fremy was not the impostor. Whatever tricks the seventh had up their sleeve, framing Fremy should prove impossible. Even if they tried, Hans would protect her. There was a chance Adlet could have escaped Mora, but he had chosen to protect Fremy instead. He would probably die as a result. But he didn't regret it—because he had done everything in his power to do what was right.

"Mora, if you're the seventh," he said, "take *that*. I ruined your plan—your plan to frame Fremy as the impostor and get her killed."

"Fremy, do not be deceived. Do not let him give you strange ideas," said Mora.

"Fremy, after I die, you find the seventh," said Adlet. "Hans is a man you can trust. Work with him."

"Don't be deceived, Fremy. You understand now, don't you? He's been attempting to ensnare you this whole time, showering you with honeyed words to gain your trust. This is simply one more piece of his plot," Mora warned. Fremy did not reply.

"Adlet." Mora clenched a fist and readied a strike. "You are quite the man. Even I thought, for one moment, that you might just be genuine."

"Don't kill me," he said. "You'll regret it—if you're a real Brave."

"This is exactly why...why you are so fearsome. If I fail to kill you now, the rest will come to trust you!"

Adlet closed his eyes. He couldn't dodge Mora's attack. Now there was no more he could do. Her fist swung down, whooshing as if to cleave the air itself. But just then, another sound cut through the mist—a high-pitched, metallic ring.

"You fool!" Mora yelled.

Adlet opened his eyes and looked behind him. Fremy's gun was up, white smoke wafting from the muzzle. The bullet had pinged off Mora's gauntlet.

"Adlet, I've hated you since the moment we met." Her expression was stony, but from one of her eyes fell a single tear. "I hated myself for feeling like I could trust you."

"Stop, Fremy! Do not be deceived!" cried Mora.

"I still hate you," Fremy continued. "The more I talk to you, the more I hate you. I end up believing everything you say, even though I swore I would never trust anyone ever again."

"Fremy!" Mora swung her first downward once more, but Adlet rolled to avoid the attack. "Enough!" said Mora. "Then I am forced to kill Adlet myself!"

Adlet picked up his sword and stood. Now that the situation was reversed, Mora set upon Adlet even more viciously. Fremy threw a small bomb at Mora and yelled, "Run, Adlet!"

As Adlet fled, he thought, *Finally. Finally, Fremy and I have come to understand each other.* But he was still far from victory. He had to show them all how the impostor could have created the fog.

Chapter 5

When All
Is Explained

"You will not escape!" Mora ran, ignoring the minibombs that flew at her. As she brought her fist down, Adlet dodged, and her gauntlet plunged into the earth like a meteorite, leaving a crater. Mora was not an opponent to be underestimated. "*Hmph!*" She grabbed a root and yanked, pulling up a whole tree. In one smooth motion, she swung her massive new club at Adlet.

"Watch out!" Fremy cried, and her bullet shattered the tree trunk.

Mora ignored Fremy, focusing exclusively on Adlet. Her attacks were relentless, and every single blow was powerful enough to kill him instantly.

Fremy cut in between the two of them and said to Adlet, "I'll hold her back. You run."

"No, you run. Mora is dangerous," he said. There was a high chance that Mora was the seventh. It would be dangerous to allow her and Fremy to fight alone.

"You're in my way, Fremy!" bellowed Mora.

Fremy intercepted her charge. Adlet stalled Mora and tried to come up with a way for him and Fremy to get away together, but that was when he sensed a bloodthirsty aura approaching from his side.

"Fremy, move!" commanded a feminine voice. Fremy jumped aside. Adlet rolled away, too. Countless white blades thrust up from the ground where the two of them had been standing.

"You're late, Princess," Mora muttered.

In the forest, Nashetania stood with her slim sword raised, a smile on her face. When Adlet saw that look, he thought, *She does smile a lot...but there's something different about her now.*

"You understand, right, Adlet?" Fremy said. She aimed her gun at Mora and a bomb at Nashetania. Adlet understood what she was trying to say—that right now, Nashetania was not their ally.

For some reason, after dealing that one attack, Nashetania didn't move. She stood there, stock-still, with her pasted-on smile. Adlet noticed Goldof behind her. He was watching Adlet, waiting for his chance to strike.

"It was fun, Adlet—those ten days we journeyed together," Nashetania began. It was as if she had forgotten they were on a battlefield. "I used to think I knew so much, but really, I didn't know anything at all, did I? I didn't know how fun it would be to set out on a journey without my coachman or maid. I didn't know the fear of my first real battle. I didn't know how confident it would make me feel to have someone beside me to encourage me," she continued. This was the calm Nashetania he hadn't seen for so long. Ever since she had found out that there was a seventh, she had been nothing but confused, frightened, and troubled. But now, her expression was bright and clear. "I am grateful for that. Thank you." A shiver ran down Adlet's spine.

"So now that I have expressed my gratitude, I'll be killing you, all right?"

"Run," whispered Fremy. "Once you get the chance, run as fast as you can. Nashetania is not acting normal right now." She, too, was afraid of Nashetania. "Listen, Nashetania," Fremy said, "Hans is safe, and Adlet is not our enemy. Mora is lying."

"She does not speak truth, Princess," countered Mora. "Adlet is our enemy. Hans has been gravely wounded. Fremy is merely under his spell." She sounded uneasy.

"Calm down, Nashetania," said Fremy. "We still don't know who the seventh is—but it's not Adlet."

"Do not fall for his wheedling. Adlet is a clever liar," insisted Mora.

Both Fremy and Mora attempted to sway her. Adlet said nothing, just watched Nashetania. He didn't want to fight. He was wounded and exhausted. The gash he'd gotten from Hans had begun to ache again. The burns he'd suffered during his battle with Fremy hurt. He didn't have the energy to fight Nashetania.

"You're listening to this, aren't you, Goldof?" asked Nashetania. "Don't attack them just yet." Her reaction was, in a way, the least desirable one. "Be careful. We cannot know what Fremy might do." Nashetania had ignored every word.

Mora chuckled, and Fremy gave up trying to convince Nashetania. Adlet prepared himself to fight again. He thought Nashetania might go for another sudden attack. But she just gazed at him, smiling. Mora seemed confused by Nashetania's lack of action.

"Adlet, what do we do?" asked Fremy.

He was unable to reply. If they could meet up with Hans and Nashetania found out he was okay, she would reconsider. But was Hans really okay? What if Mora was the seventh, or Chamo? What if the seventh had set up another trap for them?

"You can't think of anything?" Fremy pressed.

"Let's head to the temple," said Adlet. "If Hans is okay, we'll be able to regroup there."

"But if he's not okay…"

"We can't afford to think about that."

There was one other option—to prove his innocence immediately, right there. If he could reveal the seventh's entire plan, then this fight would be over. But Adlet still couldn't deduce where the fog had come from. *Think*, Adlet told himself. *It's just one last thing to figure out.* If he could demonstrate how it had been done—or even if he couldn't prove it, but could argue something convincing enough—they could avoid a fight.

"I'm trying to think, too…but I don't have any ideas," said Fremy, frustrated. He couldn't blame her. He couldn't think of anything, either.

"Adlet, I'm waiting," Nashetania said suddenly. Her cheerful tone was absolutely dissonant, considering the situation.

"For what?" asked Adlet.

"Your confession and penance," she said as she pointed the tip of her sword at him. "I know that when you catch someone who has done wrong, before they die, they confess and repent, right? I think that's what the head maid said."

Sounding exasperated, Mora chastised her. "Princess, you are somewhat ignorant in the ways of the world. Not every criminal confesses and repents."

"Is that right?" Nashetania seemed puzzled. She tilted her head and pondered the situation. "Then I may kill him, right?" Instantly, blades popped up all around Adlet.

"!" The young warrior failed to dodge the attack entirely, and his shoulder was sliced open. The blade had been so sharp he hadn't even felt any pain. One moment she'd been waiting patiently, and the next she'd gone straight for the kill with zero hesitation. He couldn't read her. He couldn't imagine what she might throw at him.

"Here he comes!" Fremy shot at Goldof, who was charging at her, spear raised. The bullet hit Goldof's armor, sending him flying back. But once he landed, he immediately began another assault.

"What *is* that armor?" Fremy was shocked. Goldof's armor was special, but Goldof himself was even more so. Fremy's gun should have hurt him despite the armor.

Goldof thrust his spear out, and Adlet and Fremy leaped off to either side. Mora took advantage of the moment to make a grab at Fremy, and Nashetania's sword stabbed toward Adlet's heart.

"Nashetania! I will hold Fremy in check! You and Goldof kill Adlet!" yelled Mora.

But Fremy would not allow that, scattering tiny bombs from beneath her cloak. The blast forced Mora back, and the smoke clouded Goldof's field of vision.

"Why are you getting in our way?" Goldof asked Fremy, though he chose not to press further and focused on targeting Adlet alone.

But Fremy instantly reloaded and fired at the knight's feet. The bullet did not pierce his armor, but Goldof lost his balance and fell to the ground. "I'll hold these two back! Run, Adlet!" she cried.

Adlet wavered. He had only just declared that he would protect Fremy, and now he was going to leave her and run off alone? But he was exhausted and had few weapons left. There was little chance he could still win a fight, even if it was one-on-one. "I *will* keep you safe, Fremy! I'm the strongest man in the world!" Adlet shouted as he made his escape.

Fremy smiled oh so faintly, as if to say, *That again?*

Adlet ran through the hazy forest. His goal was the temple and Hans.

"You won't get away!" Nashetania was hard on his heels. She unleashed attacks on him, one after another, from the earth and from tree trunks.

Adlet was headed toward the temple. Right now, Nashetania believed that Adlet had left Hans on death's doorstep. If he could correct that misunderstanding, he should be able to end the fight. He threw a smoke bomb behind him to obstruct Nashetania's field of vision and tossed pain needles to slow her down. He would use each of his few remaining tools. He just had to reach the temple somehow. Once they found Hans, this battle with Nashetania would be over.

"Goldof! Mora! What are you doing?!" Nashetania yelled over her shoulder. But she received no reply. Just as Fremy had promised, she was holding the other two in check. Now Adlet knew he could get away.

The sun had already begun to set. They had been trapped in the forest for nearly a whole day, and it had been a long battle. All the other Braves had chased Adlet while he carried Fremy over his shoulder. He had fought Hans and skirmished with Chamo, and after that, Fremy had almost killed him. Every time, Adlet had been injured. His body was nearing its limit. But this encounter would be the last. If he could get away this time, he would be able to rest for a while. He would meet up with Hans, and make Nashetania stop attacking him, and then the three of them could go help Fremy.

Adlet still didn't know who the seventh was, and neither did he know how the fog had been created. But Hans and Fremy were on his side. He could make everyone stop fighting and get them to talk instead.

After the string of smoke bombs, Nashetania completely lost sight of Adlet. At this point, he had used up nearly all the tools from his pouches. But that wouldn't be a problem. The temple was close. Adlet yelled, "Hans!"

No answer. He could see no sign of anyone near the temple.

"Hans! Are you there? If you are, come out!" *Could he be inside?* wondered Adlet, and he called out to Hans again and again. But still, nothing. "Where'd you go? Hans! Chamo! Where have you gone?!" Adlet looked at the crest on his right hand. All six of the petals were still on the flower, so all six members, including Hans and Chamo, were still alive. But where had they gone? Had they fallen for one of the seventh's traps? Or had Chamo left Hans on the brink of death?

"Who are you looking for? You're the one who felled Hans." Nashetania's outline swayed as she appeared from the forest.

"Why? Where did they go?" Adlet muttered. Or...could it be? Was Hans the seventh? Had Hans been patiently waiting for Nashetania do his dirty work?

Nashetania attacked. Adlet jumped up and ran across the roof of the temple, escaping to the opposite side. There was no time to reequip himself.

"Wait, you!" she ordered.

Adlet had to get away. But where should he run? How could he escape? He had no more tools.

As darkness gradually fell, Adlet ran desperately through the forest. But his wounds were grave, his exhaustion extreme, and he was already running out of energy.

"There you are!" Nashetania mercilessly ran him down. How long could he continue to evade her attacks? He knew he wouldn't last much longer.

"You're *still* going to run?!" she called after him.

Adlet had already given up on finding Hans. There was only one option left: to solve the mystery of the seventh, to reveal the truth to Nashetania and prove he wasn't the impostor. That was the only way. But Adlet couldn't solve the problem of the mist. He wouldn't be able to convince Nashetania unless he could explain the mystery and prove what had happened.

Adlet thought. How could they have created fog? *Fog. Fog. Fog. Fog. Fog.* As he turned it over in his mind, his movements slackened. One of Nashetania's blades pierced his side. Adlet crumpled against a tree trunk.

"I've finally caught you." Nashetania slowly faded into view.

When Adlet saw her face, he remembered the day they had departed together on their journey. He'd been surprised when he'd first seen her. He'd never imagined that a princess would pretend to be a maid to come see him. Back then, he'd figured he'd just made a good friend. He'd felt that if they were together, he needn't fear the Evil God. *Why is this happening?* he wondered. Someone who was supposed to be on his side was attacking him, and he was about to lose his life.

"Listen, Nashetania," he said.

"To what?"

"I'm your ally."

Nashetania giggled and pointed her sword at him. Its blade extended to pierce Adlet's ear. "It's far too late for that sort of nonsense." Nashetania was smiling but regarded him as if he were vermin.

I didn't know she was capable of an expression like that, thought Adlet. When they'd first met, she'd seemed so cheerful and lighthearted. But she was also a warrior worthy of being chosen as a Brave—of course she'd have fangs.

"You're a fool," she said. "If you had only surrendered and confessed, you could have had an easier death."

"I'm not gonna confess to anything. I haven't done a single thing wrong," said Adlet. He knew she wasn't going to listen.

She hadn't been like this when they first met. She had been bubbly and fun. Chomping raw carrots and half-jokingly tossing blades at him. What had they talked about then? Oh, about the Brave-killer. He couldn't have imagined that very killer would become one of his allies.

The Brave-killer. When Adlet remembered that word, something about it bothered him. But the flash of insight failed to take shape and instead instantly disappeared.

"It's no use," said Nashetania. "You won't deceive me again. You hatched a plan to trick us. You fooled us all and even hurt us. It's quite clear that you are the impostor."

"I'm not lying. You're the one getting tricked. The enemy is using you to try to kill me." But she wasn't listening. "I haven't killed any of our allies," he insisted. "I'm not scheming to trap everyone, either."

Slowly, she pointed her blade at Adlet's heart.

Can I block it? Adlet wondered. If he was lucky, he could probably survive. But Adlet's arms were leaden. If he were to block this attack, then what? It would be the next attack that would kill him, then, or the one after that. Pain and exhaustion robbed him of his willpower.

I'm cold, he thought. *I wonder why I'm so cold? Yesterday when I was traveling with Fremy, it was so hot.*

"I've told you, you shan't fool me anymore," said Nashetania. The tip of her sword was level with his heart. Adlet wasn't listening. He was just thinking about how cold he was. "You *are* the seventh," she said. The blade extended.

Instantly, Adlet's arms moved. He crossed them both in front of his body, thrusting them out between himself and the oncoming blade. He heard the sound of his flesh parting. His bones had blocked the blade. His left arm was broken, and the right had just barely stopped the attack. "...Cold?" he muttered.

"Don't bother," said Nashetania, piercing him deeper.

But Adlet pushed back. He shoved her sword back and to the side. Nashetania lost her balance, staggering. His left arm still impaled, Adlet stood and broke off the sword. Nashetania seemed bewildered by his sudden resistance.

"Sorry!" he yelled. He kicked off on Nashetania's face with the sole of his boot. She released her sword, pressing her hands where the blow had landed. He took a second step on her face, thwacking her jaw with his heel, and then he turned and dashed away from her. Life had returned to his eyes. *Why did I never notice?* he wondered.

The answer had been right there in front of him. It had been so close, he felt pathetic for having failed to recognize it. The Phantasmal Barrier was cold.

"*Ngh!* I won't let you get away!" she yelled after him.

Adlet used his mouth to extract the blade stuck in his arm. Nashetania was pursuing him, but Adlet ignored her and barreled forward. Blades came at him from the earth and the air, but he just plowed straight ahead, praying he wouldn't be hit. He couldn't prove his innocence here. If he wanted to do that, he had to run.

"Princess! Are you safe?" Distantly, Adlet heard Goldof's voice. He could faintly see the silhouettes of Goldof and Mora within the fog. He could also see that Fremy was slung over Mora's shoulder. She was struggling, trying to break free of Mora's restraints.

Adlet was glad to see that Fremy was safe. She had fought well and had managed to survive. Now all Adlet had to do was solve the mystery of the seventh.

"Don't worry about me! Follow Adlet!" Nashetania called back.

Goldof commenced his attack. He mowed down trees as he lunged with his spear. Adlet turned the thrust aside with his sword. Though he had avoided the strike, Goldof's huge frame threw Adlet backward. Adlet was grateful for that. Goldof had propelled him in the direction he'd been heading anyway. At this point, sprinting was painful.

"Run!" Fremy yelled from where she lay slung on Mora's back. She twisted her body, loosening her bonds just a bit so she could turn toward Goldof and Nashetania to fling a bomb. It slowed them down just a bit.

Adlet ran and ran. Finally, Goldof caught up to him and forced him to the ground. "This is as far as you go, Adlet," he said.

Adlet had collapsed about ten minutes from the temple. The bodies of a few dozen fiends were lying in the area. The day before, when Adlet, Nashetania, Goldof, and Fremy had seen the fiends bombing the temple, the four of them had encountered and battled fiends on their way toward the building. Adlet had broken through their lines and gone ahead while Nashetania finished off the demons. This was where that battle had transpired.

"I'm sorry, Goldof. I was unable to finish him." Nashetania jogged up to them.

"What are you talking about, Your Highness? You did a fine job running him down." Goldof gripped Adlet even tighter, and the young warrior had no strength left to resist.

"You did well, Goldof. Kill him," said Mora as she caught up to them, still holding Fremy.

"No! Stop! Please, Adlet! Get away!" On Mora's shoulder, Fremy struggled.

"Your Highness, Lady Mora, rather than killing him, we should extract information. If we kill him, we will not know who the mastermind behind this is," suggested Goldof.

"It won't work, Goldof," said Mora. "He will not speak. He is a frighteningly stubborn man."

"That's right. We should kill him immediately," agreed Nashetania.

"Let go! Let me go, Mora!" Fremy struggled as hard as she could, but she couldn't shake free.

It appeared that Adlet was cornered...but he was smiling. Why? Because he saw the silhouette approaching Mora from behind.

"...Huh?" The moment Nashetania spotted that shape, the sword slipped from her hand.

"You took way too long. Just where the hell were you?!" Adlet chided Hans, who'd finally decided to show up, and Chamo, who trailed behind him.

"Sorry. I was lookin' for ya." Hans awkwardly scratched his head. It sounded as though he knew that he shouldn't have left the temple. Well, there was no point blaming him. It had been a close call, but they'd made it in time.

"...Huh? Huh?" Nashetania was momentarily stunned. Goldof was also speechless. Nashetania forgot her sword on the ground and ran up to Adlet. "It can't be...it can't be...then..." Tears fell from her eyes.

Adlet smiled wryly and said, "Nashetania, you really are powerful. That fight was actually kinda tough. Kinda."

"What? How can this…" Nashetania covered her face with her hands and began to cry.

Goldof glared at Mora, who still carried Fremy. "Lady Mora. Explain yourself." He was gripping his spear.

Feigning composure, Mora said, "I apologize. That was a lie. But had I not done this, we would have been unable to hunt down Adlet."

"Mora, you…" Nashetania regarded her with rage-filled eyes. "Why did you lie to us?!"

"Adlet is the impostor," she answered. "That fact has not changed. Any and all means were acceptable, if they would gain us victory!"

"You're wrong! You lied! You tricked us!" Tears in her eyes, Nashetania made a grab for Mora. Goldof moved away from Adlet and cut between the two of them while Fremy escaped Mora's grasp and ran up to Adlet.

Leaning on Fremy's shoulder, Adlet slowly stood. "Hey," he said, using Fremy as a crutch and staggering forward. He spoke quietly, but the others paid close attention. "What do you think makes someone the strongest in the world?" He leaned against a tree trunk and sat himself down on the ground. Fremy pulled a needle and thread from beneath her cloak and began sewing up his wounds. "You need power, technique, knowledge, heart, and luck. All those things," he said as he gazed at the others and smiled. "The answer's simple. I am the strongest man in the world. Could anyone else make it this far?"

"Wh-what are you talking about?" Mora sounded confused and panicky.

"It's about time, isn't it? Time for me to defeat the seventh," he said.

Mora seemed stunned. Nashetania and Goldof both looked as if they had been struck by lightning. Chamo was mildly surprised. Fremy's eyes were filled with expectation as she watched Adlet, and Hans just smirked.

"I'll give you the answers. I'm going to expose the seventh's entire plan."

Then Adlet revealed his deductions. First, he told them what he had told Hans and Fremy—that Private Loren's instructions for activating the barrier had been lies and that the seventh had activated the barrier after Adlet opened the door. He faltered more than a few times during the explanation—Fremy was treating him without any painkillers.

The only ones who listened intently were Nashetania and Goldof. Mora and Chamo had both apparently already heard his theory up to this point. Most likely, Hans had told them. When Adlet finished the first half of the explanation, he breathed a sigh of pain.

"Hey, you can do this after yer done gettin' all sewed up. Or I can take over," said Hans.

"Please. Are you trying to steal my spotlight here?" Adlet said, a casual smile on his face.

"Mora. Will you be okay if he keeps going?" inquired Fremy.

A cold sweat dotted Mora's forehead and neck. "Wh-what are you talking about?"

"If you're the seventh, I think it's about time for you to surrender."

"Don't utter such nonsense." Mora turned to Adlet. "Adlet, your deductions do not hold. There is no way anyone could generate fog. It would take a powerful barrier to generate it—"

Mora rattled on, and Adlet lifted a hand to cut her off. He already knew what she was going to say. "There is. There is just one Saint in the world who could have generated that fog."

"This is absurd!" Mora groaned.

As he watched her, Adlet let out a grand sigh. He had put on a tough front for Hans, but just talking was difficult. "Mora, you said before that I don't understand the Saints' power. But let me tell you this—you Saints don't understand science. Your powers surpass the powers of science, so perhaps you might not think much of it, but science is an amazing thing."

"Science?" Mora tilted her head. It seemed she didn't even quite understand the meaning of the word.

"Do you know what fog actually is?" said Adlet. "Water vapor condenses and turns into fine particles suspended in the air—that is fog. It's the same principle that makes your breath visible in winter and makes clouds float in the sky." As he explained, he remembered his master, Atreau Spiker.

Adlet had learned cutting-edge science from Atreau in order to forge his tools—the principles of what made fire burn, the principles of the effects of poison, and even the laws governing the behavior of gases and liquids. If Adlet hadn't learned those things, he probably wouldn't have figured out the answer. Though at the time, he'd thought, *What's the use of learning all this junk?*

"The warmer the temperature of the air, the more water vapor it can contain," he continued. "If the air temperature cools suddenly, then water vapor turns back into liquid, becoming little particles that waft through the air. You get that much?"

"Nope," said Chamo.

Adlet smiled wryly. "Anyway, when the air is damp, if the weather suddenly turns cold, you get fog. That's all you need to understand."

"Roger." Chamo nodded, surprisingly obedient.

"The humidity in this forest is always fairly high," Adlet explained. "It's right by the sea, so the sea wind carries the moisture over here. If you can suddenly lower the air temperature within the forest, you could create fog instantaneously." .

"Wait," said Mora.

She just keeps interrupting over and over, thought Adlet.

"Then how would you lower the temperature so quickly?" she asked. "That would also be impossible without a large barrier created by the Saint of Ice or the Saint of Snow."

"You're a hardheaded woman, Mora," he said. "They didn't lower the temperature. They raised it."

Mora was silent for a while. And then she lifted her head as if having realized something.

"It really was a magnificent plan," said Adlet. "The scale of the idea was extraordinary. To think that they would control nature itself in order to ensnare me."

"The Saint of Sun...Leura," murmured Fremy.

Exactly right, thought Adlet.

Immediately after departing on his journey, he'd heard rumors of the Brave-killer. Famous warriors had been assassinated one after another: Matra, the master archer; Houdelka, the swordsman; Athlay, the Saint of Ice; and Leura, the Saint of Sun. When Adlet had first heard that story, one of those had felt out of place: Leura, the Saint of Sun. Though she had wielded incredible power as a Saint, she was so old, she'd have been incapable of fighting. He'd wondered why the killer would have targeted her. And then Adlet had met Fremy. When he found out she was the killer, he'd asked her, *Did you kill Leura, the Saint of Sun, too?*

Fremy had replied, *I don't know anything about that.* Of course she didn't. It had been six months prior that Fremy's fiend comrades had betrayed her. She hadn't killed any potential Braves after that. Leura had gone missing just over a month before all this began. Fremy had not been involved in the assassination of the Saint of Sun.

So then, who had done it?

"Let me ask you one thing, Mora," said Adlet. "Would it have been possible for Leura, the Saint of Sun, to raise the temperature of this whole area? I bet it would. As we all know, she is famous for being powerful enough to roast an entire castle, if she pushes herself to the limit."

"I-it would be...possible," replied Mora.

"Would she still be able to do that now, even at her age?"

"Leura's lower body has wasted away, and she can't move from her chair," said Fremy, in place of the faltering Mora. "But her power over the Spirit of Sun has not been affected by her physical decline."

Adlet nodded and then entered the crux of his deductions. "Let me explain the seventh's plan. First, the seventh and their allies abducted Leura, the Saint of Sun, and forced her to cooperate. They probably took her family hostage or something to that effect. Leura raised the temperature of the whole area, as she had been instructed. Most likely, over the course of nearly a month." Adlet looked over the faces of all present. "You should all remember that when we arrived here, you thought it was unusually hot, right? That was Leura's power." Everyone present remembered the previous day's events and nodded.

"Next, the impostor's allies attacked the fort and killed all the soldiers in it, and one of them pretended to be a soldier there. Or perhaps some of the soldiers at the fort were allies of the seventh to begin with; we don't know which. Then the mole told the Braves of the Six Flowers about the Phantasmal Barrier and gave them fake instructions."

"What if one among us knew how the barrier was really activated?" asked Mora.

"Then the plan would have failed," said Adlet. "But the chances of that were low, because the king who built it was secretive and told only a limited number of people that the barrier even existed."

"And then?" asked Mora.

"The seventh used these fiends to lure us to the temple, and when I opened the temple door, they sent a signal. At that signal, a nearby fiend and ally of the seventh killed Leura." The one who'd sent the signal was the transforming fiend that had been near the temple. Adlet figured that strange laugh had meant it was time to kill Leura. "Once Leura was dead, her power of sun terminated. The temperature suddenly dropped and the fog appeared. We were completely fooled into believing that the barrier had been activated." At the time, Adlet had felt a shiver run down his spine. But that had not been his mind playing tricks—the air temperature really had been dropping. At the time, he hadn't even considered that the change in temperature had been part of the enemy's trap.

"After that, the seventh approached the altar nonchalantly," Adlet continued, "using our confusion as cover to activate the barrier for real at that point. The rest requires no explanation. All that was left was to wait patiently until I became suspect and everyone decided I was the seventh."

"Wait! What proof do you have?" demanded Mora. "This is all nothing more than supposition!"

"I'm still not done yet," said Adlet. Fremy had finished treating him. He tried to stand, but Hans stopped him.

"You leave this part to meow," said Hans. "You just need to do the explainin'." Adlet squatted down with the tree trunk at his back. One by one, Hans searched the bodies of the fiends scattered about the area.

Adlet continued. "Now then, the final problem: Where did the seventh hide Leura's body? She couldn't have been killed far from the temple, because she had to be close enough for the killer to hear the fiend's screech that was their signal. The seventh couldn't be loitering around with Leura's body, either. There was the possibility that they would run into Mora or Hans or Chamo. They could bury it, but it still might be discovered that way—because we have Chamo." Chamo's power was the ability to control the fiends that lived in her stomach. If she had sent earthworm- and lizard-fiends to investigate the ground, she may have been able to find a body.

"This forest is big, but there weren't many places they could hide that body. Only one, in fact," he said.

"*Meow*, I found it," Hans said as he pointed at one of the fiends. It looked like a crocodile and was about five meters in length. You couldn't tell unless you looked closely, but its stomach was just a bit swollen.

"Cut it open, Hans." Adlet swallowed. This was the moment of truth: The only piece of evidence that could prove Adlet's innocence was right there. Were his deductions correct? Once this fiend was sliced open, they would know. "The only place they could hide the body was inside a fiend."

Hans drew his sword and sliced open the crocodile's stomach. The body of an old woman rolled out, soaked in the acid of the demon's stomach.

"You check, Mora. This granny is definitely Leura, the Saint of Sun, ain't she?" said Hans.

Mora timidly approached the body and then sank to the ground. "It's Lady Leura. This woman is Lady Leura."

Adlet heaved a sigh of relief. Hans took over for him. "Meow then, anybody here still thinkin' Adlet's the fake? If ya do, I'd like ya to explain why we've got this dead granny here."

Adlet didn't think anyone would still have doubts. But Mora stood up and said, "This, too, is a trap! Adlet prepared this body beforehand to convince us that he is one of us!" She continued insisting that Adlet was the impostor…but no one was listening to her opinion anymore.

"If that were the case, Adlet would have divulged his deductions long ago," said Fremy. "Just how many times do you think he almost died in order to get to this point?"

"I…I…" Mora looked down and kept trying to think of another way she might rebut Adlet. She was the only one who still doubted his authenticity. The situation had reversed. Now Adlet was the one backing the seventh into a corner. At that point, Mora groaned and admitted, "I was wrong. Adlet is not the impostor."

Still fighting the pain, Adlet sighed. The strength left his body, and his back slid down the trunk of the tree. He thought about pumping a fist, but he just didn't feel like it. "It's like I've been saying all along. I'm not the seventh."

His victory had been on thin ice. Adlet had not been entirely certain that this was where Leura's body had been hidden. The impostor could have decided to be less clever and simply buried it, or they could have killed her outside the barrier. That last part had been sheer luck.

But still, he'd won. He'd exposed the seventh's plot. *How about that?* thought Adlet. *Who else could make it this far?*

"Hey, so who killed Granny?" asked Chamo.

"Probably that crocodile-fiend. It killed her and ate her, and then it died here," said Adlet.

"Wait. More importantly, which of us is the seventh?!" cried Mora. The rest of them replied to her with silence.

Adlet still didn't know the identity of their infiltrator. He'd exposed the entirety of the scheme itself but hadn't managed to acquire any evidence as to who was actually responsible—though he felt there was nothing to discuss at this point.

"Mora, do you understand your position right now?" asked Nashetania. Her words held quiet anger. She picked up the sword she had dropped and pointed it at her fellow Saint. "Fremy, please stay close to Adlet. Goldof, do not let Mora get away."

Backing up, Mora protested. "Wait, Princess. It isn't me. What proof do you have?"

"You're right, there is no proof," she replied. "But who else could it be? You cannot intend to suggest that the impostor is Fremy?"

I should probably stop her, thought Adlet. There was no evidence. But who else could it be besides Mora? Adlet was convinced that Fremy wasn't the impostor, and neither was Nashetania. Hans had cooperated with him in revealing the plot, and Adlet had never even suspected Chamo. And Goldof? It didn't seem likely that such a loyal man would be a traitor. *It has to be Mora,* he thought.

But as he did, Chamo said, "It's not Auntie." All eyes were drawn to her. "Chamo's got this," she said, rolling up her shirt to show her stomach. There was a slate tucked under her belt. Adlet had no idea what it was. "After Auntie left, Chamo punched through the temple floor and dug down under it. There was a big box under there with a sword and slate inside."

Hans took over from Chamo and explained. "The person who made this barrier was damn well prepared. They made a spare altar for activatin' it and buried it right deep. We had a real rough time diggin' it up. Didn't you go into the temple, Adlet? There was a big hole in the floor, wasn't there?" Adlet shrugged. Nashetania had been chasing him, and it had not been the time for exploring.

"*Tee-hee.* Chamo's the one who found it," boasted the young Saint.

"Well, I was the one who got the idea there might be somethin' underground," said Hans.

"But Chamo found it."

"But I thought of it. *Meow.*"

"You can argue over who gets credit later. What's written on the slate?" asked Adlet.

Hans and Chamo smirked in unison. "There were two," explained Hans. "One was the same as the one on the altar, and the other one has this written on it. It ain't in hieroglyphs. It's somethin' even I can read." All present turned their attention to Hans—which was why nobody noticed that the expression of one among them had changed.

"'In order to activate the barrier once more, after the decorative sword and the broken slate have been removed, the procedure for activation must be repeated. In other words, grasp the sword, drip blood upon it, and then break the slate while reciting the prescribed words,'" Hans read.

"Huh?" Goldof emitted a sound. It made him sound foolish and wasn't the kind of noise one might imagine coming from him.

Adlet doubted his ears. Next, he doubted his memory. Lastly, he doubted the authenticity of the slate.

He remembered. He remembered what had happened after the four of them had set foot in the temple, before Chamo had walked in.

"Hmm? Meow then, who broke the slate? I don't know that part," said Hans.

"When Chamo came in, the slate was already smashed up," said Chamo. "So who broke it?"

Adlet searched his memory.

"The barrier has been activated. I can't believe this. Who did it?"

"I don't know. Sorry, but I have no idea what happened," Adlet had said, shaking his head.

"Well, let us deactivate it, then. Pardon." Goldof had been the first to touch it. He had pulled out the decorative sword in an attempt to deactivate the barrier.

"Give me that for a second. The previous generation of Braves made something like this before. Back then, I think they canceled out the barrier like this." The next one to touch it had been Adlet. He'd put the sword back in again, let a drop of blood fall on it, and attempted to deactivate the barrier. And then, after that...

"Nullify the barrier! Cancel it, you! You stop now! Stop the fog! I will be this barrier's master!" Nashetania had grabbed the sword. She'd shouted a bunch of different incantations and then finally grew impatient, using the sword to batter the slate on the altar. That was most definitely when the slate had broken.

"Isn't that nice, Auntie Mora? You were about to get killed," said Chamo.

"I cannot take this in," said Mora. "What does this mean?" Chamo smiled at her. Unable to keep pace with the situation, Mora could manage nothing but confusion.

"Adlet, you saw, didn't ya? Who's the one who broke the slate?" asked Hans, but Adlet couldn't reply. "Hey. Do you know, Fremy?" He turned to Fremy instead.

Fremy replied without hesitation. "It was Nashetania."

Nashetania backed away, her expression frightened. She was speechless. She shook her head very slightly, desperately asserting her innocence. "So the slate, then... B-but I wasn't trying to activate the barrier—"

"The princess, meow? That's surprisin'. I thought it was Goldof." Hans drew his sword, and Chamo put her foxtail to her mouth. Goldof stood in front of Nashetania, holding the two of them in check.

It has to be some kind of trap—or if not, then some kind of mistake. There's no way she could be the culprit, thought Adlet, and as he did, he searched his memories of the time he'd spent with Nashetania. She'd done nothing suspicious. Not when pretending to be a maid to visit his prison cell. Not when he'd been chosen as a Brave or when they'd set out on their journey together. Not when they'd saved the villagers from fiends. Not when they'd been separated and met up again later. Not when she and Goldof had attacked Fremy, deeming her the enemy. Or even when they'd approached the temple when it was being bombed.

"...Ah." A small cry slipped from Adlet's throat. On the way to the temple, the four of them had been waylaid by fiends. During the fight, Nashetania had said, *Adlet. Please head for the temple. We will take over here!*

Why hadn't he noticed? There'd been one important prerequisite for this scheme to work—and that was that one of the six Braves had to arrive at the temple first. Adlet had gone ahead because Nashetania told him to, and then when he'd arrived at the temple, he'd fallen into the seventh's trap.

"It's one thing after another, isn't it? Don't worry. I will protect you." Goldof's entire body emitted an aura that spoke of barely contained violence. He protectively shielded Nashetania behind him.

"The princess? It cannot be..." Mora was unable to act, utterly at a loss.

Hans and Chamo slowly approached Nashetania. Fremy drew her gun and stood at the ready. Nashetania drew her sword and looked pleadingly at Adlet. "Adlet, say something, please. I'm not the seventh."

No, she's not the impostor, is what Adlet tried to say, but what came out of his mouth was something else. "It can't be. Is it true, Nashetania?"

"Adlet..." When Nashetania heard that, suddenly her expression changed. She went from frightened and forlorn to empty and listless. And then she smiled. It was a dignified and cheerful display, just like the one she'd had on her face when they'd first met. "I concede," she said.

"Huh?" Adlet was stunned.

Nashetania sheathed her sword, raised both hands, and said, "Do you not understand that? I concede. It means I surrender."

None were able to speak. None were able to move. They were all taken aback by the look on Nashetania's face and her indifferent remarks. They could do nothing but stare.

"Your Highness...what are you talking about?" asked Goldof.

"Like I said, Goldof. I'm the seventh." Nashetania patted his shoulder as he stood frozen in place. It was as if she were saying, *Good job, now you can go home.* "Sorry," she said, walking around him to stand in the center of the crowd. "Perhaps I could have held out a little longer. But if Adlet doesn't believe me, I'm sure I would have been unable to convince the rest of you, no matter what I said." And then she considered the group and said, "I bungled this one. I knew that there was a backup set of ritual tools, but not that the method for activating the barrier was written on them. I should have been more prepared. But to think I would fail to defeat even one of you... I thought that, at worst, I could shave down your numbers by two." Nashetania was calm. She was not timid, not apologetic, and she was not confused. "I think the reason I failed was that I was simply not proactive enough. I had so many options open to me—I could have approached Adlet and caught him off guard, or I could have simply killed Goldof. Any number of options were available to me, but I let all those chances slip by. Up until halfway through, it was all going so well."

Adlet heard what she was saying, but her words weren't reaching his brain.

"Hans," she continued, "I had thought that most likely, you would be the most annoying of my enemies. I devised a number of ways to pin the deed on you and get you killed, but…it all came to nothing. What a disappointment. Well, I was right to predict that you would be the strongest of the lot. If you hadn't been here, I would not have lost." Smiling, Nashetania swept her gaze over the crowd. "What's wrong? You've all gone quiet."

When Adlet saw that smile, he thought that maybe Nashetania wasn't the enemy, after all. The way she was so up front about it made it hard to doubt her. He even began thinking that perhaps it had been right that she had caught him in her trap.

"Wh…," Mora squeezed out, "why did you think to kill us…? No, you really did intend to kill us, so…you were allied with the Evil God, with the intention of destroying the world…" Mora was so shocked, she couldn't speak properly.

Nashetania frowned slightly. "Perhaps all this was unnecessary. Perhaps I should have revealed everything to you and asked for your cooperation. There's no point in that now, though."

Then Goldof knelt at Nashetania's feet. "Your Highness! Please, tell me! Just what on earth are you trying to do?! I will follow you!"

Nashetania looked down at him and smiled wryly. "The truth is, Goldof, I thought you might become my ally. If you had said nothing, kept your silence, and done as I ordered, I would have told you what was really going on. But you…" She trailed off and put her hand to her mouth. A mean look on her face, she giggled. "I had no idea you would say something like that." Had something happened with Goldof? But that didn't matter.

"Chamo wants to know, though, Princess. Why'd you wanna kill us?" inquired the little Saint.

"Oh yes, about that." Nashetania put her hand to her heart and said sincerely, "I really do wish for peace. I want to create a world where the Evil God, fiends, and humans can live together without strife. That was my goal in putting this plan into action."

Adlet couldn't say a word. He didn't even understand what she meant.

"I have no ill will toward any of you," she continued. "But I must revive the Evil God. To that end, I was forced to eliminate the Braves of the Six Flowers, no matter what."

"I don't...I don't understand what you mean. What are you talking about, Princess?" Mora sounded utterly confounded.

Nashetania ignored her and continued. "I have a request for you all. Would you please withdraw? I will deal with the Evil God once it has revived. I will not allow it to destroy the human world, because I love both humans and fiends equally."

"Princess, please. Explain in a way we can understand," said Mora.

"Let me put it simply," said Nashetania. "My goal is to replace the hearts of fiends in order to force them to reconcile with humans."

That doesn't make any sense, thought Adlet. *What she's saying is absurd.* But even so, he listened. Perhaps he'd just been swallowed by the atmosphere of the moment, or perhaps it was her charisma.

"S-so...we reconcile, and then there's world peace?" said Hans. Even he was overwhelmed.

"Yes, that's right," Nashetania replied. "Though I will not say there is no danger. There will be some sacrifices. But really just a few."

"How many?" asked Fremy.

"I estimate that it will not be more than approximately five hundred thousand human lives." Nashetania rattled off the figure as if it were a simple matter of course. Her voice was filled with confidence.

I don't get it, thought Adlet. He couldn't understand any of it—not what she was trying to do, not what she was thinking. What he saw there was a monster with a charming form. "Hans. Fremy. Mora. Chamo," he said. He turned to his dazed allies. "Kill her!"

Roused by Adlet's words, Hans drew his sword and dashed forward. Chamo put her foxtail in her mouth and spewed up fiends. Mora clenched her fists and threw a punch at Nashetania. The first attack to connect was Mora's fist. She smashed Nashetania's head in one hit. But...

"So trying to explain it to you was useless, after all." Nashetania stood there, her head caved in as if it were nothing. Her body crumpled. Armor, clothing, and all, she transformed into something mud-like. "What a disappointment." The voice came not from the mud that had been Nashetania, but from the forest around them. "Good-bye, Goldof. It's really a shame we couldn't go together."

"What was that...?" trailed off Goldof.

"A fiend technique. And that of a high-level fiend, too," said Adlet.

"And Fremy," Nashetania continued. "I feel that perhaps you and I could understand each other."

"*Meow!* She should still be close!" said Hans.

"Let us see each other again sometime," the voice finished.

Hans ran in the direction from which it had been emanating, chasing after Nashetania alongside Chamo's fiends.

"Fremy! Take care of Adlet!" Mora said, sprinting into the forest. Goldof, who had been momentarily frozen, ran off, too. Only Adlet and Fremy remained behind, alone.

"No way...Nashetania? I can't believe it," Adlet moaned. The moment the identity of the seventh had come to light and he could relax, pain had assaulted him.

Fremy moved Adlet from his perch against the tree and laid him down on the ground. "Don't speak, Adlet. You've pushed yourself too hard."

"Pushing myself too hard...is my special technique." Adlet smiled.

Fremy's face hovered just above his. "You've lost too much blood. Hold on. This isn't much, but I have some tonic."

"You've gotten a lot nicer... You should've been like this from the start."

"I told you not to talk," Fremy ordered, fishing within her cloak.

As Adlet watched her, he thought of when they met. When he'd first seen her, he'd found her beautiful and wanted to protect her. There had been no logic in those desires. Even now that he knew she was the daughter of a fiend, knew she was the Brave-killer, those feelings had not changed. "Hey, Fremy. Do you like me?" he asked.

The hand that had been searching beneath her cloak stopped. Fremy looked at Adlet and said, "I hate you." She averted her eyes as she spoke. But she didn't sound upset.

"Why?" he asked.

"When I'm with you, I want to live."

When Adlet heard that, he smiled. *I won't let you die,* he tried to say. But the words wouldn't come out, and his mouth wouldn't move right.

"Adlet!" His vision suddenly narrowed. Fremy was slapping his cheeks. She seemed to be yelling something, but he couldn't hear.

"No...on't di...me......"

Don't worry, I'm just closing my eyes for a bit, he tried to say, but his lips would move no more.

Something soft touched his lips. A stimulating liquid poured into his mouth, down his throat, and into his stomach. And then Adlet's consciousness fell into darkness.

Epilogue

The
Next
Mystery

When Adlet opened his eyes, it was painfully bright. The light of the morning sun was shining on his cheeks. The fog had cleared.

"…" Adlet looked around. He was inside the temple, and sunlight streamed in through the broken door.

"So you've awakened." A voice came from the direction opposite the sunlight. When he turned his head, there was Mora. "Sorry. I am not Fremy," she said.

Sarcasm? Come on, thought Adlet. But he probably actually would have been gladder to see Fremy beside him.

Adlet looked at his body. What seemed to be a dark-green poultice was wrapped all over him. He didn't remember Fremy using something like that when she'd treated him, though.

"Those are medicinal herbs imbued with the essence of the mountain," said Mora. "With injuries of that sort, you should recover in two days."

"Really?" marveled Adlet.

"The power of the mountain is the power of healing. Believe in my abilities."

Adlet sat up. It hurt quite a lot, but he could move. The previous day, he'd been prepared for the very real prospect that he'd never be able to fight again. *The power of the Saints is unbelievable*, he thought.

"Adlet, I apologize." Suddenly, Mora placed her hands on the ground and bowed her head. "I failed to realize that you were really a Brave. Truly the greatest mistake of my life. My foolishness caused you such injury…"

"What's done is done. Go apologize to everyone else, instead." Adlet made Mora lift her head.

Then, from near Adlet's feet, Hans said, "She already has. She was grovelin' and everythin'."

"Oh…then that's good enough." Adlet lay back on the floor. It seemed that Mora and Hans were the only ones inside the temple. Where were the others? And where was Nashetania?

"We let Nashetania get away. Sorry," said Hans.

"Is everyone safe?" asked Adlet.

"Of course. Chamo, Fremy, and Goldof are outside," Mora confirmed.

Adlet breathed a sigh of relief. As long as they were all okay. They had overcome that fearsome plot without losing a single member. That was enough reward.

"Adlet, I shudder to consider what might have happened had you not been with us," said Mora. "Nashetania would have deceived us all. How many of us would have fallen?"

"Feel free to keep relying on me all you like," Adlet encouraged.

"Normally, I would laugh off such remarks and say, *Oh, since you're the strongest man in the world?* But you *are* different. You really did do so much for us."

"Hey, hey, meow," Hans said. "Yer not gonna show me any thanks?"

"Oh yes. You did fine, too."

"*Meow!* Why am I not gettin' the same level of appreciation here?" Hans protested. "I did a lot, too. I was the first one who figured out that Adlet didn't do it. We even beat up Chamo together. And I was the one who convinced Chamo 'bout everything and made her search under the temple."

"I—I understand," said Mora. "You did much for us, too. Thank you. You have my gratitude."

"That'll do," said Hans.

As Adlet watched their exchange, he thought, *Hans really did do a lot for us.* Adlet was alive because Hans had seen the truth. Hans had also been the one to finally pin down Nashetania. "Hans, you figured out Nashetania's plan, didn't you?"

"Yeah, but only half of it," Hans admitted. "I didn't figure out where she'd been hidin' the body." He didn't seem to be lying. Adlet was wholeheartedly glad that Hans was not his enemy.

"Hans, you really are an amazing guy. I've never met anyone else I could count on like you," he said.

"Hmm?" Hans suddenly started acting funny. He blushed, looked all around, and scratched his head.

"I'll be counting on you from now on, too," Adlet finished.

"H-hey. It's embarrassin' when you flatter meow like that."

"What is with this man?" muttered Mora. Adlet didn't really know, either. Then Chamo came into the temple.

"How is Goldof, Chamo?" inquired Mora.

"He's hopeless. He won't talk, no matter what you say to him," Chamo said with a shrug.

Adlet felt sympathy for him. Goldof had been cruelly betrayed by the very princess to whom he'd been so loyal. Would he be able to handle it at his young age?

"Let's just leave him behind," said Chamo. "He's not gonna be useful like this."

"No, he must recover, even if we must force him. The battle has not even begun," said Mora.

Adlet's cheer dissipated. She was right. Their goal was to destroy the Evil God, and they hadn't even set foot yet in the Howling Vilelands. Adlet pushed himself up and then stood.

"Huh? Can you stand, Adlet?" Chamo asked.

"I'm just gonna go get some air," he said. It did hurt a bit, but he could manage walking. He left the three of them behind and went outside. Basking in the light of morning, he passed through the pillars of salt. He noticed Goldof there, balled up and leaning against one of the columns.

Adlet figured he should leave him alone, so he distanced himself from the younger man.

It wasn't long before Adlet found the person he was looking for. She was a little ways from the temple, in the forest. "You're awake," Fremy said shortly. Her manner was completely changed from how it had been the day before. Her expression was cold.

"Yeah." He stood beside her. *Now then, what to talk about?* When he looked at her, nothing came to mind.

"It's too bad. That Nashetania was the seventh, I mean," she said.

"What's that supposed to mean?"

"That's what's been on your mind, right?"

"Why'd you have to put it that way?" Adlet pouted. It wasn't that he'd considered Nashetania special. *I just felt like I got along with her pretty well. So, well, I guess it is too bad.*

"Sorry, but can you not talk to me?" Fremy looked away. Her attitude confused him. She had fought so hard to protect him just the day before. Where had that gone?

"I don't really know…," she said, "…how I should talk to you. I don't know how to look at myself."

"…"

"So I'd like a little time."

Adlet sighed. "Fine. Then I'd just like to ask two things." Fremy nodded. "You're coming with us, right?" he asked. "You're taking back what you said about wanting to fight alone?"

"Yes. I've given up on that. Even if I were to insist on leaving, you wouldn't listen, anyway."

She just can't be honest with herself, thought Adlet. "And is it true…that when you're with me, you want to live?" Fremy blushed and glanced down, then gave Adlet a spiteful look. She nodded very slightly.

"Let's do it," said Adlet. "Let's beat the Evil God. And all of us are gonna come out alive."

Fremy nodded and then turned away, as if to say, *Are we done here?* That was when it happened.

"...?" Adlet saw something—something that looked like a person approaching the temple from the direction of the fort.

"What is it, Adlet?" Fremy asked. She then quickly noticed, too.

The one approaching was a girl, her small frame encased in iron armor as she trotted toward them. Mora and the others noticed the sound and emerged from the temple. Goldof lifted his head and looked at her.

"Um, pardon me!" The girl bowed her head deeply. She wore tiny glasses and looked like the quiet type. She had a timid expression, like that of a little squirrel. The thick armor she wore clashed completely with the impression she gave off.

"Rolonia, is that you?" asked Adlet.

The girl raised her head. When she recognized Adlet, she beamed. "Addy! I haven't seen you for so long! So you were chosen, after all!"

"Y-yeah, I guess... It has been a while, but, uh...," Adlet stuttered. The girl proffered a handshake. Confused, Adlet accepted it.

From behind him, Fremy murmured, "Who is she?"

Adlet released her hand, flustered, and the girl noticed the looks everyone was giving her. Then she bowed her head. "I—I'm so sorry! I haven't introduced myself!" The girl—Rolonia—bowed her head again, multiple times. "I'm Rolonia Manchetta, the Saint of Spilled Blood. I'm very sorry I'm so late!"

Mora called out to her, making her lift her head. "Rolonia, why are you here?"

"Lady Mora, I really am sorry for being so late!" she said. "But when I tried to rendezvous with you all, the fog appeared, and I couldn't approach the area."

"That was not what I meant...," said Mora.

"Um...I know I'm not really powerful enough to be one of the Braves, but I'll do my best!" Rolonia added. Adlet felt as if the breath had been knocked out of him. A shiver went down his spine. Mentally, he was staggering.

"Could you show us proof?" requested Mora.

"Y-yes—here it is. The proof I am one of the Braves of the Six

Flowers." With that, Rolonia removed her breastplate to show them the crest near her collarbone. It was the same as the one Adlet had—the same as the one the others had: a real Crest of the Six Flowers. "Um, sorry, but this has been bothering me for a while now..." Rolonia looked over the shuddering group and asked, "Why are there six of you?"

None of them could reply.

Adlet understood—their fight with Nashetania had been nothing more than a preliminary skirmish. The real battle had only just begun.

AFTERWORD

To everyone who read my previous series, *Tatakau Shisho* (*Fighting Librarians*): long time, no see. And to those who have not, it's nice to meet you. I'm Ishio Yamagata. How did you like *Rokka: Braves of the Six Flowers*? I hope you will stay with me for many years to come.

It's been so long since my last series ended. I've caused grief and trouble for a lot of people. I'll do my best to ensure that won't happen again. I felt lost for quite a long time, but lately, I've come to feel that whether I'm lost or not, I just have to write. Have I made some progress? Or is that a step back?

I suppose I'll report on my current state of affairs. I'm the type who's fine when it's hot out but terrible at dealing with the cold, so in summertime, I've always been troubled by air-conditioning sickness. But this year, I've been keeping the air-conditioning low because of the power shortages, so I've been healthier than in previous years. But even so, I left the fan on too long and caught a summer cold. I was out for three days. The same day I recovered, I took a cold shower, and the cold came back, wasting another day. Will I never be able to manage my impossibly poor health? This is actually causing me legitimate concern.

I plan to contribute a portion of the royalties for this book to the Fukushima Decontamination Committee, a citizens' group working to remove radioactive material from Fukushima. It won't be much, but I hope I can be of some aid in the recovery, however small.

Finally, the acknowledgments. To Miyagi-san, who illustrated this book for me: Thank you very much. To my managing editor, T-shi: I apologize for all the trouble I caused you this time around, too. And to everyone in the editing department: Thank you so much for your help with everything.

And to all my readers: I hope I will see you again.

Regards,

ISHIO YAMAGATA

Nashetania

Fremy